The Research Project

Sarah Fawcett

To my mom
and her collection of romance novels
that I read over and over again.

Acknowledgements

Thank you to Rob, you're never allowed to read this book or any others I write, but keep believing in me and giving me the opportunity to write my heart out and we'll travel this road together.

To Margaret for educating me about feminism, rotten politics and life outside my little box through her incredible posts and for the smart advice on a genre she doesn't read.

To lil Sarah for being a great friend and making this process more exciting by giving me the positive feedback I so desperately wanted.

To Sarah T for her logical and technical approach to my imagination and for her endless support.

To Corey for the guidance regarding flying a Cessna. God speed.

The Research Project

1.

My body immediately consumes the stored heat from the inside of my car when I sit inside. The short walk to the car chilled me and I am thankful that the warmth from the day's sun wasn't able to escape my little car. Shivering, I quickly shut the door and start the engine. I'm surprised by the cold night. It was beautiful this morning. I guess autumn in Toronto is here. I'll have to remember to bring a coat tomorrow. I pull my wraparound dress tighter to me and flick the button to turn on the heated seat. The two dots on the dashboard light up and I sit back, waiting for the heat to appease me.

Out the window, I can't really tell if the leaves on the trees are turning colours yet. There aren't many trees in this neighbourhood where I work. I don't even have a tree in front of my practice and my front walk is cement. There's a few blowing on the road, but I don't see the reds and yellows of the fall.

My office is a late 19th century semi-detached house, which was one of the most popular architectural styles during the Victorian era. It was refurbished on the inside years ago, but the distinctive mansard roof and the detailing on the red brick has remained the same.

I smile at the sign that hangs over the front door: *Colleen Cousineau. Child Psychologist.* It took me nine years to become a child psychologist and when I leased this office, I very proudly commissioned a local woodworker to make that sign. It's a marvelous feeling each and every time I walk through the door.

The heat is roasting my back now, so I pull out and drive home. I could technically walk to work every day, but I never know if I'm going to be carrying files or text books with me. I'd hate to lug heavy bags wearing heels. The route home is absolutely scenic and is considered to be the largest continuous area of preserved Victorian housing in North America. Maybe I could bring a pair of running shoes to work. I could change into them and enjoy the changing of the seasons.

As I pull up to my house, I notice that the shrubs around the property are overgrown. They need to be trimmed one more time before winter hits. They look awful. I grab my purse and briefcase and get out of the car, walking directly to the bushes to inspect them. Yes, they definitely need to be cut.

After unlocking the front door and walking inside, I drop my keys into the little glass dish on the entryway table. Oh? Where are Steve's keys? I peek through the window on the front door and look for his car. I didn't even see it on the street. I was too busy worrying about the bushes. I guess he's not home. Well, I won't bother him about trimming the shrubs. I'll call the gardener instead. If Steve's not home now, he must be working late again, so he deserves a break. I chuckle to myself. Even if he was here, his keys wouldn't be in the dish anyway. They'd probably be on the floor or on the stairs. He's always losing them.

I open the closet door and hang my purse on a hook. I see a piece of lint on my arm and pick it off, but then scrutinize my entire dress. I grab a sticky roller from the top of the closet and give my dress a good once over. I step out of my black heels and put on my sheepskin booties. Oh, they feel nice. I don't care if they don't go with my dress, it's better than tracking in dirt and city grime all through the house. No one is home. There is no one here to impress. I nod resolutely, pick up my purse and make my way into the kitchen.

I place my purse on the white and gray marble counter and head toward the fridge. As I start to open the door, I spot something dark and sticky on the handle. I inspect it closer and it looks like jam. I immediately get a disinfecting wipe from the broom closet to scrub it off. I don't eat jam. Steve must have had it on his toast this morning. And now I see his used plate, knife and coffee cup in the sink. I sigh. I usually leave for work before him in the morning and I always seem to clean up his messes when I get home. I finish sanitizing the fridge door and stick his dirty dishes in the dishwasher.

I kick the dishwasher door closed, throw the wipe in the garbage and catch my reflection in the kitchen's sliding glass door. My mane of light brown curls looks wilder than usual and I try to pat them down, but give up. I pull the ends of the belt on my blue wraparound dress a little bit tighter. The dress shows off my slender, toned body, but the booties look ridiculous. I smirk and continue to get the last vanilla yogurt out of the fridge. When I close the fridge, I grab the pen stuck to the magnetic shopping list and write *yogurt*.

I open my mail with a letter opener and click on the banking application on my smart phone to pay my hydro and utility bills. When I finish, I neatly file the invoices in my metal filing cabinet under the kitchen desk. I rinse out my yogurt container and place it, along with the empty envelopes and junk mail, in the recycling bin under the sink, and stick the spoon in the full dishwasher and turn it on. Finally, I grab a glass of water and head to my home office to finish up the day's work.

My home office is small compared to my practice, but I've decorated it to my own personal style and find it very comforting. My bright yellow leather rolling chair puts me in a great mood whenever I see it. The walls of my office are pale yellow, with white wainscoting on the bottom. The framed prints are bold and bright, except for the one black and white photo of Steve and me, on our wedding day. This is my favourite room in the house and I enjoy my time in it.

My schedule is busy; I often work ten hour days, but I love it. I keep a professional distance from my patients, but sometimes I just can't let their problems go and I will diligently research until I find a new theory or practical application to try. Children have such young, moldable minds and I need to do everything I can to help them through their difficult issues. I had a particularly problematic session with one patient today, so I sit down and review my notes and record them into a recording device. I'm thoroughly involved in my work when Steve barges in.

"Colleen, we need to talk," Steve says, standing with both hands on my desk.

Steve is good-looking man, thirty-five, with brown hair that is slightly thinning in the front. To be honest, he's lost a lot of muscle in the last couple of years and it disappoints me. He is a pharmaceutical sales representative and it requires many hours of legwork and dedication for it to be rewarding and lucrative. He often leaves for days at a time, travelling to Ottawa and Windsor. He has even travelled to the United States for business. It leaves him very little time to do much of anything, much less work out. While I appreciate his work ethic, I've always had a thing for muscles and it is quite unfortunate. However, I love him dearly and would never let that small fact ruin my feelings for him. My marriage means everything to me. I gently remind him from time to time that he needs to exercise. He might just need another push. Maybe we can go to the gym together like we used to when we were in university.

Steve seems wound up again. "I'm recording my last session, honey. You know that when my door is closed, I'm working. I'll be out in ten minutes." I brush my hand in the air to wave him out.

"I'm not a child. Don't dismiss me. This is important." He stomps his foot.

I remember the last time he stomped his foot. It was when he wanted a new seventy-five inch LCD television. I was against it because just two months earlier, he had bought a seventy inch OLED television. He has always liked to research online for the next best thing and has been extremely liberal with our money in the four years that we have been married. I found it completely absurd to get an LCD television again, simply because the technology is old, even with the advancements that have been made. I like the OLED. It has lower power consumption. Besides, we didn't need another television! I voiced my opinion, he stomped his foot, and he bought one anyway.

I realize that he buys new things to reward himself. He treats himself to these luxury items to justify the amount of hours he works, but right now I'm not interested in hearing about another new gadget that he has to buy. He doesn't need my permission. I just want to finish my work, have some tea and go to bed.

I keep my head down and say sternly, "Steve. Not now. I'm busy. Please."

"Colleen, I'm not leaving until you put your damn recorder down! Look at me and listen to what I have to say," he demands.

"I do not want to hear about an iPod, iPad, or how the Xbox One is better than the Play Station. I don't want to know how much your next endeavor is going to cost. I don't want--"

Steve cuts me off, "I'm leaving you."

2.

"What?" I place the recorder gently on the desk and look up slowly.

"Yes, I figured it would come as a surprise to you and your extremely organized life. You didn't have *marriage over* penciled into your agenda, did you?" he chides. "Maybe if you didn't schedule our weekly sex dates, we wouldn't be here." He pulls a couple of books off of my shelves and drops them onto the floor.

"You're saying that you are leaving me because I schedule sex? You never told me that you didn't like that or that you weren't happy." I am confused. I thought he liked Saturday night sex. "And why are you doing that to my books?" I run over to them, and start picking them up.

"You never listen to me! If you don't have something written down in your agenda or if there's not some sort of alert on your phone, it must not exist. Right? Isn't that your philosophy?" He rolls his eyes, walks to my desk and pushes some papers onto the floor now.

He is right, but he can't be leaving me because I'm organized. I can't think straight. My papers are everywhere.

"You're too mechanical. You don't have any time for spontaneity or any sort of a real life and that includes me. I don't want to be stuck with a thirty-two-year-old, boring robot."

Robot? "Why are you messing up my office?" I ask. I'm not able to focus on his argument. I look at him strangely. He is out of control.

"I have been unhappy for most of our marriage, starting with you not taking my last name! You're too controlling! I've had enough."

"Not once have you indicated that you were unhappy. We were just planning our five year anniversary trip together. You know that I looked on the internet for hours for the best deal! Why would you let me do that if you didn't want to go? I've already paid for it!"

9

"That was your idea, as usual. You didn't ask for my opinion. I can't stand being told what to do. I'm not a child. I'm going to pack a bag and I'll get the rest of my things later." Steve starts to leave my office.

I look up at him. "That's it? I don't even get a chance to talk to you about it? To fix it? I *am* a therapist, Steve," I plead.

"I know that you are a god damned therapist. But you deal with children. You don't listen to adults. You don't even listen to your own husband."

"I'm listening now," I whisper. I stop cleaning and look up at him.

"I'm done trying to talk to you, Colleen. Live in your perfect, little world… In your immaculate house… And with your pristine possessions." He takes another swipe at my desk and more papers sail into the air and onto the floor. "You can fix this mess in your office, Colleen, but you can't fix us."

"There are tactics and strategies for these sorts of problems. We need to sit down and figure out a solution."

"I've had enough of your psycho bullshit. You can be as mechanical in bed as you want with the next poor sap. I'm done." Steve stomps out and slams the office door.

I stand up to go after him, but I don't how to handle the outburst. I love Steve, but he is acting like a child again. He always makes rash decisions and it's normal for him to demand things and be over dramatic. I usually tell parents to ignore this type of behavior and not feed it. Parents should only intervene during a temper tantrum when there is a threat of violence or bodily harm. But am I supposed to ignore the threat of separation?

I don't understand where any of it is coming from. First of all, he knew that I wanted to keep my last name from the beginning of our relationship. I've always been up front with him. And hyphenating Cousineau-Bellacicco was just too long and too… Too rhyming. If he had a problem with it, he should have told me when we were engaged.

As for our marriage, how can he say that he's unhappy? I think it's an ideal marriage. We enjoy each other's company and have the same interests. Our work doesn't give us a whole lot of time to be together, but that's why I started scheduling our sex dates on Saturday night. It brought us together once a week and kept things alive. But he just criticized that too.

And he criticized me. I can't believe the words he used to describe me: controlling, a robot, methodical in bed. It makes me sick. I shake my head and sit down in my chair. I like our Saturday night sex. Steve is great in bed and I look forward to it each week. I thought he agreed that it was a good idea and liked our routine. But maybe that's why he mentioned I lack spontaneity. Where did our marriage go wrong?

Could it be a mid-life crisis? No! He's too young! But he does buy toys, gadgets and other useless items. Could his excessive consumerism be related to boredom? Does he think his life is stale? Is he trying to compensate for something he thinks is lacking? I don't think our marriage lacks anything.

I hear Steve stomp down the stairs, open the front door and then slam it shut. I start to go after him, but stop. Maybe he just needs to calm down and he'll be back tomorrow. I clean up the mess he made and go to bed, but don't get any sleep that night.

3.

One month later, I am at my practice, sitting at my chestnut desk, waiting for my next patient to arrive. This office is not as cozy or as pretty as my home office, but I think it's decorated professionally. The children seem to like the large, colourful prints of far-off places, like Egypt and the Amazon. It's painted a sky blue with thick royal blue curtains over white wooden blinds. The clutter of children's games and toys constantly bothers me though. I'm constantly tidying up the shelves, trying to put the books in alphabetical order and the games in some kind of neat stack. Once a week, I have someone come in and clean the office from top to bottom, carpet to ceiling. They know how I like my shelves.

I straighten my notepad in front of me, take the lid off of my pen and turn the handle of my coffee mug to the right. I brush a lock of curls away from my face and roll my blue-gray eyes. My hair always drives me crazy. It's one thing that I cannot control.

My secretary, Margie Malone, knocks on my door and walks into my office. Margie has been with me since I opened the office. She is a mother of two, but her children are in college. She's a petite woman who types like a fiend. The best thing about Margie is her friendly smile, which makes her perfect for greeting children. She hands me the file for the next patient.

"Are you ok?" she asks, her eyes worried.

"Yes, I'm fine."

"You look upset."

I open up the drawer of my desk and start tidying its contents distractedly. The push pins should not be in the same compartment as the safety pins. Margie knows that Steve and I have separated, but I haven't divulged much more. I don't really want to share either.

"I know that you're the therapist, Colleen, but you can talk to me anytime. You can tell me anything. I won't judge you and I won't tell anyone."

I shut the drawer and look up. "Thanks Margie, but really, I am doing well. I do need some paperclips, though."

Margie nods. "I'll order some more." Before she closes my door, she says, "I'm here if you need me for anything else."

After Steve left that night, I didn't take a single day off. I actually extended my hours and threw myself into my work. As a therapist, I know I should talk to someone about my situation, emotions and feelings, but I'm just not ready.

Margie buzzes the intercom, "Your ten o'clock appointment is here. Carrie Swiftwood."

Finally. "Please send her in, Margie." I'd rather listen to Carrie and fix her problems.

My morning patients are a delight. They are very receptive to my different approaches and methods. I play a card game focusing on shyness with Carrie. The game helps children communicate their feelings and develops insight into their problems. Carrie has never even looked at me. She usually keeps her eyes on her hands in her lap, even after the several sessions we have had.

In the middle of the game, I am pretending to swim with dolphins, something I've always wanted to do, and Carrie starts laughing. She actually looks at me for the first time and says, "You're funny." Progress.

In my next session, I read a story to one little boy named Seth, who hasn't talked to anyone since his mom died recently. The book is about the love between a little boy and his dog. When the dog dies, the boy starts telling the dog every night that he will always love him. Seth surprises me by asking if he should tell his mom that he loves her every night before bed. It is such an achievement. I tell him that it's important to tell people how you feel, even if they are in heaven. When our session is over, I give him the book to take home and he smiles at me.

Another patient, a teenage boy named Jesse, who initially came to me as a result of his bullying, has come so far with being able to deal with his control issues that now, he mentors children who are the victims of bullies. We have our last celebratory session today. At least I can help someone else, if I can't help myself.

4.

At lunch, Margie has to do an errand, so I sit at my desk and eat the quinoa and beet salad that I packed for lunch.

I pick up my calendar and realize that it's been thirty-three days since Steve moved out. I sigh. I'm still upset that he didn't give me a chance to talk openly about his reasons for wanting to leave. He just left. And he won't even take my calls. He has always been childish, but this is cruel and heartless. I can't stop thinking about the situation, I have anxiety all the time and I jump every time the telephone rings.

With the addition of longer work days, I also book up any free time I have with interesting clubs and workshops. They help to relieve my stress and let me feel some sort of normalcy. I usually learn something and enjoy it, but mostly the activity helps me to take my mind off everything.

I enrolled in a cooking class on Mondays at the Culinarium, off of Eglinton Avenue East. I've always liked cooking and I'm excited to learn how to make different cuisine each week from different chefs around Toronto. Last week, I made empanadas, Spanish rice and sangria. It was easy and it was delicious. I genuinely enjoy the steps and the focus needed to cook intricate dishes. The end result is very rewarding.

On Tuesday nights, I play co-ed volleyball at the University of Toronto. I've actually been in the same house league since I completed university. Since Steve and I played together in university, he would come with me occasionally, when his work permitted. The other players come and go, but they all seem to be my age, fit, and have the inane desire to keep the glory days of college volleyball alive. It can be pretty competitive.

On Wednesdays, I go to an art class and work with mixed media at the Art Barn School on Eglinton Avenue West. I used to paint in high school, but my academic education took precedence. I didn't have time to focus on or explore my creative talents because art was an elective that would not help advance my career. However, I am really appreciating the experience. In class yesterday, we used water colours to create a rural landscape. I couldn't get the brush stroke on the wheat grass quite right, so my instructor showed me how to hold the brush in a different position. I was just getting the hang of it, when the class ended. He said I could stay after to work on it, but it was late and I still had to do my daily recordings.

Today is Thursday and I am going to a book club meeting around the corner at the local community centre. I've been going for a couple of weeks and we're just finishing *Lady Chatterly's Lover* by D.H. Lawrence. It's a famously controversial novel about sexual freedom and sensuality. My minor is in English and it's stimulating to recall the knowledge that I learned, but haven't used in years. I also enjoy the intelligent banter between the members of the club.

And on Fridays… I look at my calendar carefully. It looks like Fridays are open at the moment. I have been thinking about looking into flight school. Learning to fly a plane would be exhilarating and a rather significant conquest. A pilot's skills are so precise and logical. It would be a great challenge. I pick up my pen and write on my *To Do* list in my agenda, *Call the local airport/flight school.*

"Your next patient is here, Dr. Cousineau. Jeremy Sampson," Margie buzzes, interrupting my daydreaming again.

"Give me a minute to clean up and then you can send him in." I put my empty lunch container in my thermal bag and push my calendar to the top corner of my desk. I'll fly through the clouds another time.

5.

Before my last patient, I check the phone messages that Margie has written down, and I see that my best friend Christine Beckham, is in the pile. I have known her since university, when she was in my Psychology 101 class. She was always late to class, wore the tightest jeans and smelled like the fragrance department at Macy's, but she surprised me with her intelligence. We debated nature versus nurture, with her taking the stance that our lives are shaped by experiences, and she was tough. I couldn't make my genetics argument stick. We hit it off immediately.

"Call Christine back before you go to your boring, old book club." I look at Margie and ask, "Did she actually say this? Or did you add the 'boring, old book club' in yourself?" I smirk.

Margie smiles, "Nope, Christine said that. But I was thinking it."

I stick out my tongue. "Thank you, Margie." I can let loose once in a while.

Before I close my office door, I hear Margie say, "So professional."

I laugh and poke my head out. "I work with kids. I'm allowed to stick out my tongue." I close the door and pick up the phone dialing Christine's number.

"It's about time!" Christine answers.

"What? No hello?" I say.

"Why don't you bail on the bookies and come out for a drink with me, Ci-Ci?" Christine begs, calling me by my old college nickname. She always gave people nicknames, depending on what they excelled in or how they acted. She called Steve, Hammer, because of his volleyball skills, but she used only my initials to name me. I asked her why and she said that Ci-Ci reminded her of Coco, as in Coco Chanel, and just like the designer, I'm classy and sophisticated. I couldn't argue with her logic.

"I can't do that. I've made a commitment and they need me there to make notes." I shake my cup of pencils.

"Notes? Really?" She laughs. "You can meet me afterward. I'll be down the street from where you'll be. It's a bar called The Blue Iguana."

"Who will be there?" I have known Christine since university and she has always been an extrovert. She used to drag me to parties and bars, to all school social and sporting events and she even got me to join the spirit committee. I put my foot down when she asked me to try out for cheerleading. Not surprisingly, she excelled at being a cheerleader. We are complete opposites, but we get along really well. Christine brings me out of my shell and I somehow ground Christine with common sense. I used to make her study for hours and she still acknowledges that she couldn't have gotten great grades without me.

"I'll be with some of my co-workers. They're really laid back, nice people. You'll like them," she says. Christine works at a health insurance company. It seems like a boring job for a girl of her caliber.

"I won't know any of them. I won't know what to say." I start organizing my pencils in the cup, pencil lead up. I like to see if they're sharpened before I take them out.

"Ci-Ci, when have you been at a loss for words? It's what you do for a living. And anyways, you'll be with me. We haven't been out in forever, so I'll probably ignore them."

"I don't know," I protest. I stick a pencil in my electric sharpener. Then blow on it when I take it out.

"Ci-Ci, quit sharpening your pencils! You are coming with me tonight or I will pull you out of that meeting by your book bag! You need this and I need to see that you are doing okay," Christine softens.

A week after Steve left, I told Christine what had happened. However, I didn't open up to her about his harsh comments or my part in the separation. I'm too ashamed to admit that I failed as a wife and a lover.

"You talked me into it. I will come to your Blue Iguana. Is nine o'clock too late?" I hope.

Christine snorts, "That's when things are just getting started!" She hangs up.

I hang up the phone and shake my head. She's crazy. But a smile tugs on my lips.

6.

"Thank you, Dr. C," my seven-year old patient Lucy says.

"Goodbye, Lucy. I'll see you next week." Her blonde ponytail bobs up and down as she runs to her mom's arms. I nod to the girl's parents and close the office door.

It would be so nice to have that young and carefree attitude, but I immediately frown and look down at Lucy's file. Poor Lucy. Lucy has major separation anxiety, mostly brought on by the stress of new children and teachers at school. I've gotten Lucy to the point where her parents can leave the room while Lucy and I talk, but she needs more exposure techniques, so she can eventually go back to school.

As an only child, I was the opposite of Lucy. Both of my parents died when I was young and I was brought up by my mother's sister, Anna Cousineau. Aunt Anna was strict and extremely scholarly. She was a professor at the university and earned her doctorate while I was in high school. I lead a life of studying, knowledge and no-nonsense because of my aunt. I welcomed change and new experiences, but only if it benefitted my schooling. The more I could learn, the happier I was. I loved Aunt Anna and eventually took her last name. She died of breast cancer two years ago.

"Goodbye Colleen," Margie says, as she peeks her head into the office.

"Did you file my stationery receipts under taxes?"

"Yes, Colleen."

"Is the answering machine on?"

"Yes, Colleen."

"And the--"

"The paper cups for the water dispenser? Yes, I refilled them."

"Thank you, Margie. I appreciate you more than you know." I smile at her.

"Have a good time at your book club. I'm glad that you are going out. Good night."

Before packing up my briefcase with the day's patients' files, I check out my image in the full length mirror that I keep in my office. I try to smooth down my curls, but they just want to go where they please. I'm wearing a navy, knee-length pencil skirt and a white and blue striped form-fitting shirt. I hope I'm not overdressed for the Blue Iguana. I suddenly feel nervous. I haven't been out socially in a very long time.

I use this mirror for children with self-esteem issues. I have them look straight into their own eyes and talk to themselves confidently with positive affirmations.

I look myself in the eyes and say aloud, "I am a smart, strong woman. I can work through my problems and have a happy life again." I lower my eyes, "Pffft," I scoff.

I put on my coat and lock up the office. It's a beautiful fall evening, the air is unseasonably warm and there is no breeze. Bright orange and red leaves now litter the pathway that I walk on to get to my car. I'm happy to have found such a quaint and private area to have a practice.. I especially like that I always have convenient parking right out in front of my office.

I place my purse and briefcase on the back seat and then climb into the driver's seat. I see my book on the passenger seat and I sigh. I don't mind the novel or the meeting, but it reminds me that I only signed up for it to keep me sane. That saddens me. The meeting is on Church Street, three blocks down. I could walk, but then I'd have to trek back to my office in the dark.

After parking in the lot of the community centre, I walk to an adjacent café and order a chai tea latte. I decide to sit down on a wooden bench facing the children's park. A handful of kids are playing on the jungle gym, sliding down the slide and climbing up the ropes. They are screeching and laughing and I can't help smiling. It's been hard to smile lately.

Steve has not come to see me at the house since that last night we talked. However, a week ago I came home one evening to find that he had cleared out his clothes and toiletries. I was surprised to see that he had left all of his treasured televisions still hanging on the walls. I left him a long, rather detailed message that night, begging him to explain himself, but I'm still waiting for an answer.

I actually call him daily, numerous times, leaving pleasant to irate messages. He has not once returned my call. I need to know what exactly made him leave. I replay our last conversation over and over in my head and it's not enough information. Something is missing. I do agree that I have obsessive-compulsive tendencies when it comes to my profession and my home. I like things to be tidy and organized. Who doesn't? But for him to leave me for those reasons seems asinine. I don't believe that I carried my idiosyncrasies into our marriage. But then, I scheduled sex, so maybe I did. Perhaps I should schedule that therapy appointment for myself.

I notice another book club member hanging around the entrance. His name is Dave, I think. I've been to two meetings and he just joined last week. He is a good looking man with brown wavy hair, slim build and wearing a button down shirt, suit jacket, and no tie.

"Hi, Colleen," he says, as he walks over to me.

He has nice teeth. "Hi, Dave." I sip my latte.

"Nice night." He sits down beside me.

"Yes, it is."

"Can I ask you something? I know that I don't know you very well, but I've been wondering something about you since last week. I can't figure it out," he tilts his head looking at me.

I turn to him. "What is it?"

"What makes a woman like you come to a little community centre like this for a book club?"

That's a strange question. "First, I'd like to ask, why *a woman like me*?"

"I guess I have a stereotype of what book club attendees look like, and you have definitely raised the bar for clubs everywhere."

I think he's flirting, but I'm not sure. "It's really an easy explanation. I went to school with Maryanne." Maryanne is the club leader. We've kept in touch since university, but she has three kids and is usually too busy to socialize. "She has been asking me to join the club for months."

"Oh, I thought that you might be a librarian." He smiles.

"Uh. No." I shake my head. "More like a child psychologist who needs to get out at night." And forget about how horrible a wife I am.

"I could pick a bunch of better places than a book club to enjoy my time."

"You're probably right, but this suits me for now. Why did you join the club?" I turn the attention to him.

"It's a long story. Maybe I'll tell you later," he winks. "It's almost seven. Let's go inside."

I don't like his wink. He holds the door open for me and I walk through, and into our meeting room. I turn to ask him if he finished reading the book, but I don't, because he's looking at my behind. I blush furiously and turn back, hurrying across the room, trying to get away from him. Why do men do things like that?

In university, Christine would constantly tell me how pretty I was and would positively comment on my lean, fit body. Then she would try to set me up on dates. It was like she was trying to convince me that I was meant to date, but I just didn't care for the boys. I didn't see why it was necessary and I definitely wasn't interested in the boys who wanted to date me. They were immature, unfocused and somewhat unintelligent. I had a volleyball scholarship and played that and other sports with boys, but that was the extent of my relationship with them.

Then I met Steve. Steve was on the men's volleyball team. At first, we just trained together, lifting weights and running on trails. We would grab a protein shake after our workouts and sit in my dorm room and talk about volleyball and the other teams that we had to compete against. We would share our hopes and dreams for the future too. Until one night, Steve took the shake out of my hand and kissed me long and hard on the mouth. I was completely surprised and I stepped back from him, looking at him. He started to apologize, but I stopped him by leaping at him, and kissing him for what seemed like hours. Christine applauded me when I told her what happened. It's about time, she had said.

Thankfully, I've never had to deal with any other men if this is the kind of treatment I would get. I shake my head furiously and sit down. I hope he doesn't sit beside me.

7.

It is five minutes after seven and it looks like everyone is here for the book club, except Maryanne. I hate it when meetings start late.

We are in what I assume is a multi-use room; red, orange and brown paper leaves are stapled to the bulletin board with the word *Autumn* across the top and the cursive alphabet circles around the entire room. I sit back in my chair, with my legs crossed and I tap my pen on the desk. I'm ready to make notes in the club journal, if the meeting would ever begin. Where is Maryanne? Just then, she rushes through the door.

"I'm sorry I'm late," Maryanne says and she takes a seat beside me. She has physically changed since university, but that's what happens when you have children, I suppose. She hasn't lost all of the baby weight yet, but I don't know how old her kids are either. Her hair is messy, falling into her eyes, and her shirt is half tucked in. She's frazzled. I nod to her, but don't say anything because she is busy organizing herself and I don't want to distract her. I just want the meeting to start.

It figures that Dave is sitting on the other side of me and I tentatively glance at him. He catches my eye and feigns a yawn. I look away. He's not taking this seriously.

Maryanne takes a deep breath, "Just to recall, the story concerns a young married woman, Constance or Lady Chatterley, whose upper-class husband, Clifford Chatterley, described as a handsome, well-built man, has been **paralyzed** from the waist down due to a war injury. In addition to Clifford's physical limitations, his emotional neglect of Constance forces distance between the couple. Her **sexual frustration** leads her into an affair with the **gamekeeper**, Oliver Mellors."

A woman named Miranda interrupts, "The novel is about Constance's realization that she cannot live with the mind alone. She must also be alive physically. This realization stems from a heightened sexual experience Constance has only felt with Mellors, suggesting that love can only happen with the element of the body, not the mind." Miranda is a thirty-something librarian who is really into books, conveniently. She has gorgeous auburn hair and green eyes. She looks like a cat.

Maryanne continues, "What types of themes do we see from the author?"

Miranda, once again, speaks up, "Lawrence argues for individual regeneration, which can be found only through the relationship between man and woman." Her voice even sounds like she is purring.

"Sometimes man and man," Dave says teasingly. He was referring to the author's fascination with the theme of homosexuality.

The group chuckles.

"Love and personal relationships are the threads that bind this novel together," Miranda ignores the laughter. Meow.

Maryanne interjects, "What kinds of relationships are explored?"

"There's the brutal, bullying relationship between Mellors and his wife Bertha, who punishes him by preventing his pleasure. There is Tommy Dukes, who has no relationship because he cannot find a woman whom he respects intellectually and, at the same time, finds desirable," Miranda rattles off.

"There is also the perverse, maternal relationship that ultimately develops between Clifford and Mrs. Bolton, his caring nurse, after Connie has left," Jane says softly. Jane is an older grandmother and joined when I did. She has a cute pixie cut and looks younger than her sixty-five years.

"Good one, Jane," I say. Jane smiles and sits up straighter.

"Now, what can we say about the mind and body theme?" Maryanne asks.

"The contrast between mind and body can be seen in the dissatisfaction each has with their previous relationships. Like Constance's lack of intimacy with her husband who is all mind," Mark says. Mark is a math professor at the university. He has longer, scruffy hair and large glasses. He kind of looks like a beagle.

A tiny blonde woman, whose name evades me, speaks up, "This is a novel that raised censorious hackles across the English-speaking world." Esther. That's her name. She is a tiny thing, with a British accent. "Lawrence describes sex and orgasm, and whose central message is the idea that sexual freedom and sensuality are far more important, more authentic and meaningful, than the intellectual life."

The way she says orgasm, reminds me of the old Benny Hill television show. She is embarrassed saying the word and covers up her mouth as she says it.

I look down at the blank page and tune them out. I think about the last Saturday night sex date that I had with Steve. I had reminded him during breakfast that I would be waiting for him at exactly eight-thirty in the evening, in the bedroom. Steve had seemed aloof and uninterested, but I had just thought that he had work on his mind. I had booked a couple of patients that afternoon, and after my last one, I had texted him another reminder about our date. I hadn't received a response, but had thought nothing of it. When I had gotten home from work, Steve was not home yet, so I had eaten dinner alone, finished my recordings for work and had gone upstairs to take a bubble bath.

When I had heard the front door close, I got out of the bath and dressed in a sexy, black and red teddy, garters and high heels. Steve had always liked my legs in stilettos. At eight-thirty on the dot, I had called for him from the top of the stairs, laid on the bed with candles lit and had Norah Jones playing. Ten minutes later, I had almost gone to yell for him again, when Steve had come into the room. He had looked at me, taken off his clothes and climbed on top of me without a word.

"What are you doing?" I asked. "You know that I always start on top." Steve climbed off of me and I straddled him. I reached down and had found that he was only semi-aroused. "What's wrong, Steve?"

"Nothing," he said quietly.

"It's you and me time. Forget work and let me make my baby feel good."

I rubbed the length of him, slowly, and pushed my breasts in his face. He started to get hard and I pulled my thong out of the way and placed his tip at the entrance of my moistness. I sat up, pushed my way back onto him and started moving my hips and lifting up and down. It had felt wonderful.

"Steve, rub my nipples." Steve reached up and tweaked my nipples, almost mechanically. I wanted him to enjoy it, but I couldn't force him to forget about work. I just kept pumping my hips and rocking back and forth. The rhythm was good and I could feel him deep inside me.

"Oh that's good. I'm going to come." I started moving faster and the build-up began. The wonderful pleasure increased and the feelings overwhelmed me. I exploded and cried out, shuddering with pleasure from my orgasm. I collapsed on Steve's chest and when I caught my breath, I sat straight up and smiled at him.

"Your turn, Steve." I knew what he liked, so I reached down behind me and started massaging the rocks between his legs. I lifted up off of him and came down hard, faster and faster. It took him longer than usual, but his breathing quickened and he climaxed.

"That was great." I got up immediately to clean myself off in the bathroom. When I returned, Steve was already gone.

"Steve?" I didn't an answer and figured that he went to eat dinner. I shrugged my shoulders and continued to get ready for bed.

Now that I think back to that night, I can see that Steve probably wasn't as happy or as satisfied as I thought. I was just doing my job as a good wife, having sex with him on Saturdays. It's not about being a good wife. It's about being a wife that is in tune with her husband's needs all the time. Why couldn't I see that before?

8.

I try to push away those thoughts and concentrate on the book group.

Dave is talking, "Not only do men and women require an appreciation of the sexual and sensual in order to relate to each other properly, they require it even to live happily in the world."

Wow. The book echoes my life.

"Great point, Dave," Maryanne says and stands up. "That was a great meeting. Thank you for continuing to meet here. Your dues can go in the jar by the door. Remember, this money will go towards purchasing books for Central Public School's library. See you next week."

How much did I miss? Where did the time go? I fumble and put my notepad away. So much for note-taking.

"Goodbye, Colleen," Jane says.

"Goodbye, Jane."

I turn to Maryanne. "How are you?"

"Crazy busy. I have to get home. Little Grayson just cut a tooth and my husband can't handle the crying. The rambunctiousness of our twin two-year-olds doesn't help either. It's too much for him," she sighs. "I'm not sure if I can keep doing this book club. Maybe you can take it over?"

I now understand the weight issue and her frenzied state. "Give me a call. Let me know for sure."

"How do you do it, Colleen?"

"Do what?"

"You have a booming practice, you come out to the book club, among other activities, and you have a husband. You have it all and are always so put together.

Do I tell her that looks may be deceiving? "Oh. I--."

She cuts me off, "I'm sorry. I have to go. My husband just called me for the fourth time in fifteen minutes. I've only been gone an hour for god's sake. Women truly are the caregivers."

Maryanne hugs me. "See you next week." And she's gone.

She'd be surprised to know how utterly a mess I really am. I may not show it, but I couldn't even concentrate for the last hour. I'm not going to tell her that.

Dave walks up to me, "Those were some exciting insights to Lady Chatterly."

"Yes. It is a novel which has had a profound impact on the way that 20th-century writers have written about sex. Sex couldn't be ignored as a crucial element in a relationship anymore," I babble, suddenly realizing that I missed his sarcasm.

Dave stares at me. "You really like the book? I was just making small talk."

"I thought you were asking for my opinion. I really do like the novel." I turn to get my coat, blushing profusely. Why is he even here, if he doesn't like the book?

"I can see that." Dave smiles. "But your opinion is correct. Sex could never be ignored."

Typical. I shake my head and grab my purse and book.

"A couple of us are going to The Blue Iguana for a drink. Would you like to come?" Dave asks.

Are you kidding me? "Oh." How do I handle this? "I'm actually going to meet my friend there right now, but I haven't seen her in a while and I really want to catch up. So I don't think I can sit with you. I'm sorry." I don't want to go there with him.

"We're both going to the same place. Could I at least walk with you?"

I'm annoyed and a little flustered. "Y-y-yes. Sure." I was not expecting this, but we are just walking there. It's just a walk.

Outside, Miranda and Mark see us and wave, but they start walking ahead of us. Dammit. I don't even get the comfort of a group dynamic. One-on-one. Great. I focus on the walk. It's an Indian summer this year. After a couple of cool nights in September, they've warmed up for October. I walk with my head up, looking through the tall buildings at the stars. As I start to appreciate the beauty of the night sky, I stumble over a crack in the sidewalk, and I'm about to go down. I brace myself for the impact, covering my face.

"I've got you," Dave says as he quickly grabs my elbow with one hand and I can feel his other hand on the small of my back. I get goose bumps. "You ok?"

I am stable on my feet again. "Yes. I'm fine." I pull away quickly and straighten my coat, putting my purse back over my shoulder. Stupid shoes. We start to walk again and I see that Dave has put a little distance between us. I feel guilty.

"I'm sorry." I feel awkward, but I should tell him something. "I've recently separated with my husband and I don't know how to act around men anymore." I try the straightforward approach.

"I'm not trying to make light of your situation. I am truly sorry that you're going through a separation, but I just saved you from breaking an ankle. I don't want to get married." Dave chuckles.

I look up and give him a shy smile. "You're right. You didn't need to know that."

"That's ok. Now I know not to propose to you," he teases.

I smile. "So, Dave, tell me why you joined this book club." I move to the other side of the sidewalk to avoid another couple walking hand in hand towards me.

Dave falls into place beside me. "Quick to change the subject, I see." He laughs and points to Mark and Miranda. "Mark is my friend. He just separated from *his* wife, and he joined this book club to meet women. I am here for moral support."

Wow. The dog and the cat are a couple. "Why go to a book club?" I would think that a bar or nightclub would be a better place to meet women, not that I'm an expert in that field.

"That's what I said! But his colleagues at the university talked him into it. They convinced him that he might pick up a hot librarian." He laughs, "Who knew that he would actually pick up a hot librarian."

"That is funny. Is that why you asked if I was a librarian too?"

"Maybe. And really, what are the odds that both Mark and I would meet someone at a book club." He smiles at me.

Odds might be in his favour, but not mine. I am not here to meet men. "I overheard you say that you are a dentist?" I change the subject.

"I am an orthodontist. My office is on Parliament, although, you don't need to know that. You have a beautiful smile." He looks at her. "You definitely do not need my services. Not those particular services anyway."

What services is he offering me? I don't think I want to know. "You're right. I've never needed braces, so I won't need your services. However, I can always refer my patients to you. Remember? I'm a child psychologist." I try to change that subject too.

"That would be great. I would appreciate that tremendously. Here's my business card." He reaches into his jacket pocket and hands me a silver embossed card with a sparkly molar in the top right hand corner. *Dave Chemello. DDS, MCID.* "Could I have one of yours?"

"I don't have any with me," I quickly lie. I don't want him to know my information. I don't need some random guy calling my office. Margie would be all over that.

"Oh." His face falls.

"We're here," I say thankfully, standing at the front door of the Blue Iguana.

Dave nods to the bouncer and opens the door. A waft of stale beer fills my nostrils and I am instantly reminded of the bars in university, the ones where Christine dragged me. I haven't been to a bar like this since I was first married.

My eyes adjust to the darker ambiance and I see a crowd of thirty-somethings standing at the bar and sitting in oversized booths. Some music that I've never heard before is playing loudly from an actual juke box. No one is dancing, but I see many couples standing together, talking. It's a dating scene. Steve and I didn't go to places like this. If we went for a drink, it was at a restaurant or lounge. This place is for singles.

Someone pokes me in the arm. It's Christine. She looks more gorgeous than ever. Her blonde hair falls in soft waves at her shoulders. She is wearing gray dress pants that hug every curve of her voluptuous body. And her blue blouse is loosely open, showing just a peak of her perfect double D's.

"Hey! Ci-Ci!" Christine says tiptoeing to reach my ear as she hugs me. She's about five foot two. "Who's the hottie?" Her blue eyes look in the direction of Dave. Hottie? Does she mean Dave? I guess he's a hottie. I didn't notice.

I tap Dave. "Dave, this is my friend, Christine."

Dave smiles and offers his hand to Christine. She shakes it and looks up through her lashes. "Nice to meet you," he says.

"You too." Christine looks at me and raises her eyebrows. I look at Dave and then back at Christine.

"Listen, I don't want to interrupt your girl's night. You two catch up. I'll go sit with Miranda and Mark. Maybe we can chat later?" Dave looks at me and I see that his eyes are green.

"Great. Yes. I need to talk to this girl. I haven't seen her in ages. Go see Mark and Miranda. I'll talk to you later," I spew out.

Dave smiles at me and nods at Christine, then walks away.

9.

Christine whistles. "I could have had him hook, line and sinker, but he likes you. He couldn't take his eyes off of you. You should do him."

Do him? Christine loves men. She uses them at her disposal and never regrets it or feels guilty about it. She is not arrogant or egotistical about it and she is obviously safe and protects herself against disease and pregnancy. Sex is a game to her and she enjoys the conquest. At first, I thought that Christine had self-esteem issues, but when we roomed together in our second year, Christine revealed that her parents had a volatile separation and divorce. She was subjected to many of her father's indiscretions that, as a young girl, she should not have been. She was daddy's girl and it hurt her tremendously. She thought that he could do no wrong. Now, Christine doesn't want a relationship because she saw how hurt her mother had been.

I used to watch, in worry, as Christine dated man after man, but she has remained strong and unscathed. She's not hurting herself or anyone else, so I never question her. It's unfortunate that society views promiscuity as unacceptable for females. I'm pretty sure that I couldn't be capable of playing the field, but for Christine, I can see why it would be liberating.

"Christine! Did you say that I should *do* him? He does not like me. We are in a book club together. And I will not *do* him. I'm not in college anymore," I protest.

Christine takes me by the hand and we walk to the bar, trying to squeeze our way to the front. "From what I remember, Ci-Ci, you didn't *do* anyone in college, except Steve. Now that you're not with him, you need some experience. I think it would be good for you to date a little. And you don't have to be in college to have casual sex."

"I don't know. I don't think I can have casual sex." I don't even know how to have regular sex apparently.

"This is the perfect time to have some fun, date a little and get funky in bed." She elbows me playfully.

I look around to see if the crowd around us overheard her. "I don't know. Besides, I still want Steve back. I can't start sleeping around. What if he finds out? I know he said some hurtful things, but I think he might be right about me. I need to change first," I say thoughtfully.

"Change? What are you talking about? You don't need to change. He hurt you! He left you!" Christine argues.

"He left me because I wasn't a good wife. I have issues. I need to learn how to relax and be exciting. I don't even know the first thing about being spontaneous. I need to become a better woman." How do I begin to do all that?

"I think you are perfect the way that you are, Ci-Ci. I don't know how you can think those things."

"Trust me. I need to change. I didn't fulfill Steve sexually." I barely look her in the eyes.

Christine stares at me and shakes her head. "I know that you are a smart woman and you wouldn't just make something like that up." I nod. She puts her arm around me. "Well, let's figure this out. You said that you need to change. It seems to me that the change you are looking for involves dating men."

"You're right." I sigh. I'm not going to learn these things without dating.

"Don't worry. I will be here to support you in any way that I can. Dating is my specialty."

"Thank you. The thought of meeting men and getting shot down really scares me," I confide.

"You? You get shot down? You have never known how utterly beautiful you really are, Ci-Ci. Boys were dying to date you in college. They always asked about you and you were just too into sports and studying that you didn't even notice or care. Then Steve scooped you up and your experience started and ended there. You need to find out how much you have to offer someone. You need to date and see what's out there. I think you'll surprise yourself," Christine says with sparkle in her eye.

We finally find an opening at the bar and Christine squeezes herself in between two men. They both look down and check her out.

I stand closely beside her. "Where do I even start?" I just made a huge decision. My stomach is moving around, kind of flip-flopping everywhere, and my heart rate has increased considerably. I'm nervous and excited and I really need to think about what I've just agreed to undertake.

"If this is what you really want to do, you can start with that tasty treat, Dave, over there. He is really into you. Before you leave tonight, set up a date with him," Christine suggests and she tries to wave down the bartender.

I can see Dave sitting in an oversized booth, drinking a Heineken. My stomach churns nervously. "That's easy for you to say. You know how to talk to men. I don't even know what to say to him."

Christine turns to the cute bartender, "Two vodka-waters, please". The bartender looks at her and then her breasts, gives her a lopsided grin and saunters off to make the drinks.

Christine turns to Colleen. "Let's not worry about that now. Get a couple of drinks into you and we'll come up with a game plan." Christine pays the bartender and tips him generously. He rings a bell at the bar that signals to everyone that he got a great tip. The bartender holds up his hand for Christine to high five him. She climbs on the brass step under the bar and just barely reaches his hand to comply. He winks at her and she smiles seductively.

Christine whispers to Colleen, "It's going to be a good night." She has found her next conquest.

We sit at a table away from Christine's co-workers and where I still have an unobstructed view of Dave.

"If you're going to play the field, you are going to need a bit of a makeover," Christine says.

"What do you mean?" I touch my hair. What's wrong with me now?

Christine laughs. "Not that kind of makeover. You're beautiful. You need to change the way your mind works. You seemed a little awkward with Dave and you don't have to be. He likes you and he already likes what he sees, but you do have to relax and flirt a little."

Flirt? I roll my eyes. "How do you do it?"

"Here's what you need to do with Dave. Touch him a little more, maybe on his arm." She touches my arm lightly with her fingertips. "You have to laugh at his jokes and maybe flip your hair back at the same time." Christine giggles and her hair sashays around her shoulders. "Oh, and keep eye contact with him for a little longer than normal when you're talking to him."

"Oh, that's all?" I play with the straw in my empty drink. It seems like a lot of stupid things to do, just to get a guy's attention. How am I going to add it all in?

The bartender comes over with two more drinks. "On the house," he says.

"Watch this," she whispers to me. She turns her head quickly to look at him and her blonde hair swishes around her face like before. She touches his hand, "Thank you so much." She gazes at him and he's the one who breaks eye contact. He looks almost shy, but he's not leaving. He's interested in her.

"You are very welcome. Now, don't you leave without saying goodbye."

"It's too early to leave." She laughs and tosses her hair off of her shoulder.

He walks away and looks back at her one more time. So, that's how it's done. She makes it look so easy.

Christine turns to me. "It might seem weird to you at first, maybe a little robotic, but it gets easier."

There's that word again. "Do you find me robotic?"

"No. You can be logical and sensible, but not robotic."

"Are you sure?"

She cocks her head to the side. "You're worrying too much. You have the great ability to adapt and change when you learn something new. I was worried that you would never meet someone and fall in love, but when you met Steve, you figured it out. He was your first kiss, your first boyfriend, and your first everything. You learned pretty quickly how all that worked. I'm sure you will ease into flirting and dating too, once you learn the basics."

"The last thing Steve said to me, before he left, was that I was a robot and I was methodical in bed," I admit quietly and take a sip of my second vodka water.

Christine looks at me sadly. "That bastard! That was immature. Now, I don't know how you are in bed because we never talked about sex in college. Well, *you* never talked about it. Do you think you're a robot?"

I blush and toy with my straw. "I think I might be."

"Why?" She looks stunned.

"I am just like you described me. I am logical and sensible. I live my life with those traits. You saw how I was in school. Everything in its place and everything has a place. I followed the perfect career path. My house is spotless. I'm organized to the extreme. My cell phone alerts me all the time, reminding me when to eat, drink water, exercise and to even have sex! I know I took these obsessive compulsive tendencies to the bedroom." Tears spring to my eyes.

"It couldn't have been that bad." Christine touches my arm.

I always start on top. I shake my head and look down. "Yes, it was that bad." I wipe my eyes with a bar napkin.

"Now I understand why you want to change. Do you like sex?"

"Yes! I loved it when Saturday came around. We had our Saturday night sex date. I would get new lingerie, light candles and think about it all day."

"Saturday night sex date? You only had it on Saturday nights?" Christine is in shock.

"Um... Yes. Believe me. I now see how robotic I am and how my obsessiveness with organization basically ended my marriage."

"How did sex become a one night scheduled session?"

"I don't know. He worked a lot and I worked more, and we weren't spending any time together, so it just seemed the smart thing to do. I was doing the only thing I know how. I organized my life. I didn't know that was wrong." I groan.

"You're not wrong. Organization is good to a point. You just need to allow a little spontaneity into your life, especially in the bedroom. That's where you need to let loose and create chaos!" Christine laughs.

That word chaos makes me nervous. "I'm not a chaotic person. Could we tone it down and maybe start with creative or open to suggestions?"

"Oh Ci-Ci! You definitely need to experience a one night stand. Casual sex will be liberating for you."

I laugh and relax a little. "I guess I'm talking to the right person. You should be a sex therapist."

"I want to *have* sex, not talk about it!" We laugh together. "Cheer up. What I do know about you is that when something is wrong, you fix it. Your degree is in what again?" She teases. "Psychology! You can do trial runs, hypothesize, and use placebos! Do whatever knowledge that psychology degree gave you to get experience."

"You know nothing about psychology, Christine." I laugh. "But I see where you are going with this. Einstein said that the only source of knowledge is experience. I can only get better at sex if I research and practice."

"Listen to yourself! Practice? You don't practice sex. You just do it. But that's my philosophy and a popular running shoe's slogan too. Maybe you need to find your own way. Psychology is your thing. Use it to your advantage to get the sexual experience you need."

"This makes sense to me. I can do this."

Just remember that sex is supposed to be fun. You need to loosen up," Christine teases.

I smile. "I guess. I'll do it for the love of science!" I raise my glass.

She pulls my hand down. "Before you do anything, take off your wedding ring."

"Oh," I say. I twist the platinum band that has three, two-carat diamonds, around my finger. "I guess I should do that." I pull it off and attach it to my key ring. I suddenly feel depressed.

"Shake it off, girl." She rubs my back. "Here comes Mr. Sexy Pants. Say yes when he asks you out, because he's going to ask."

10.

I freeze and watch Dave walk towards us. "Hi, ladies. Catch up on gossip?" He smiles and places his hands on our table.

I was so aloof and uninterested before. How do I switch modes? I stuff my key ring back into my purse.

Christine stands up. "Yes, we have. I just need to visit the ladies room. I'll be right back." She touches my shoulder and whispers in my ear, "Just say yes."

Dave slips in beside me on the bench seat. "You two were so animated talking to each other. I totally wanted to be a fly on the wall. What were you talking about?"

I blush again. "The usual girl stuff. Were you having fun with Miranda and Mark? I'm sorry that I didn't come over to see you yet."

"They're hitting it off, I think. Who knew that the book club would be such a dating gold mine? I honestly thought it would be like the movie, Revenge of the Nerds." Dave laughs.

I laugh, and try to tilt my head back sensually. "I love that movie." That was awkward.

"You have a beautiful laugh," he says. His green eyes gaze at me appreciatively.

He liked that? "I am a big nerd at heart, Dave." I briefly touch his arm.

He looks down at my hand and then looks into my eyes. "I like nerds."

I pull my hand away and quickly break eye contact. I have to work on that one.

He takes a deep breath. "Would you like to have dinner with me tomorrow night?"

Just say yes. Christine's words echo in my head. "That sounds nice."

"Awesome. You have my card, why don't you call me tomorrow?"

I dig into my purse, take a pen out and write on a napkin. "No. Here. This is my cell number. Call me tomorrow between twelve and one o'clock. That is during my lunch. I will not be available again until after five o'clock. We can confirm plans at that time. If I don't answer, I may have had an emergency client…" I trail off. I'm being controlling. "Forget what I said." I crumple up the napkin. "You're right. I have your number. I will call you tomorrow."

Dave laughs. "Will you?"

"I'm sorry. Yes, I give you my word." I'm barely listening. I'm trying to figure out how I would begin this type of research. If I'm going to learn something about sex, I need to have a game plan.

Christine takes that moment to return to the table. "Who wants another round of drinks?" Christine says, enthusiastically.

"I'm sorry. I have to go home. I work tomorrow at eight." I look at my watch. "Don't you have to work too, Christine?"

"Nope. Day off. I'm going to stick around a bit with my co-workers." She leans in close to whisper, "And work my magic with the bartender."

I shake my head. "I need your confidence."

"You have confidence, you just need to focus it." She turns to Dave, "Are you leaving as well?"

"Yes I am. I can walk you back to your car, Colleen," Dave suggests.

"That would be perfect," Christine butts in. "You can never be too safe." She winks at me.

"Thank you, Dave. I appreciate it." I glare at Christine. I really need some time to figure out how I am going to approach Dave.

Christine hugs me and whispers, "Call me tomorrow, Ci-Ci. And please just relax."

"I will try." I am in a completely new and foreign situation. My first date ever and I have no time to prepare for it. I am freaking.

He nods his head to Christine. "Nice to meet you."

"You too," Christine says, sweetly. Dave walks toward the door and I look back at Christine. Christine gives me two thumbs up and a big smile.

I shake my head, smiling. I catch up with Dave and he opens the door for me and we walk out.

"She's not too obvious, is she?" Dave asks jokingly.

"Christine definitely isn't shy, but she's just looking out for me. I have only been with one man my whole life and now, being separated, she is trying to help me experience life," I explain.

Dave is quiet. Did I say something wrong? I look down at my feet as I walk.

37

He clears his throat. "Do you always say what you're thinking?"

"Always," I say. Why wouldn't I? "Oh no. Christine has always told me to filter my thoughts. Did I share too much again?" I clench my fists tightly and shake my head. I feel so stupid. I want slap myself in the head.

"No, Colleen." He stops me. "I like that you are straightforward. It's refreshing in the dating world. Believe me. You are an intelligent woman and I like that you can tell me anything."

I keep looking down. I'm embarrassed and don't know how to react. I'm not used to compliments from anyone other than Steve.

"And right now, you are being pretty shy and sweet. I find that very appealing too." He gently lifts my chin up with one finger.

He finds me appealing. Interesting. I avoid his eyes. "I wouldn't say that I'm shy. Maybe inexperienced."

"You've only been with one man your entire life?" He asks incredulously.

I look him straight in his eyes. "Yes." I am a brave and strong woman.

He tips my chin up a little higher. "Can I kiss you?"

Oh. My stomach flip flops. I didn't see that coming. I can do this. For research, I tell myself. "Yes, you may."

Dave looks right into my eyes and steps closer to me. His hand is still at my chin and his other hand reaches softly past my neck and cups the back of my head. Still looking into my eyes, he comes closer, nose to nose. I close my eyes. I can't look at him. I immediately feel his lips on mine and they are soft. I open my mouth slightly and I feel a quick, gentle touch of his tongue on mine. It actually feels nice. My heart starts beating faster and I experiment with my tongue. I flick my tongue out to meet his, matching his every movement. This is surprisingly easy.

Both of his hands are behind my head now, but one hand tangles in my curls. I should make bodily contact too. I reach up and put my hands on his chest and slide them up to the back of his shoulders. I can feel his muscles through the material and I assume that he exercises, probably daily. I let the feeling of his lips and tongue and the closeness of our bodies override my thoughts. The kiss becomes more heated and our breath is ragged. He takes one hand down my back and pulls me closer. Our bodies are crushed together and I can feel his hardness against my hips. How can this feel so good? I don't remember feeling this way when I kissed Steve. I have never kissed Steve like this. I pull away from Dave and try to catch my breath.

"What's wrong?" Dave asks. "Did I go too far?"

"No," I say. I feel like I'm cheating on Steve. I look around and the streets are empty. This is happening way too fast.

"Then why did you stop?" Dave reaches for my hands. "I mean, this is not the best place to be making out, here on the sidewalk. But, I like it."

Relax. I smile up at him nervously. "It was wonderful, but I just need to slow down and think."

"I understand."

"If we are to go on a date tomorrow, I have to remind you that this is new to me. I don't have any experience dating at all."

"You'll be fine. If I make you feel uncomfortable or anything, just tell me."

"Are you sure that you still want to have dinner with me?"

"Absolutely."

He takes my hand and we start walking again. My brain is in overdrive. I have to cut out major emotions if this is going to succeed. I need to formulate objectives and conduct an informal experiment. Obviously Dave is my first sample, but I'll need a wide variety of subjects and environments.

"You better call me," Dave says.

"I said I would." He interrupts my thoughts. "This is me." I point to my car and dig my keys out of my purse.

Dave keeps his eyes on me and moves closer. He's going to kiss me again. Flip flop. He puts his hands on either side of my face and kisses me deeply. Our tongues, slowly and tantalizingly, move together. Oh my. This time he stops abruptly. Did I do something wrong? He takes the keys out of my hand, unlocks my door and opens it for me. "Drive safely," he says.

Oh. "Good night, Dave."

I get in my car and he before he closes it, he says, "Sweet dreams," and walks away.

I analyze what just happened. First, I automatically assume that I did something wrong because he stopped kissing me. Then I was disappointed that he stopped. So I lack confidence in my ability to kiss and I am a hypocrite. I tell him that I want to take things slow, but would've kept kissing him if I had the chance. I need to get my shit together.

I look in the rearview mirror and see that my face is flushed and my lips are swollen. I touch my fingers to them and remember the kissing. The car is cold, but my body is broiling. How can a stranger do this to me? I don't even know him, except that he is handsome, a nice person and he kisses extremely well. Can I use him for the experience? I wonder if he would mind. Do I even tell him? Probably not. I wouldn't want to make him self-conscious of his performance. I know how that feels. If he kisses well, can I assume that he's going to be good in bed? I hope so. I don't want to waste my time. If that's all that I need from him, then he should be able to teach me something, right?

Wow. I did not think that this is how my day would turn out. I go from being scared to change and not getting Steve back, to making out with a guy and scheduling a date with him. It feels like a dream, but I'm proud of myself and excited for the outcome.

I wonder how long it will take for me to become better in bed. How many men should I see? How many encounters should I experience? What will define the new, more relaxed, sexier and experienced me? The thoughts keep coming one after another. I don't know how I'm going to fall asleep.

11.

I actually do sleep well and wake before my alarm, completing eight miles on my treadmill easily. I drink my usual protein shake with one banana, one scoop of whey powder and one cup of coconut milk, while deciding what to wear. Getting dressed today is anything but normal. I might not be able to go home before my date with Dave, so I have a dilemma: Do I dress professionally for work or somewhat appealing for Dave. I take out many outfits, but finally decide on a sleeveless and backless, low-cut pale blue dress that hangs just below my knees. To make it appropriate for work, I add a light-weight knit top that buttons up to my sternum. I can take it off before the date. It works.

I am out the door at seven sharp and pull into my parking space fifteen minutes later. I feel energized and seem to have a zip to my step. My hair bounces as I walk tall towards the corner coffee shop. I don't think I need the caffeine, but I stop to get a latte anyway.

I order a vanilla latte and wait in line, with the other patrons, for it to be made. I can smell cinnamon rolls baking and I see the barista put a fresh tray in the glass display. I am tempted to go back and buy one.

"Colleen?" A voice says.

I look up. It's Jack Fraser, my husband's friend from work. Oh god. Not now. "Hi, Jack. How are you?" I smile politely.

"Good, Colleen. How about yourself?" He raises an eyebrow.

He is obviously referring to my mental state post-separation. "I'm fine, Jack. Really, I am." I avoid his eyes.

Jack has been over at my house more times that I can count, for dinner parties, work events and even birthday celebrations. His unshaven face, blonde hair and blue eyes make him a ruggedly handsome man, but he's Steve's friend. I could never look at him any other way. I wouldn't want to anyway because there's just too much history. I have laughed with him, finished off bottles of wine with him, and met his many girlfriends. He's quite a player and tends to primp in the mirror just as much as his girlfriends do. I see him like a brother. I don't even want to think about what Steve has told him about me over the years. I know that men gossip too. How embarrassing.

"You were always a strong woman. Don't let Steve's infidelity get you down." Jack touches my arm.

"What do you mean by infidelity?" I ask confused.

Jack stammers, "Oh, uh, I mean... Shit. You didn't know?"

"Know what?" I am angry, knowing that what Jack is about to say will hurt me tremendously. My body goes rigid and I can feel my teeth clenching tightly together. I think I may pass out. I've never felt this fluttery feeling in my chest before. It makes me want to scream.

"Maybe we can sit down and talk? I don't have to be at work until ten," Jack suggests.

I breathe deeply, thinking. Shoot. I have an appointment right at eight. "Give me one minute." I get my cell phone and dial the office. Margie answers immediately.

"Margie, something has come up. Please reschedule my eight and nine o'clock appointments.

"What? Are you ok?" I know Margie is shocked. I have never done this before.

"Yes. I'm ok. Something has come up."

"Are you sure you're ok?"

"Yes. Please just apologize for me and I'll be there for ten." Silence. "Margie? Did you hear me?"

"Yes, I'm just worried about you."

There's that fluttery feeling in my chest again. "I am fine. Trust me."

"Ok... I'll see you at ten."

I hang up. I have never rescheduled my appointments before, but this could be the key I've been looking for. This could be the *something* that never added up when Steve left.

"Let's talk, Jack." I turn to the barista and take my latte from her.

We sit down and I notice that he's playing with his coffee cup and avoiding my eyes. "Listen, Jack. I realize that you're Steve's friend, not mine, and I understand that it might be hard to divulge secrets that he may have disclosed, but--."

Jack cuts me off. "Colleen, I'm not afraid of losing his friendship. I lost all respect for him a long time ago," Jack says. "Why do you think I stopped coming over?"

"From what I remember, you got a big promotion and you were too busy for him." I try to recollect, "That's right. Steve said that you were a hot head and that your ego wouldn't get through our door anymore. His words, not mine. I believed him."

"Typical Steve," he mutters. "He's been a real dick. Listen, I'm more afraid of hurting you further than he already has. What has he told you? What were his reasons for the separation?"

I blush. Maybe Jack doesn't know everything. "He wasn't happy. He had issues with me and he just didn't want to be married to me anymore."

"He blamed you? That's just great. Colleen, he doesn't deserve you and you don't deserve this pain. He is a liar. You need to know the truth."

"Ok. Tell me." I brace myself.

"Steve is dating someone and he has been for about six months. He was cheating on you." Jack watches me, "With his secretary."

My heart drops in my chest and I feel nauseous. I put my coffee on the table because my hands are shaking. I'm deflated. My entire body feels heavy and if I let it, I would fall toward the ground. I can't hold myself up much longer. I gulp for air. His secretary? I met her numerous times. At his work parties and dinners with his boss. She's so young.

"He wanted me to cover for him the last time he travelled to Ottawa, but I wouldn't do it. I think you wanted to meet him for the weekend in Ottawa, but he was with her, so he needed an excuse. He wanted me to vouch for him and tell you that he had important meetings all weekend or some stupid story like that."

"I remember that. I didn't end up going because his secretary called me…" My voice trails off. The same secretary he's screwing. I am so stupid. I clear my throat, trying not to cry. Six months? I didn't even know he was unhappy. How could I have pushed him away into the arms of another woman?

"I am so sorry. There was no way that I could lie to you and when I told him how I felt, that he was wrong and that he should be honest with you, he didn't want to hear it. He became angry with me and we haven't talked since."

I have to shake this off. This is definitely the *something* that I needed to know about. "I'm sorry that you were put in that position," I say, thinking out loud. "Thank you for trying, but I may have caused him to cheat. I wasn't the best wife." I take a napkin and wipe the table in front of me. Yes, Steve wouldn't have cheated if he was content.

"What? That's not true. You can't make someone cheat."

"He was unhappy in our marriage. I don't blame him for trying to find happiness elsewhere." I fold the napkin in half and place it under my latte. This makes more sense. How stupid am I?

"If he was unhappy in your marriage, he should have told you and you could have worked on it together," he scolds and shakes his head angrily.

"Maybe he couldn't talk to me. Or maybe I wouldn't listen." Steve did say that I don't listen to him.

"Why are you defending him? Every time I was at your house, you were charming and attentive. You made sure that everyone was comfortable. You are an amazing person, extremely sweet and funny. God, you did anything to please everyone, Steve included. I don't know how he could have been unhappy." He grabs my hands.

"You obviously don't know everything," I say sternly.

"Colleen, it's not your fault! Fuck! I didn't want to tell you this, but after seeing your reaction, you have to know. The woman that he's seeing now is not the first woman that he's been with since you've been married." He avoids looking at me and takes his hands away.

"You're just saying that."

"No I'm not. I would never lie to you. It kills me to tell you this."

"How many do you know of Jack?" I ask.

"Three or four," he says quietly.

I gulp and try to swallow the bile that is rising up my throat. "How do you know?" I manage to say.

"He had meetings with women behind locked office doors and I know they weren't clients. He was late for meetings and showed up frazzled with lipstick on his face. He said it was yours, but you don't wear lipstick."

"I could have."

"Colleen, you don't. I know you."

He's right. I never wear lipstick. "But he never admitted his affairs to you, so how can you be so sure?"

"We're friends. I'm a man. I just know."

"When did you first know?"

"It was before he got his promotion to regional manager."

I do the mental math. Three years ago. We've only been married for four years.

"I don't mean to be the snitch. I'm not looking for you to find solace in me. I'm so sorry, Colleen. I always wanted to tell you because I respect you, but it wasn't my place." He touches my hands again.

I ignore his comforting words and look down at my latte. It's not that he met this woman and now it's true love. He's just a habitual cheater. I'm not sure if that's better or worse. I put my elbows on the table and my hands over my face.

"You deserve better." He moves his chair closer to me and touches my shoulder.

I look up. "No. No. I made him do this." We used to be in love and then I messed it up. I shake off his hand. Steve was just trying to relieve his sexual frustration from only having sex once a week. It's worse than I thought. I'm worse than I thought. I loved him so much, but he only saw how I controlled the sex in our relationship. I controlled everything. I emasculated him. How could he even look at me or respect me when I treated him as my subordinate.

"You can't make someone cheat! He's just that type of guy. You keep saying that he wasn't happy with you, but I think he's always going to be in pursuit of the next best thing. Nothing or no one can make him happy. It's not you at all. Nothing is wrong with you. Please believe that. You are a smart and beautiful woman. You are amazing. He is the idiot who didn't know how good he had it with you."

"Really? You think he had it good with me? Didn't he ever talk about his sex life with me? I bet he never admitted to you that I was a robot or methodical in bed," I blurt out.

"Never Colleen," his voice is low. "And I don't believe any of that for a second." He takes my hand. "He only told you those lies to make it easier for him to leave you. He already had a new girlfriend. He's not going to tell you that he's screwing around on you. He told you something to make him feel better about leaving you"

"He's never lied to me before. I just don't believe it."

"Jeez Colleen. You're doing exactly what he wants. He wants you to feel bad and take the blame."

I shake my head. "I do take the blame." I stare blankly at the customers coming into the coffee shop. How many of them just lost the love of their life? How many of them are at fault? Well, I'm going to own up to my mistakes.

"Come on, Colleen. I know it's difficult right now, but try to realize that he is scum," he says gently. "You are not responsible for the end of your marriage."

I am at fault, but it's not the end of my marriage. I know what I have to change and I'm going to reconcile with him. I push my chair out and our connection breaks as I stand up. "I have to go to work, Jack. Thank you for telling me this. I appreciate your honesty. Take care."

Jack stands up. "Colleen, please don't leave upset. I have to know you're alright."

"I'm fine. I promise." I give him a half-hearted smile and hastily leave the coffee shop. Don't cry. Shake it off. I'll use this information to fuel my motivation to get the experiment started.

12.

As soon as I get to my office, I quickly say hello to Margie, ignore her questioning look and close my office door. I begin to research infidelity. If I pinpoint why he cheated, then I can gear my research towards specific sexual goals. *Research studies indicate that twenty-two percent of men and thirteen percent of women cheat in a marriage.* That seems pretty low. *Signs that he is cheating include: working late a lot, taking trips that the other spouse can't go on, credit card bills for unexplained gift-type items and distance, anger and pickiness.* While a lot of those points ring true, I skip to the section about why mean cheat. There are ten reasons, but five are inane. Really? Steve wouldn't cheat because he was bored or because he lacks male-bonding.

I write down some of the realistic reasons in a fresh notebook.

1) *He is immature.*
2) *He is addicted.*
3) *He is insecure.*
4) *He wants out.*
5) *He has unrealistic expectations.*

I look at the five reasons and assess each one as it relates to Steve. While Steve can be juvenile by buying trivial toys and gadgets, and spending too much on something that he could have gotten cheaper, he is definitely not immature. This reason is pretty illogical too. He is a smart man. He has always had pursuits and a lot of ambition. While his professions over the years have changed quite a bit, his present career is something that he excels at and enjoys. He's never been a ladies man. I don't think he counted the notches on his belt. That's what immature men do. I don't believe this is the reason as to why he cheated. I cross it off the list.

I can't fathom Steve being an addict either. Someone with an addiction would show signs just as an alcoholic or drug addict would. I'm sure that he would have showed signs early on in our relationship, like using sex to self-soothe or escape. He could have been hiding it all along, but that would make me incompetent as a psychologist. I am educated to perceive those types of signs. I don't know why I wrote this one down. I scribble out number two.

Is he insecure? He has never required compliments or an ego boost from me or anyone else. He was above that. He had quite the self-esteem in university, but he was an amazing volleyball player and deserved to boast and be proud about that. He excelled at every job he obtained and has been the top sales representative since being at his present company. His pride is too great to succumb to an extramarital affair just to feel better or feel desirable. However, if I emasculated him by unknowingly making him my subordinate, that would have crushed his ego. Maybe he cheated to build himself up again. Why didn't I see this sooner? I made him a weak man.

Number three leads to number four. I made him feel impotent and that lead to cheating, which leads to an easy end to our marriage. He wanted out. What other reason would there be for him to want out? My stomach ties up in a knot. There are all of those reasons he told me. Unhappiness. My controlling issues. I can't relive it again.

The next one sits heavy in my mind. Did he have unreasonable expectations about our relationship and marriage? Was I supposed to be the doting wife? I did work a lot of hours. Perhaps I should have been there for him for him more. I obviously didn't meet his every sexual and emotional need. I was too focused on my career and even brought it home with me. I failed him and he felt entitled to seek intimate attention elsewhere.

The last three reasons make sense and it proves the need for my research. The first goal of my research will be to focus on my date with Dave. It seems simple, but I need to prepare emotionally and mentally. Actually, first I need to confirm our date. After the few morning appointments I have, I call Dave on my lunch break.

"Good afternoon, Dr. Chemello's office. How can I help you?" A friendly voice asks.

"May I please speak to Dr. Chemello?" I ask politely.

"Whom may I ask is calling?"

"Colleen Cousineau." And then I'm put on hold. Loosen up. Flirt. Have fun. I repeat Christine's words. Within a minute, I hear Dave's voice.

"Good afternoon, Colleen. I'm happy that you called," Dave says.

"Why wouldn't I, Dave? I'm looking forward to having dinner with you this evening." Did that sound too forced? I try to giggle. It sounds weird.

"Great. Me too. What time are you free?" He asks.

"I'll be finished with my last patient at six." I line up my notebook so that the bottom of it is two inches from the edge of my desk and perfectly straight.

"Well, I'm done here at five-thirty. I can swing by and pick you up, if that's ok?"

"Yes, that's fine. My office is at 324 Charles Street," I say. "I'll lock up and meet you outside." I am too formal. I knock the notebook sideways and try giggling again.

"Perfect. I can't wait to see you," he says.

"Yes. Me too. Good bye, Dave." I suck at this.

"See you soon."

Time passes by slowly and, of course, my last patient cancels. Margie left already and I have over an hour to wait for my date. I start researching again. The articles I read about women and casual sex provide no new insights. I already know that the female brain is not biologically set up to have casual sex. Women react with bonding, attachment and love after sex. It seems that all of these articles focus on the negative aspects of casual sex. Women tend to feel regret, disappointment and even depression after one night stands. I become doubtful and scared. That is not what I need. I need to know how to feel detachment and indifference. How does Christine do it? I give her a call.

"I would have called you first thing this morning, but I figured you were either hung over or preoccupied with a certain bartender," I tease.

"Try both. But apparently morning sex cures a hangover too." She laughs and then moans. "I'm still not ready to laugh yet. Head still hurts."

"Was it worth it?" I need to know.

"Definitely. He was a Grade A specimen. I do know how to pick them."

"Is he still there? I need to ask you a question."

"No, he's gone. I kicked him out first thing this morning."

"This is what I wanted to talk to you about. How do you not form a connection with the men you have sex with?" I ask.

"It's not difficult. I like men, but I don't need the romance. I hook up with a guy based on great chemistry and the desire to be... Sorry Ci-Ci, I have the desire to be fucked."

I'm glad she can't see me blushing. "Is fucking the same as making love?"

"Probably not. I have no desire to love the guy I'm fucking. I don't exchange information with him or go out on a date, and I don't want to see him again," Christine says.

"You have a different brain than most women," I mutter. I alphabetize the psychology magazines on my desk and stack them, lining up their spines. "Most women hook up with men to eventually find someone to marry. It's our evolutionary drive."

She laughs. "Not me. I am in constant pursuit of pleasure, not settling down. If I hooked up with a guy thinking that I wanted to find a life partner, then I would probably be in a relationship."

I pause to think. "I think I understand you. By changing a small factor in the way that I think, the outcome will be different." Could it be that easy? "If I believe that casual sex will help me get experience, then I will be able to participate and benefit from it."

"Right on, Ms. Psychologist! But try not to be so scientific. Go on your date with an open mind. If something happens, trust your instincts. Live in the moment. And don't feel guilty for getting lost in the experience," she coaxes. "You have needs too."

"I think I'm ready to experience sex without a commitment." I'm trying to convince myself.

"Good luck and call me tomorrow to tell me how your date went."

"I will."

13.

I walk over to my bookshelf, scan the titles, and pull out two books: *Qualitative Research* and *Self-Determination Theory*. I scan the chapters, open each book to a specific page and start scribbling in the same notebook that I used to dissect infidelity:

Goal - *To become more sexual for my husband*
- *I am inexperienced, mechanical, controlling, "methodical", a "robot".*
- *I want to relax and experience/learn different styles of sexual behavior: foreplay, intercourse, flirting, role-playing, et cetera!!!*

Research question development
- *What does existence of feeling or experience indicate concerning the phenomenon to be explored:*
    - *I am nervous, unknowledgeable and shy (about sex).*
    - *Never dated a man, where do I meet them?*
    - *No self-confidence, will I be able to meet men? Please them?*
    - *No set standards or benchmarks.*
    - *Only been with one man in 32 years.*
    - *Only know 1 position and how to pleasure a man 1 way.*
- *What are necessary & sufficient constituents of feeling or experience?*

- Need to be bold, outgoing and confident.
- Open to new experiences.
- Meet all types of men.
- Obtain a new outlook on casual sex
- What is the nature of the human being?
  - To follow a moral code, no promiscuity, be monogamous/have a relationship.
  - However, if the motivation behind the choices I make are for the 'right' reasons, then it is healthy and appropriate.

Method

- No clearly defined steps to avoid limiting creativity of researcher.
- Sampling & data collection.
- Seek persons who understand study & are willing to express inner feelings & experiences.
- Describe experiences of phenomenon.
- Direct observation.
- Audio or videotape?

Data analysis

- Classify & rank data
- Sense of wholeness
- Examine experiences beyond human awareness/ or cannot be communicated

Outcomes

- Findings described from subject's point-of-view
- Researcher identifies themes

If I believe I am doing this experiment for the right reason then, according to the self-determination theory, my well-being will thrive. Basically, if I can convince myself that casual sex is appropriate, then I should excel at it or become better. I am satisfied with this guideline for my research. Hopefully this will keep me focused.

14.

    I look at the time and realize that I only have minutes before I have to meet Dave outside. I check out my reflection in the mirror and try to primp quickly. I add a dab of lip gloss, try to smooth my unruly curls and I pop a mint into my mouth. Almost forgetting, I unbutton the knit top and take it off, revealing the low-cut neckline. My goal is to get experience. Let's do this.
    I step into the waiting room, reach over the reception desk to turn off the mini light that Margie always forgets to shut off, and I hear the front door open. I turn around to see Dave standing there. He looks athletic and toned in a pale blue polo shirt. The shirt compliments his green eyes.
    "You look stunning. That is a beautiful dress." He eyes me appreciatively.
    "Thank you. You look great too. I thought I was meeting you outside?" I question, but then quickly say, "Not that I mind." I have to stop being so bossy.
    "I figured I could help you with your coat." He takes it from me and as he helps me into it, I feel his fingers graze my bare shoulders.
    Flip flop. "Thank you," I say again, as I turn around.
    "You're welcome." He's looking intensely at me.
    "Shall we go?" I squeak. We walk outside and I take a deep breath to calm down, while locking the office door. I can do this.
    He takes my elbow and guides me down the path. "I thought we could go to *Il Fornaro* for dinner. Do you like Italian?"
    "Yes, I do. And we can walk there, it's so close." It's another pleasant October evening.
    "That's what I was thinking, but I didn't know if you could walk in those heels." He points at my six inch pumps. "After last night's potential fall, I'm not sure how steady you are."

"Don't worry. I'm well-trained, but I do prefer my running shoes." I smile at him. "However, I'm pretty sure that I could run five miles in these heels."

Dave laughs. "You must be a runner to have legs like yours." He's flirting. This is to be expected.

"Do you work out, Dave?" I already know the answer, remembering the solidness of his pectorals and deltoids, but I should give him a chance to boast about himself.

"Yes, I have a membership at one of the squash and racquetball clubs. They have weights there too. I used to play tennis in university and now I just try to keep in shape. I usually go after work, so I am blaming you for missing my workout today, Dr. Cousineau," he teases.

Would he consider sex a workout? Wow. Where did that come from? I'm getting way ahead of myself. "I used to play volleyball in university," I say quickly. "Well, I still do. I play on a co-ed team at the university. And I workout at home or run outside, usually early mornings. I know what it feels like to miss a workout, so I'm sorry I'm taking you away from that tonight, Dr. Chemello." I look at him and smile.

"I don't mind missing a workout. It's nice to indulge once in a while." There's a sparkle in his green eyes. "Wouldn't you agree?" He flirts.

"Absolutely." This is going well, but this is the easy part.

Our walk to *Il Fornara* is only seven blocks, past a lot of taverns and bars. It's Friday night and there are crowds everywhere. The sidewalks are starting to get busier, restaurant patios are still open and people are pushing their way around us, almost separating us. Dave grabs my hand and pulls me right beside him.

"I don't want to lose you in this crowd," he says. I smile. Body contact is acceptable.

We arrive at the restaurant and Dave opens the door for me. Inside, I look at all of the pretentious Italian décor. The checkered tablecloths, images of grapevines, and a large mural of major Italian tourist attractions create the right atmosphere, but I find it so fabricated. Thankfully, Dave has a reservation for an outside table on the patio and we are lead out another set of doors to the gated area in the front of the restaurant. A few eight foot tall propane heaters are lit up. It's very cozy.

Dave pulls out my chair, and when I am seated, he runs his hand along my bare back. Flip flop. He bends to whisper in my ear, "I've wanted to touch your skin since I met you in your office tonight." He sits down beside me, inches away. "You look incredible in that dress."

I am at a loss for words. I lightly rub my stomach, trying to calm it.

"Are you hungry?" He's referring to my belly rubbing.

"Um no… I mean, yes," I stammer. I start lining up the forks with the placemat, and then push it away, messing it up.

He cocks his head and smiles. "Which is it?"

I take a deep breath. "I have butterflies when you touch me. I'm trying to get them to settle down."

Dave takes my hand. "Butterflies, eh? I won't tell you what you're doing to me. It wouldn't be appropriate," he murmurs.

Oh my. Is he referring to his… his… nether parts? He is taking flirting to the next level.

"Let's get some wine to calm your butterflies." He signals the waiter to come over. "Would you like white or red?"

"Red, please."

He turns to the waiter. "Could you suggest a bottle of red, please?"

While Dave chooses a red, I think about a time I was on a patio having dinner with Steve. It was romantic, with candles and wine, but he kept leaving the tale to take calls from work. A big deal was going through at work and he had to make sure all the details worked out perfectly. I didn't mind because it was a beautiful night and I was in love. He could do no wrong. But it seemed like every time Steve went to take a call, the waitress was nowhere to be found. I overheard some patrons getting upset over this fact. They wanted another glass of water or they wanted to pay the bill. The last call he took, lasted a very long time and the waitress never came out. I finished my dessert and a third glass of wine. When he finally came back, his tie was askew and his hair a mess. He said that the call got heated, but the deal was done. The waitress came by with our bill and I swear they exchanged a glance, but I thought I was being crazy. Now, I'm not so sure.

"You are quiet," he states and takes my hand. The waiter is gone. "I don't want to overstep my boundaries or scare you, and maybe I shouldn't have alluded to how you arouse me, but you are an extremely beautiful woman. Ever since we kissed last night, I can't stop thinking about you and what you do to me. I hope I am not being too forward." He looks at me questioningly.

Flip flop. "I'm not afraid," I say, bravely looking into his eyes. "I'm just not used to this type of attention or flirting. And what my body is feeling is definitely new too, but I am certainly not afraid."

Dave starts to lean in. I think he's going to kiss me.

"Here is your wine, sir." The waiter uncorks the bottle, pours a little in the glass, for Dave to taste it.

Dave sits up straight and takes a sip from his glass. He does all of this without taking his eyes off of me. He says to the waiter, "It's fine."

The waiter pours me a glass, and fills the rest of Dave's, and the waiter says, "I'll be back soon to take your order."

Dave is really forward. I pick up my glass and take a sip. I need to pick up the pace and predict some of his moves. I can't be shocked or embarrassed every time he flirts or compliments me.

"Here's to you, Colleen, and a memorable evening," Dave says and we clink our glasses together.

Dinner is wonderful and I actually settle down. It could be the wine relaxing me, but our conversation flows nicely and I momentarily forget about my main goal. We eat slowly and talk about our time at university, our practices, and some of the patient woes we endure.

Dave brings up my marriage. "How long have you been separated?"

"Just over a month."

"That's not very long at all. How long were you married?"

"Almost five years."

"Just a blink of time."

I quickly turn the conversation to him. "Have you ever been married?" I don't want to get sad and depressed.

"No, I was engaged once. It didn't work out."

"I'm sorry," I say.

"Don't be. I was too young. Lately I've been dating quite a bit, but I'm not a player, and I'm definitely not looking for a wife at the moment." He laughs. "I am learning about what makes women tick."

"Have you figured it out?"

He laughs again. "No, I haven't. Every woman is different. I do know that they wanted to be treated with respect and they just want to be happy. If I can do that, even just on one date, then I know that I'm doing alright."

This man is safe to be with. I relax even more.

Another bottle of wine is ordered and we talk about volleyball and tennis and where we have travelled. I try to touch his arm or hand during the conversation. I want to show him that I'm interested. He reciprocates and squeezes my hand often.

The waiter clears our empty dishes and hands us dessert menus. As I peruse the menu, Dave places his hand on my upper thigh, "I love your curly hair. You are incredibly sexy." I can feel the heat from his hand through my dress.

The waiter asks us if we would like anything. Dave gazes at me, his eyes travel down my body and up again. "Colleen, would you like dessert?"

I give Dave the same sensual gaze. Game on. "No, thank you. I don't think that there's anything on the menu that I want." I can't believe I just said that.

Dave's mouth opens slightly and his eyes darken. It works. Such an old pick up line and I pulled it off. Now I'll have to pay the consequences.

The waiter looks at us, takes out the bill from his apron, places it between us, and says, "Have a good evening." Did I make the waiter uncomfortable?

Dave slowly pulls his eyes away from me and reaches into his back pocket for his wallet. He looks at the check, throws a couple of one hundred dollar bills on the table and says, "Let's go." He stands up and pulls my chair out, and helps me put my coat on. He guides me to the door with his hand on my lower back. I'm getting nervous, but excited at the same time.

15.

Outside, we walk only a little way past the restaurant when he grabs my hand and pulls me into a dimly lit alleyway beside the restaurant. Before I know what is happening, his lips are on mine, hungrily. Flip flop. More surprises. His tongue is soft, but urgent, and I let mine react, matching his intensity. One of his hands goes through my open coat and I can feel his fingers grasping the waist of my dress. His other hand is behind my head, fingers tangled in my curls, massaging my scalp and neck. His hips are pressing into mine and I feel his hardness. It feels so sensual.

I gently push back, testing, and I hear him groan. I guess that was a good move. He steps back an inch, while gently holding onto my upper arms, "Would you like to come to my apartment?" His voice is husky.

And so it begins. "Yes," I say. I am incredibly anxious, but I try to focus on the outcome of my research.

We walk back to my office holding hands, but in silence. He stops at a black Volvo and opens the passenger door. I scoot in, but he doesn't close the door. I look up and he's eyeing me. "Damn, you have gorgeous legs." He winks and closes the door.

I am beside myself. I don't know what to expect. I don't know what to do. Can I do this? I'm starting to perspire a little, and my heart is beating out of my chest. Am I going to pass out? Just breathe.

He gets in the car and we pull out and drive down the street. His Volvo is manual, so it keeps his hands busy, but at a red light, he reaches across the stick shift and touches my thigh. It tickles and I get goose bumps all over my body. I think I'm holding my breath. We just look at each other, not saying a word, and then the light changes to green and he releases my thigh. I finally exhale. I don't know if I can go through with this.

About ten minutes later, we are at his apartment on Queen's Quay. He parks out front and gives a valet his keys. He takes my hand and leads me through the automatic door. We walk past a front desk with a doorman, who says, "Hello, Dr. Chemello." Dave just nods and keeps walking, with me in tow.

The lobby is very striking and almost imposing. The dim lighting and lavishness of dark wood give the space a dark, masculine atmosphere. I look behind me and the entrance doors soar upwards for almost two stories. I feel very small and out of place. We stop at the elevator and he pushes the button.

Dave asks, "Are you ok?" I nod timidly.

"No, you're not." He smiles. "Listen, we are just going up to my apartment. We'll have a glass of wine and relax." The elevator door opens, we step in and he presses the number eleven. He turns to me and takes my face in his hands, "It got a little heated, but we can calm things down again." He gives me a peck on the lips. I take a deep breath. I feel better, but I'm only going to see this man once. Things can't slow down. That isn't the plan. I don't want a new boyfriend. I need to sleep with him. *Get it together, Colleen.*

The elevator door opens and he takes my hand again, to walk me to apartment 5501. There are only three other doors on the floor. He selects a key from his key ring and opens the door. I walk into an expansive living room, decorated in browns and tans. It features a gas fireplace with a marble hearth and mantle, and a large beige rug made of wool and silk partially covers the gorgeous oak hardwood floors.

"Here. Let me take your coat." I turn around and he helps me out of it and he slides open the closet door to put it away.

I walk to the large windows overlooking Toronto Harbour. It's hard to make out the water in the dark, but the light from the moon makes Lake Ontario sparkle. The docks and patios are still brimming with people. This city never sleeps. The Harbourfront Centre is my favourite place to go when I have free time. On Sundays, I often walk along the water, grab a salad and find a bench by the water's edge to people watch.

"Make yourself comfortable," I hear him say. "I'll get you a glass of wine."

I sit down on the joint of the L-shaped brown suede couch. "Your apartment is beautiful and the view is spectacular. How long have you lived here?"

"About seven years." He must be in the kitchen. "I love summertime in Toronto. I always visit the different ethnic festivals at the Harbourfront. There's great food and music." He appears, with two glasses of wine, "What am I saying? You live here too. You must go to the festivals, right?" He offers me a glass. I take it,

"Yes I do. I like the Greek festival best." I take a large sip of wine.

"Souvlaki and ouzo... Mmmm." He smiles and sits right next to me, putting his feet up on the marble-top coffee table that has a large stump of wood as the base.

I scrunch up my nose. "Not so much the ouzo, but I'll take the baklava."

"You like sweets? I never would've thought that considering what an amazing and fit body you have. And you didn't have dessert tonight either."

"Trust me. I like sweets. What woman doesn't? You must have learned that dating." I smile. "Like you said before, it's nice to indulge once in a while, but I believe you have to pick your indulgences." I didn't mean anything by that statement, but I quickly realize my own double entendre. So does Dave. He stares at me and smiles. I blush and I'm about to rephrase and explain myself, but Dave beats me to it.

"You didn't mean that statement to be bursting with sexual innuendo, did you?"

"Not that time." I laugh.

"That was funny. You don't look very comfortable," he says, putting his feet down and placing his wine glass on the table. "Please sit back." He gestures to the corner of the back of the couch. Ok. I start to get nervous again, but I wriggle back.

He reaches down and picks up my feet, very gently, and looks at me for permission. I nod. He smiles at me, and holding both feet, he proceeds to take off one shoe and places it on the floor, followed by the other. Still holding both of my feet up, he slides down the couch towards me, so that my calves end up resting on his lap.

I am very aware that my skirt has travelled slightly up my thighs and I'm not sure if I should pull it down. I don't know if my panties are showing. His hands start to come towards my thighs and I panic and start to sit up. Already? But he just grasps the hem of my skirt and gently pulls it down to its length. I relax and sit back. This is nice. I can handle this. I take another sip of wine.

Dave looks at me and grins, but positions his hands on my knee, the one furthest away from him, and he starts massaging my knee in a gentle, rotating motion. He continues to slide his hands slowly down my leg, feeling the shin, and sides of the calf and down to my ankle and the top of my foot. He lifts my foot slightly off of his thighs and kneads my foot with his very capable hands. His thumbs rest on the top of my foot and his fingers press into my arch, from my heel to the ball of my foot. He takes his time and it feels wonderful.

He squeezes my big toe. "Pressure on the big toe is supposed to affect your head. Do you feel anything?"

"Not specifically. You are relaxing me entirely, not just my head. Do you know about reflexology?"

"I studied it briefly and it has always interested me." He squeezes the top of my arch on the outside of the sole of my foot. "What about now?"

"It feels good. Where am I supposed to be feeling it?"

"Your spleen."

I laugh. "Nope. I don't feel it."

"How about here?" He squeezes the inside of my heel, close to the arch of my foot.

"My esophagus?"

"I must be doing it wrong." He massages the same spot gently. "Now?"

"I give up."

"Hmmmm. This stuff doesn't work. You were supposed to feel it... uh... in your..." He stops and smiles at me.

I blush and giggle. "You definitely missed that spot."

"What man can ever find it?" We laugh together.

He continues to slide his hand up and down the outsides of my foot with gentle pressure. "I figured that you deserve this massage for wearing those shoes." Dave lifts my leg a bit higher, surprising me and bends down to kiss my big toe. This could be considered foreplay. It's very sensual and erotic and I am sexually stimulated by it. He places my foot back on his lap and repeats the same process, starting at my other knee. I sit back and close my eyes. I am enjoying his touch, but I start to realize that it's not going to end at the foot massage. I begin to tense up again. I feel him lift my leg higher and I open my eyes, he's kissing my other big toe. He lifts both of my legs up from his lap and slips out from beneath them. He stands up and takes the glass of wine from my hands and places it on the tree stump table. Here we go.

He sits down beside, looking at me. "I just want to kiss you."

Flip flop. He's asking permission. It's now or never. I take another breath, place my hands on either side of his face and pull him down to meet my lips. I didn't know I could be so bold. His mouth explores mine and I search his with my tongue. His lips are soft and I can taste wine. I like kissing him.

I'm partly lying on the couch with my head resting on the cushion and he's half-turned towards me, holding himself up with one hand. His other hand is on my hip, pulling me toward him. Our kissing deepens and it sends electric pulses down between my legs. His hand travels up my body and comes to rest on the back of my neck. His lips leave mine and he gives me fluttery kisses on my cheek, my ear and then down my neck. I tilt my head to the side to give him more access because it feels so nice. One of my hands is on his still on his face, feeling the stubble on his cheek. My other hand has grabbed on to his polo shirt and I notice that I'm breathing heavily. My hips are twisting towards him involuntarily. I still can't believe that kissing does this to me. It feels wonderful. When did this connection disappear with Steve? I know he used to have this effect on me. I guess I didn't try to make it work. I fell into a boring old scheduled routine.

I need a break. "I'm sorry. I need to um…"

"The washroom?" He smiles and points down the hall. "It's the first door on the right."

I stand up, smooth my dress down and walk down the hall. I turn into the first doorway and turn on the light. It's the bathroom. I close the door. I turn on the sink, put my hands on the counter and look at myself in the oval mirror.

I can't be thinking about Steve when I'm with Dave. I'm not going to get the desired data for my research if I keep that up. It's pep talk time.

I start whispering to myself, "Look how nervous you are. You need to get over these insecurities and fears and learn something that you can take back to your husband. You need to be a good wife. He left you because you are horrible in bed. Dave can help you. You can do this." I wash my hands, turn off the faucet and dry my hands.

I look at myself one more time. "You can do this."

I slowly walk back to the living room, taking deep breaths, and sit beside Dave on the couch.

"Are you ok?" Dave asks gently.

I nod and look up shyly at him.

He leans towards me and gently kisses me. Flip flop. His hands touch the bare skin on my back and he pulls me close. I give into his soft lips and searching tongue and melt into his arms.

All of a sudden, Dave stops and he puts his hand out for me to take, "Come with me," he whispers.

Where does he want to take me? Where are we going? I'm not sure if I should go. I trust him and everything he is doing feels amazing and I feel comfortable with him. Stop questioning. Relax. *You can do this.* I take his hand.

He starts walking down the hallway of his condo, with me in tow. He kicks open a door with his foot and we're in his bedroom. Oh dear. I wasn't expecting this. But, really? What did I expect? His bedroom is all browns and beiges again. The bed looks soft and inviting, with a lot of pillows. But I am panicking. I've only been with Steve. How can I do this with another man?

I try to buy time and walk to his dresser and pick up a bottle of cologne. I smell it. It's the kind that he is wearing tonight. I look around the room. There aren't any pictures or artwork. What do I do now? I turn to look at Dave and I freeze.

Dave walks up to me and puts his arms around me, his hands rest on the back of my shoulders. I put my arms around his waist and my cheek on his chest. We stand there, holding each other, for a few minutes. It's nice and soothing. I miss this kind of comfort.

He pulls away and looks at me. "I will stop if you tell me." And he kisses me again. I start to relax in his arms. It feels so nice. I put my hands on his chest, feeling the outline of his hard pectoral muscles. His hands are gently caressing my bare back and dipping low towards the waist of my skirt. He reaches lower and pulls me closer by grabbing my bottom. Oh. He didn't waste any time. This is surprising. Maybe he's testing me. I almost push him away. I'm not sure if I can do this. But his hands rise back up again to my back.

His tongue feels so velvety in my mouth and it makes my legs weak. Our hips are pressed together and I can feel how hard he is, the length of him is pushing into my pelvis. Intense desire overpowers me. My body has surrendered. The ache between my legs gets stronger. I can feel my panties getting damp. His effect on me is unbelievable.

Dave's hands are at my waist again and he's found the zipper to my dress on the side of my waist. How did he even find it? He undoes the zipper and his hands travel back up to my shoulders, taking the straps off my shoulders. Oh no. I hold my breath. As the straps fall down my arms, to my elbows, my whole dress starts to slip off, and I keep my hands at his waist, stopping the whole thing from dropping to the floor. I'm naked from the waist up. Why didn't I wear a bra? Should I stop him now or keep going?

He pulls me close to him, his arms encircle my back and my bare breasts are pressed against his polo shirt. I hold him tight, afraid to reveal my breasts. I am shaking. Am I scared? Or am I excited? His mouth is devouring mine and I cannot stop kissing him. I feel him inching me backwards and then the back of my knees hit the bed. He stops kissing me, and locks his eyes on mine. He pulls away from me and takes my hands. This is it. He straightens my arms for me and my dress falls to the floor. I'm standing in front of him, wearing nothing but my white lace panties. Steve has been the only man who has seen my bare breasts. I am mortified. I need to cover myself up. I also want to pick up my dress and put it on a hanger, but I quickly brush that thought aside. I am half naked. What do I do next?

Dave gently coaxes me down onto the bed by touching my shoulders. He crawls beside me and has me lie down completely. I quickly bring my hands up to my breasts, but he grabs my hands and says, "You are beautiful. Let me please you."

I don't know where to look. I look into his eyes and it seems too meaningful, too momentous. I want to keep the emotions out of this.

Dave releases my hands and leans over and kisses me hard, pushing his tongue into my mouth. I lose my breath. But then he is gone, kissing my neck and clavicle. He reaches over my body for my arm, and lifts it, making it rise over my head and onto the bed. He tickles my arm with his fingers, as his hand comes back down, to my underarm and over to my breast. He cups it in his hand and uses his thumb and forefinger to squeeze my nipple making it hard. I moan and close my eyes. He knows what he is doing. Then I feel the warmth of his mouth on my other breast, his tongue circling the nipple, his teeth gently biting. I have never felt anything like this before. I arch my back and lift my hips, giving into the sensation. Both of my breasts are being tortured in such a pleasurable way. I am on the brink of an orgasm. I squeeze my knees together, trying to relieve the pressure accumulating between my legs.

"Does that feel good?" He asks softly, his fingers still toying with my nipple.

"Yes," I manage to say.

I feel Dave get up from beside me and I open my eyes. I bring both hands to rest just under my breasts. I want to cover myself up. Where is he going? He takes off his shirt and throws it to the floor. Oh. He looks hard and lean. He crawls onto the bed and straddles my thighs. He bends over me and kisses my neck and uses both hands to squeeze my breasts together. He nibbles on each nipple, toying with them.

I put my hands on his shoulders and slide them down to the backs of his arms. I like feeling the outline of his triceps. He slides down lower on my thighs and kisses my rib cage. I feel his tongue outline both of my bottom ribs. His lips are soft on my taut stomach and I feel him lick my navel. He's kissing every inch of me. My fingers run through his soft hair. I feel his chin stubble grazing my lower belly, and now his lips are at the waist of my white lace panties. What's he doing? My hands freeze in his hair. His tongue slides slightly under the lace at the top of my panties. What? He's going down there?

He changes our positions slightly; he moves between my legs and pushes my legs wider, so that his head is at the apex of my thighs. I sit up slightly, panicked. I yank his hair. I want to tell him to stop. Steve never did that. But then, I feel his hot breath there, over my panties. Flip flop. I moan and lay back down. His mouth presses lightly on my sex. I moan louder and he pushes my legs wider. I feel his finger slip under my panties from the side and he starts to gently probe the entrance of my wetness. More hot breath and I feel his finger enter me. It takes my breath away. His other hand pulls my panties out of the way and now his finger and tongue are on my sex. My hips contract and I push them up to meet the erotic intrusion.

Every muscle in my body is tense. His tongue swirls around and around and teases my clitoris. His finger is rhythmically pushing into me, deeper and deeper. I think he has two fingers inside of me now. I'm panting and my body is writhing, uncontrollably. I am pushing my sex into his face. I can't help it. I feel tremendous pleasure build up, deep inside me, and I can no longer contain it. My body goes rigid and the orgasm rips through me. I cry out loudly as it continues, it doesn't seem to stop. I can't catch my breath.

I feel Dave move and get up, but I can't move to watch him. I can't even open my eyes. I am paralyzed with satisfaction. That was plenty of experience for one night. I hear him rummage around beside the bed and then he's back beside me. "I have a condom," he says. He's not done? Should I tell him that it's too much? This is crazy. But I can't deny him his release. That wouldn't be fair. I'm still thinking when in one swift movement, he is on top and easing into me. But I'm always on top. I don't dare to tell him that. It feels wonderful, gentle and full.

He thrusts tenderly at first and I groan. My clitoris seems more sensitive from the oral stimulation and each time he pushes into me, my insides tighten and pulsate. It feels amazing. He gradually starts plunging harder and faster into me and the pressure deep inside me increases once again. I can't control my body. I wrap my legs around his and move my hips to meet his. A low growl escapes from his throat. "Come for me." His voice is coarse.

"Yes," I breathe. My insides tighten up, my muscles flex and I shatter to pieces, moaning loudly as I come, and as he continues to drive into me.

Not soon after, I hear Dave. He groans as he reaches his climax and his body shudders on top of me, burying his head in my hair, until he is still. After a minute, he moves up onto his elbows to look at me, green eyes sparkling.

"That was amazing," Dave says.

I blush under his gaze. "Yes it was." Unbelievable.

Dave eases out of me, and we spoon, my back to his front.

"You can stay here tonight. I don't mind."

I hadn't even though about sleeping arrangements. I probably should leave. Dave's arm is around me and he is so warm. I feel so content. Satisfied. I miss this kind of embrace. I miss sex too. I have to remember every detail to write down in my notebook. I start to go through the evening in my head, but drowsiness overcomes me. I don't fight it. I fall into a deep sleep.

16.

I see a bright light through my eyelids. I stretch and open my eyes. Where am I? And then I remember. My stomach drops. I slowly look beside me and Dave is not there. I'm relieved. But there's a note: *Colleen, I work on Saturdays 7 to 11. Feel free to stay in bed or grab a coffee using the Keurig in the kitchen. If you wait around, maybe we could have brunch together. Last night was incredible. Dave xo.*

I put the note down, sit up and hug my knees. What do I do? His bedside clock reads eight o'clock. I have three hours to decide what to do. I need advice. Where's my phone? I get up and grab the bathrobe that's hanging on the back of his bedroom door and pad out into the hall. I find my purse on the couch and pull out my phone. Christine had better answer.

After the sixth ring, I hear her voice. "Who is calling me so early?" She growls.

"I'm sorry but I need your help, sunshine," I say.

"Ci-Ci? It's not even nine. I had a super late night. I think I just got home an hour ago. You know I need my beauty sleep. Why do you need--." She stops. "You had a date last night." She's excited now. "What happened? Tell me now!"

I don't know how to start, "I... uh..." I walk over to the window and look out at the boats in the harbor. I'm too embarrassed to tell her. I don't want to tell her details about my sex life.

"You fucked him!" Christine yells into the phone. "Woohoo!" She cries.

I roll my eyes and blush profusely. "Yes I did. Now what do I do?" I vaguely recount the night's events and tell her about the situation that I am in at the moment.

"So it was good sex. Do you like him?" She asks.

"It was great sex and, sure, he's nice. But that's not the point. Remember?" I continue, "I want experience, not a new boyfriend. I still want Steve back and Dave just put me a step in the right direction."

"Oh, so you learned a few things?"

I blush again. "Yes. A few. I learned a lot actually."

"Glad to hear it. I wasn't sure if you could pull it off."

"Pull what off?"

"Casual sex. I guess I forgot who I was thinking about. You always seem to excel in new situations."

"I haven't pulled it off yet. I'm still here."

"Ok. This is what you have to do. You're actually in the perfect position to keep the control. You need to get out of there now. Leave him a note, saying that you have a bogus meeting or whatever and get out of there," she orders.

"Shouldn't I wait for him and tell him the truth?" I ask.

"Hell no! It was a one-night stand!" She howls. "If he comes back and you're still there, it'll be harder for you to say goodbye."

"Why? I'm a pretty straightforward person. It can't be that bad." I feel guilty for not being honest with him.

"Believe me. You don't want a face-to-face confrontation. He'll tell you how beautiful and special you are and probably talk you into another date. You won't be able to ignore his puppy dog eyes."

His puppy dog green eyes. "And another date is bad?"

"Yes! If you want to keep it casual sex, you need to play by its rules. No second dates!"

"Oh. Ok." I take it all in.

"And if he calls you, don't answer. He doesn't need any explanations" she says.

"He doesn't have my number. I have his," I say. "He might call the office, but Margie screens all of my calls."

"Wow. You are better at this than you think." She giggles.

I smile. "What did you do last night?"

"I met a guy at a cigar bar. He took me to his penthouse and we had fantastic sex."

"Can I ask how you feel now?"

"I feel proud, desirable and fulfilled."

"Oh." How does she do it?

"Why? How are you feeling now?"

"I do feel empowered and satisfied, but I also feel a bit of regret and loneliness. I miss Steve. The experience wasn't bad at all. I just hope he doesn't find out." I'm sad that one of my favourite parts from last night was the cuddling.

"Put thoughts of Steve aside for a minute. During your encounter, did you focus on yourself and make sure that your needs were met?"

"Yes, I think so." It was very gratifying. I was content after my orgasm. The second one was a bonus.

"Did you worry about your partner at all?"

"No, not at all." I really didn't. He seemed to be enjoying himself immensely.

"That's casual sex. Get as much out of the experience as you can. It'll be good for you."

"Thanks Christine."

"You really ought to start paying me."

"It's true. Now I have to get out of here."

"Call me later."

I put my cell in my purse and quickly go back into the bedroom to put my clothes on. I find my white panties on the dresser beside the bed and my dress on the floor where I left it, at the end of the bed. I put the robe on the back of the door and I start to make his bed. I put all of the pillows at the headboard and then I pause, pull the sheets back, and mess the bed up. I also throw a pillow on the ground. I am not a perfectionist. Grabbing his note, I walk out of the bedroom.

I find a pen in the kitchen and scribble a note on the back of his: *Dave, I have an appointment at noon. Thank you for last night. It was incredible. Take care.* I drop it on the kitchen counter, slip into my shoes, and get my coat out of the closet. Before I leave, I go back into his bedroom and pick up the pillow that I flung and place it on his bed. I'm not a slob either.

I scramble out of his house and catch a taxi on the street to take me to my car. In the taxi, I pull the key ring out of my purse and kiss my wedding band. I'm one step closer to getting Steve back.

17.

While I drink my protein shake, I flip through this month's *Journal of Human Sexuality* and I find an article about one-night stands. It confirms Christine's opinions that sex with a stranger can help a person focus on the physical act, pleasure and experimentation. The conclusion states that casual sex can lead to more fulfilling sexual experiences. This makes me feel better. Now I just have to figure out how I can brush aside my existing reservations about sleeping around and the idea of promiscuity.

I need to get out and think. I decide to go for a run downtown by the water, but not by the Harbourfront. Actually, I go in the opposite direction, toward Ontario Place. Just to be safe. I don't want to bump into Dave.

It's sunny and a little chillier today, but it's a great day for a run. I open my drawer of running apparel and smile. It's my favourite drawer. The shorts, sports bras and spandex are all folded into neat piles and lined up front to back. It's all so bright and colourful. I grab my new electric blue shorts, an orange sports bra and a long sleeve spandex shirt. I stick my iPod in the sleeve pocket of my shirt, tie up my bright orange and blue running shoes and I fly out the door.

Even though it's not a perfect day, a lot of people are out sightseeing and sitting by the lake, making the most of their Saturday. Some even have blankets on the grass, trying to soak up the last sun of the season, but their hot coffees and sweaters give the temperature away.

I run through the maze of people and listen to my music. The rhythm of my feet puts me in a trance and I feel alive and free.

I start to think about Dave and what I learned from our experience. He was so intimate with me and I only knew him for, basically, one night. How did that happen? We were comfortable talking to each other. We had a lot in common. The chemistry was there. When he kissed me, I melted. And my body surrendered to him. I gave him the right vibes, the right signals. I gave him the green light, so to speak.

But how did he know that he could proceed? Was he so intuitive of my need to gain experience that he moved forward? I was hesitant, but I was ready for whatever he was willing to give me. I kissed him back. I touched his body. Oh, and the flirting probably helped. *"I don't think that there's anything on the menu that I want."* I'm sure that made him confident.

The environment, consent and desire were present for relations to occur. But with Steve, we were married... those three variables always existed. Isn't that what marriage is? What stopped Steve and me from having mind-blowing sex?

Dave did things that Steve never did. Steve never went down on me. He never tried or even asked to do it. I didn't know that I could achieve orgasm from it. If I had known that it was so... effective, I would have asked Steve to do it a long time ago. But I never went down on him, either. I shake my head. I don't know why I never did it. I guess we just got into such a routine, that it just never happened. I liked touching him and feeling his hardness in my hand. He used to touch me down there with his fingers before we were married. When did that stop? More importantly, why did it stop?

Steve wasn't a very creative or overly sexual man. Did I control the situation and set the road map and he just followed? But why did he cheat if he wasn't sexual in the first place? When did he change and why didn't he take control?

I am getting mad, fuming actually and I start running faster. I'm such a control freak. Why couldn't I see that I was pushing Steve away? I'm an idiot. For a few seconds, I close my eyes to block out the words in my head and I suddenly slam into something or someone and I trip and fall onto the grass, landing on my hip.

"Why don't you watch where you're going?" A man's voice says.

I start to look up, seething, "Are you kidding me? You ran into me!" I screech.

"Colleen?" I see that it is Jack Fraser. He extends his hand to help me up, but I'm still too angry to let him. I swat his hand away and get up by myself. "I am so sorry. I was trying to avoid some people and I looked back and didn't even see you coming. Are you ok?"

I calm down a bit. "I didn't see you either. I was in the zone. Where did you come from?"

"That path." He points. "We ran right into each other."

"I ran right into a brick wall." I laugh.

"At least you fell onto the grass. No scrapes." He smiles.

I smile back. "Are you ok?"

"No worse for wear."

We start to walk, and I feel a pain shoot through my hip, down to my knee. "Argh," I cry out and limp over to a bench.

"You are not ok." He follows me. "Sit down." I sit and start rubbing my hip. He stands in front of me and stares at me. His blonde hair falls into his eyes as he bends down to pick up my leg. What's he doing? I stop rubbing. He raises my sore leg up to hip level and slowly turns my foot outward. I look at him curiously. But when he turns my foot inward I wince.

"You need ice." He puts my foot down, looks around, and jogs over to a hotdog vendor. He talks to the vendor and the vendor points to his cooler. Jack jogs back over with a plastic bag full of ice. Who knew that Jack was so thoughtful and attentive? I always thought he was a womanizer, and just cared about himself.

"Put your leg up on the bench. You need to elevate it," he orders.

"I'm fine, Jack. I can do this when I get home," I say.

"Do it now," he says, looking at me intensely.

I do as he says and he puts the bag of ice on my hip. "Hold it there." He looks satisfied. "Do you want some water?" Without waiting for an answer, he goes back to the hotdog vendor and pays for two bottles of water. He returns, opens the cap on one of the bottles and hands it to me.

"Hydrate," he demands.

"Ok," I yield and take a swig. "You're bossy."

He looks at me and his eyes soften. "Sorry. I'm just worried about you. I know you love to run and I hope I didn't put you out of commission."

"I'll be fine." I cock my head. "How do you know that I run?"

"Are you kidding? I started running because of you." He smiles shyly. "I was over for dinner one night and you showed me all of your marathon bib tags. You gushed on about how running makes you feel, the total body benefits and the adrenaline of crossing the finish line. My date was pissed that I left her in the dining room and ignored her."

"I'm sorry." I don't even remember that night.

"Don't worry about it. I swear the look on your face was reason enough for me to start running."

"Really?" I didn't know I had that kind of influence on anyone.

He looks at me and runs his hand through his hair. "You really motivated me. It was a difficult start, but now I see what you mean about running. My mind takes over and I feel like I can run forever. It's an unbelievable feeling."

"Euphoria."

"Pardon?"

"When you run, your endorphins increase. They are hormones that elevate your mood and thus, you get a euphoric runner's high.

"That's what it is. A runner's high." He sits down beside me. "I've been training for my first marathon. It's in the spring."

"That's great." I smile.

"Maybe we could run together some time. I need to challenge myself and speed up. I'd like to match your eight minute mile pace," he says.

"I'll have to slow myself down then," I tease.

"Ha. Ha. Make fun of the beginner."

"I'm kidding. I'll run with you anytime."

"I hope you're able to run at all." His eyes sadden and he looks down at the ice bag on my hip.

"I'm fine. Can I get up now?" I ask.

"Of course." He takes the bag of ice from me.

I stand up and take a few steps. It hurts, but I can walk on it.

He looks at me carefully. "Are you ok?"

"Yes. It's not like I sprained an ankle or broke a bone. It's just a bruised hip. I can handle it." There will probably be a colourful contusion there tomorrow. We start walking along the pathway, staying on the right side, so that joggers and rollerbladers can cruise by easily. I start to dread the long walk home, I had been running awhile.

"Do you want to share a taxi home?"

He read my mind. "That would be great." I look at him. "I know you know where I live, but what about you? Are you close by?"

"Sure, it's close," he says. "How are you holding up, by the way? Emotionally, I mean. The last time I talked to you, I had given you some shitty information to mull over."

How much do I tell him? "Actually, I'm glad you told me. It opened my eyes and now I have a game plan. I'm headed in the right direction now. I feel good."

"Care to share?" He elbows me.

About my sex life? "No, I'd better not."

"You're blushing! You must have a good plan."

"I can't tell you."

"Hey, I just want to remind you that I don't talk to or hang out with your ex anymore. Any conversations that we may or may not have will not be divulged to that clown," he says seriously. We're on the edge of the street now, and Jack is searching for a taxi.

"I would rather just keep it to myself for now. And that clown is still my husband," I say with my hand on my hip. He can't talk about Steve like that.

He stares at me. "You still want him back?"

"He's my husband," I burst out. "Now and forever. It's in our vows."

"You'd be willing to forgive and forget about his adultery?" He asks incredulously. I nod. "I knew you were an angel, but this is unbelievable. You are a far better woman than he deserves." He shakes his head in disbelief.

An angel? "Like I explained before, I was not the wife that I should have been. My plan is to be better," I say quietly.

He takes a hold of my hand. "I'm not sure where you got your information, or how you got off track, but you need to realize that you are an amazing woman. You don't need to change at all. I definitely don't see you in the fucked up way that you do. I wish I could open your eyes and show you." We lock eyes, but I pull mine away first.

I raise my hand up in the air and step out onto the street, "Taxi!" I yell. Instantly, a taxi comes rolling to a stop in front of us.

Jack shakes his head. "You're good at everything, aren't you?" He opens the door and I climb in. He slides in next to me.

"What are you talking about?" I'm horrible at sex and keeping a marriage alive.

"You have no idea how amazing you are." Jack turns to the taxi driver. "58 Seaton Street, please."

That's my address. He thinks so highly of me. Why? "You seem to know so much about me, Jack, and I don't know anything about you. Are you still with the same pharmaceutical company as Steve?"

"I left that company about six months ago and I opened a clinic on Isabella and Yonge," he says.

"A clinic?" I ask, surprised.

"A physiotherapy clinic."

"I don't understand. Do you own the building?"

"No, Colleen. I'm a registered physiotherapist. I just wasn't a practicing one. I went to the University of Toronto too, but when I graduated, my first job was in pharmaceutical sales. I stomached it long enough to make a down payment on my own clinic."

Wow. I never would've guessed. "I don't know you at all," I say wistfully.

"No, you don't."

"It's strange because you came over a lot, almost every weekend. All I know is that you dated a lot. You came to our house with a new girlfriend every time. They always seemed to be in love with you."

He sighs. "Don't remind me."

"Blondes. Brunettes. Redheads. You were a busy man." I laugh.

He looks out the window. "I couldn't find the right one, I guess," he mutters. Then he turns to me. "Colleen, I always wanted to tell you about Steve. You didn't deserve the way he was treating you. You have such a big heart. I hated the idea of breaking it."

"I don't want to get into it with you again, Jack." I shake my head. "I am married to Steve and only he and I know how our relationship really was... or is. I will get back with him again because it's my choice."

We are both quiet. I look out the window and see people window shopping on the familiar streets near my home. Steve and I used to wander the streets of Toronto, looking in stores for special items to bring home and sitting at new cafés drinking lattes and eating scones. A Sunday at Kensington Market was one of my favourite pastimes with Steve. We would browse through the antiques and collectibles while holding hands and trying to make deals. I wonder what Steve is doing right now. Does he miss me too? I hope I'll be able to convince him that I have changed when the time comes. Will he take me back?

Jack suddenly grabs my hand. "I'm sorry, Colleen." I look at him. "I don't want you to think I don't respect you or your decisions. I care about you and I just don't want to see you hurt." His blue eyes ablaze. "You deserve to be happy."

I squeeze his hand. "It's ok, Jack." The taxi is slowing down and we are pulling up to my house. "I'm a big girl and I'll figure it out." I suddenly realize that I don't have any money to help pay for the taxi. I let go of his hand and pat the pockets of my running shorts. "Jack, I didn't bring any money with me on my run. I expected to run home," I explain.

"That's ok. You can owe me," he says. "Maybe we can run together next weekend, when you're all healed up."

"That would be fine. I still have the same home number. Give me a call," I say.

"Hold on," he says. I sit and he gets out of the taxi. I realize that he's going to open the taxi door for me. He really is sweet. I've never seen this side of him before.

My door opens and I step out. "Take care of yourself, Colleen." He winks at me.

"Thanks, Jack. You too." I smile and walk to my front door. I look back and he's watching me walk away. I wave to him and he waves back. I fish the single house key from the tiny pocket in my running shorts and unlock the door. As I close the door, I see his taxi pull away.

18.

I spend the rest of the afternoon sitting on my chaise lounge, icing my hip and completing menial tasks. I don't want to move around too much because I want to take care of my hip. Running is my escape. I don't know what I'd do if I couldn't run. I record Friday's notes on my recorder, browse a few magazines that I bought last month and never read, complete the crossword puzzles from the entire week and watch some television.

By dinnertime, I am bored. I need to get up and do something. I scrub the kitchen floors and use a toothbrush in the corners and along the baseboards. When they're dry, I get a fresh bucket of water and scour the façade of my kitchen cabinets and then polish the wood. I'm about to vacuum the crumbs out of my dining room chairs when I notice my notebook that holds my qualitative research about my sexual goals. I take it out and sit down at the table. I complete the data collection outline filling in my experience with Dave.

Data Collection

Sample #1
Seek persons who understand study & are willing to express inner feelings & experiences
- *Man, aged? (in his early 30's), orthodontist, tennis enthusiast*
- *Brunette, green eyes, hard body*

Describe experiences of phenomenon
- *I had to change my view of Sample #1 from being a nuisance to a possible sample. When I did that, I had an instant*

connection, especially when he kissed me the first time. (He walked me to my car). On our date, we flirted and had open conversation, with much in common. He would look at me in such a way, or touch my hand, or say something provocative and I was aroused and ready for any experience that he would show/teach me. I had 'butterflies' in my stomach, which I can only explain as nervousness and anticipation. I let him touch me in ways that I have never been touched. I allowed it and I consented to it, non-verbally.

- Foreplay consisted of kissing, foot massaging and breast manipulation (heavy petting).
- He performed cunnilingus on me and I climaxed.
- Then we had intercourse (with a condom) and I climaxed again.

<u>Direct observation</u>

- What is needed to be more sexual: Open communication, a common desire or goal, consent, physical attraction, commonalities in character, and <u>confidence</u>.
- Cunnilingus is amazing; tongue and finger simultaneously is erotic and extremely stimulating.
- Future goals: fellatio

<u>Audio or videotape?</u> n/a

<u>Data analysis</u>

<u>Classify & rank data</u>

- 5 out of 5
- 1st Sample, no ranking available (#1 for now!)

<u>Sense of wholeness</u>

- *I feel strong in my convictions and believe in my research. I am doing what is right. I still want Steve back and I am learning what it takes to get him back. I want to be everything to him.*
- *I do need to be more confident in bed, being naked and with my samples.*

<u>Examine experiences beyond human awareness/ or cannot be communicated</u>
- *Will I miss Sample #1? Maybe. It was a strong connection. Maybe if I don't obtain a Sample #2 and Steve won't take me back, I may give him a call.*
- *Guilt. Not calling Sample #1.*
- *I feel morally wrong using Sample #1 for research. I believe in monogamy.*
- *Do I feel guilt/bad/slutty or is it because society says I should feel this way?*
- *Remember my new moral code/ 'right' motives:*
- *I want to explore and learn about my sexuality. I believe that it is an important experience to have.*

My last notation is forced. I feel like I am talking myself into this research. I'm still not sure if I can continue to violate my own morals. The good old double standard still looks down on women, but glorifies men who have casual sex. How can I overcome and ignore society's standards? It is surprising, however, that I haven't thought about Dave until this moment. That's a good sign. I have relived the experience over and over in my mind, but none of the guilt. It really was casual sex. And it was good. I'm kind of proud of myself. I close the notebook and put it back into my briefcase.

I am about to call Steve when my cell phone rings. "Hello?"
"Ci-Ci, what are you doing?"
"Nothing."
"Get dressed. We're going out."
I roll my eyes. "I don't want—."

"And I don't want to hear it! Get some jeans on and a nice shirt. I'll be there at eight." She hangs up.

Christine has always been able to talk me into things. In university, I'd be studying for an exam and only she could pull me away from something so important, to go to a party with her. Whether it is her domineering personality or just the fact that we have fun together, I always seem to comply.

I put on jeans and a cowl neck shirt, finishing the outfit with brown high heel boots. I put on some lip gloss and try to smooth my hair down.

At eight, I start pacing my hallway. At quarter after eight, I hear Christine honking her car horn. She's fashionably late, as usual. I rush out to get in her car and I cringe and let out a tiny whimper when I sit down.

"What's wrong with you?"

"I hurt my hip today, but I'm fine. Where are we going?"

"It's a surprise. You look great."

"Thanks. So do you." She's wearing jeans and a tight, fuchsia v-neck sweater.

"How is Project Sex?"

"Project Sex? You named it?" I laugh loudly.

I reveal a little more about my night with Dave and she tells me about her bartender.

"We've never done this," she says.

"Done what?"

"Talk about our conquests!"

I giggle and smile. "No, we definitely have not." I have never told her about my sex life with Steve. I should have opened up more, earlier on, and maybe she would've told me that I'm abnormal. I could have fixed the problem sooner or not have let it happen at all.

"I like it. Not so much about hearing your dirty details, but sharing our lives a little more."

"Me too."

"I really haven't seen you since you've been married. I've missed you."

"I know. I'm sorry. Thank you for still being here for me. I promise that when I get back with Steve, we'll go out more."

"I'll take whatever I can get."

Christine pulls into the driveway of a large, unfamiliar building and parks. "You ready?"

"For what?"

She opens the door of the building and there's loud music and bright lights. I can barely make out anything. When my eyes adjust, I see tables with women around them and a stage.

"A strip bar?!" I screech.

"We are the celebrity judges."

"Are you kidding me?" Naked men? I'm supposed to judge naked men?

Christine takes my hand and pulls me to the front of the bar. She talks to a man briefly and then turns to me. "Colleen, this is Luca Simpson. He owns this bar."

He extends his hand and I look up at him. He is very good looking. I take his hand. "Thank you so much for helping me with this hot body competition. One of the judges backed out at the last minute."

All I can do is nod. I am totally out of my element.

"When Christine said she would bring someone, I didn't expect a beauty like you." He holds onto my hand. "It's a pleasure to meet you."

I blush and pull my hand away. Christine stands beside me. "Where do we go?"

Luca takes us over to a table in front of the stage and I see that our names have already been put on the table. I look at my chair before I sit down, take a napkin from the table and wipe it off. I'm sure the dirt and bacteria in this place has to be atrocious. Bodily fluids. Yuck. My germ phobia is kicking in.

Luca leaves and I attack Christine. "You brought me to a hot body competition at a strip bar? What makes you think that this is a good idea? I have my reputation to uphold. I don't know if I can stay." I work with children. I can't be here!

"Look at your name plate."

I pick it up. *Colleen Condreau. Psychic Advisor.* I start laughing. "Thank you for that, but what if there are pictures?"

"I already asked and the press is not going to be here."

I feel a bit better, but not about the filth. I am about to put my purse on the table, but I squint at the surface and it looks questionable. I can't bear to do it, so I put my purse on my lap. I also have to get over my initial distress of bare naked strippers. I've never been to a place like this before. I have only seen two nude bodies before, and only one up until yesterday.

Christine pats my back. "It's only naked men. If this won't bring you out of your shell, I don't know what will. Let's order a beer!" She waves over the half-naked server and orders two beers, "Keep them coming!" When he turns to leave, Christine bursts out laughing.

"What?"

She points to the server. I turn around and see that he's wearing a g-string. His butt cheeks are bare. I did not want to see that. I close my eyes and shake my head, trying to get the image out of my mind.

"Come on, he's got a rockin' body."

I bury my face in my hands. "This is too much."

"It's only going to get better." She laughs and pats my back.

"Welcome to the Hot Body Competition!" A voice booms over the speakers. "Put your hands together for the celebrity judges!" Women in the crowd cheer and applaud. There are three other women seated at our table and the host introduces them first, they stand up and wave. "We have Christine Beckham, an insurance agent at State Shield Insurance." Christine stands up on her chair and bows. "And finally, we have Colleen Condreau, she is a Psychic Advisor." I stay seated and wave. The spotlight hurts my eyes.

"Ladies, we have our first dancer. What girl doesn't love a teddy bear? How about a teddy bear that is not only cuddly and cute, but one that also dances and transforms into a gorgeous male stripper? Put your hands together and welcome Teddy!" The crowd erupts into screeches and wolf whistles.

A man in a teddy bear costume and oversized head walks out and does a pirouette and some other silly ballet steps to children's music. It's pretty tame, but I know he's here to take his clothes off. The server comes back with our beer and I take a long drink.

The music changes to a thumping, tribal beat and he picks up the pace and rips off his costume in one motion, keeping his massive head on. He is only wearing a brown, furry bikini bottom that shows every bulge of his manly package. His perfectly shredded body is oiled up with every magnificent muscle glimmering in the spotlights. I try not to focus on that too much. He strikes poses all over the stage, thrusting his hips into the audience. The music changes once again to a techno beat and he pulls his teddy bear head off. He's very cute and plays the audience well, smiling and pointing to the different women.

He starts pulling his bottoms away from his skin, looking down into them and pulling them side to side. He suddenly rips the bottoms away from his body and I close my eyes. I hear 'boos' from the audience and I look again. He pulled the furry bottoms off, but he had another black bikini bottom on underneath. I breathe a sigh of relief.

He dances up to the judges table and poses in front of us individually. He gets to Christine and she waves a rolled up twenty dollar bill in front of him. He kneels down in front of her and she pulls his waistband away from his hard stomach and tries to peek down inside. She gently places the bill into his pants and he takes her hand and makes her cup his manhood. She laughs and sits back down. I would be mortified if he did that to me. Thankfully, he skips me. The sight of money must have distracted him.

He dances to the middle of the stage and as his third song ends, he rips off the black bikini bottom and his erection springs free. I quickly look at Christine and she's yelling and screaming.

"Judges, can we have your scores, please?"

The first judge holds up a seven and the next two hold up eights. Christine holds up a nine and I hold up a seven right in front of my face, so I don't have to look at his penis anymore. She looks at me and shakes her head.

The screams die down and Christine turns to me. "You gave Teddy a seven? That was the best of the best. You have some pretty high standards."

"He was all right."

"I'd like to see your version of a ten."

The server comes over and brings us another beer. "On the house." He points to the bar and Luca and another man in a baseball cap raise their beers to us. We raise ours in return.

I've relaxed a little. The strip bar is not so bad. I thought I would have more penises flapping in my face. During the break, Christine and I talk about Teddy and the crazy audience and someone taps me on the shoulder.

I look up and it's the man with the baseball cap from the bar. He's wearing a plaid shirt and has light blonde facial hair under his nose and on his chin. He's pretty cute.

"Hello, Colleen."

I stare blankly at him. "Hi?" I don't know him.

"I'm Charlie Cooper. But you should know that because you're a psychic."

I smile and shake my head. "I'm not exactly a psychic. I just would like to remain anonymous."

"I'm sure that's what all psychics say. You don't want to be bothered. I understand. I bet people ask you, 'What am I thinking?' all the time."

Is this guy serious? "No really. I'm not a psychic."

"That's what I was thinking! I knew you would deny it." He's smiling now.

"Charlie, I'm a child psychologist." I start laughing.

"And I'm a respectable businessman. We can lie to each other all night." He takes a drink of his beer, his eyes smiling. He's cute and funny. "I don't think a child psychologist would be caught dead in here. It's not very professional."

"That's what I said." I look at Christine and start to get nervous again.

"I'm kidding. It's ok. You're allowed to be human and have fun."

Christine elbows me and I turn to her. "Charlie Cooper, this is my friend Christine Beckham." Christine holds her hand out and Charlie shakes it.

"Are you the next act?" Christine asks.

"No I am not."

"Too bad." She winks.

She's right. He seems to a have a pretty fit body. I can't really tell how muscular he is under the loose shirt, but his jeans hang nicely on his waist. When he reached across to shake Christine's hand, his bottom looked pretty firm. I blush to myself.

"I work with Luca, but not in this industry." He looks at me. "I have respectable employment too." He pulls up a chair beside me. Why is he sitting beside me? "I thought I'd sit with you during the rest of the show."

"Why?" I ask dumbfounded. "You want to get a better view?"

"Not of the show." He cocks his head to the side and smiles. "I was watching your reactions and you do not like this, do you?"

Is he flirting with me? "Um. No. I mean, it's ok. But this is my first time coming to a place like this. Christine told me to get dressed. I didn't know where she was taking me."

"It is objectionable. Male strippers are disgusting. You shouldn't watch this."

"You're kidding again. Right?"

"Yes. You're quick. I kind of figured that you're not too comfortable here. I came over because I thought I could help you." He looks over at Christine. "She looks kind of busy."

I turn to see Christine putting a rolled up bill in the server's thong. I quickly look away. "Yes, this is her kind of environment." I laugh.

"Ladies, we have the second contestant ready to entertain you." The women go wild, screeching and whooping it up.

Charlie leans in, "These women are insatiable. I hope my mother is not here." He smells really good. I laugh and smile at him. He has a great smile.

Charlie makes jokes while the stripper woos the crowd. The stripper tries to make the audience clap to the beat and Charlie comments that he looks like one of those wind-up monkeys banging cymbals together. When the stripper tears off his thong during the last song, Charlie covers my eyes. "You don't need to see that. It's not real. I don't want you to be deceived. That's not how big they are on the average man." I take his hands down and pretend to take a peek. "Oh, you missed it. You'll have to score him based on his abilities alone." I laugh loudly.

The host is asking for our scores and I hold up an eight, the same as Christine.

"An eight? I would have given him a seven. He couldn't even do the splits," Charlie jokes. "I'll be right back."

"You're having fun," Christine looks towards Charlie.

"He's very funny."

"And very cute. I love a little facial hair on a man."

"You're not angry at me because I'm talking to him, are you?"

"Not at all. It's what I want for you, to get out and have fun. If that means talking to a good looking, sexy man, then I'm happy." She eyes the servers barely covered behind as he walks by. "Besides, this place is fun for me. I like the eye candy."

I suddenly realize that this is another opportunity for me to practice flirting and possibly get more experience. I find it funny that I didn't recognize it sooner. How could I not see it? Charlie is interested in me. Why else would he be talking to me? I've got to work on reading nonverbal communication.

Charlie steps between us and hands us two more beers. "You two must be thirsty from all that heavy panting. Ogling men can be a tough job."

"Somebody's gotta do it," Christine says and holds up her glass. We all clink our glasses together.

The host comes out of stage and the women automatically start hollering and whistling. "All right ladies, we have our third and final, sexy contestant."

I don't watch a lot of the act because Charlie and I talk about our education and professions. He is an entrepreneur and he and Luca own a few businesses in the downtown core.

"Seriously, I can totally see why you want to remain unidentified, Colleen, but don't feel guilty for being here. Everyone needs a release. What else do you do for fun?"

Do I tell him that I am just recently separated? No, too soon. "I work long days, so it doesn't leave a lot of time for play." I fiddle with the label of my beer bottle. I need to muster up some courage.

"Play? That's a word with a lot of different meanings." He pokes me playfully. "What do you like to play?"

I blush, but take the chance. "I like to engage in new experiences." I want to look away, but I hold strong and look him in the eyes.

He's about to say something when Christine pokes me. "He's going to take it off!"

I look up at the very same time the stripper rips off his bikini briefs and I swear he's staring right at me. He's pointing at his erection, mouthing, "You like it." I shake my head furiously and look away.

Christine is laughing. "He deserves a ten."

"Judges, you scores please," the host says.

The first three judges hold up eights, Christine shows a ten and I put up a nine. It looks like contestant number three won the competition. He dances up to the first couple of judges and shakes their hands.

83

Christine sticks another rolled up twenty down his pants and he gives her a kiss. I just shake his hand and quickly wipe my hand on my jeans. I need hand sanitizer.

Charlie puts his arm around me and laughs. "You are too funny."

"I'm going to find Luca and thank him for everything," Christine says.

"I'm eager to continue our conversation," Charlie starts. "You said that you like to engage in new experiences. Can you expand on that?"

I finish my beer. "I am at the point in my life where I would like to try new things and keep my mind occupied."

"Why now?"

"Why not?" I smile.

"You are very mysterious. I like it. I am an open book. Plain and simple."

"Oh, I doubt that you are plain or simple. You make me laugh and that is rare. People just aren't funny anymore."

"I doubt that people come to you to tell you jokes. You're line of work would be pretty serious stuff. How about this? Knock Knock."

"Who's there?"

"ADHD."

"ADHD who?"

He doesn't say anything. He just looks off to the side.

"ADHD who?" I ask again.

"Oh sorry, I was bored. I already went to the next door."

I laugh loudly. "That was ridiculous."

"You have an amazing laugh," he says staring at me.

"Thank you. And thank you for making me laugh. I don't know when I've had this much fun."

"Can I ask you straight out if you would like to come home with me tonight?"

Flip flop. "You can ask," I laugh nervously. I'm buying time. Do I want to go home with this stranger? He is pretty cute and funny. I'm attracted to him. Should I?

Christine walks up to us. "That was a fun night. I'm ready to go home."

I look at her and then at Charlie. "I'm going to have another drink with Charlie, if that's ok with you, Christine?" I see Charlie smile. I just agreed to go home with him. Who am I?

Christine smiles and hugs me. "No problem at all. Have fun. And you," she says to Charlie. "Take care of her."

"I will."

"I'll call you tomorrow," I say and Christine leaves the bar.

He stands up, pulls me to my feet and when I take a step, I limp slightly. "Are you ok?"

"Yes, I'm just a little stiff from running today."

"I live another couple of blocks down. Do you mind walking?"

"Not at all." It gives me a chance to get this nervous energy out of my system. I need to keep an open mind. I know I'll learn something else, just like with Dave. I need to let go of inhibitions and try to enjoy the experience.

19.

We walk in silence down the street, but we are holding hands. I feel him squeeze my hand twice quickly. I do the same and he looks at me and smiles. At a red light, we stop on the corner and he turns to me. "Just to be sure," he says. He takes my face in his hands, bends down and kisses me gently. I feel the rim of hat hit my head, but then quickly focus on how soft his lips are. His facial hair is surprisingly soft too. It feels nice. I dart my tongue out and feel his tongue touch mine. The kiss deepens and I put my hands on his chest for support. He pulls back. "Yup, I'm sure." He lets out a deep breath and we walk across the street.

We walk into the hypermodern lobby of an apartment building and go to the elevators. It looks like Studio 54 with pendant lights hanging throughout the area reflecting on a beautiful wall of sparkly tile. The metallic surfaces and dark woods also make the space feel manly. Charlie has style.

He pushes the button and the elevator opens immediately. Inside, he looks at me. "Who knew that I would meet someone as amazing as you in a male strip bar?"

I'm amazing? I don't know what to say. "You already know how I feel about strip bars, so it is very surprising that I met someone like you there too."

"You mean someone without germs?"

I laugh. "Exactly." Humour relaxes me.

We stop on the fifteenth floor, and we walk across the hall to his door. There are no other doors on the floor. He unlocks the door and I am welcomed into an immaculate and very manly condo. It is deep blue, with brown leather couches and touches of gray. Over the fireplace is a large abstract painting with random slashes of siren red paint. The place is massive. I see the kitchen and living room and a hallway in both directions. A large brown Labrador retriever trots up to Charlie. He sniffs me, but would rather see his master.

Charlie scratches behind both of his ears. "Go to bed," he tells the dog and it saunters off. Charlie takes my hand again and leads me to a sitting room off of the living room. "This is my favourite place to sit." He takes off his hat and we sit on an oversized, gray velvet couch. I take a quick look to see if it's covered in dog hair, but it's not. When I look up, I realize why he likes to sit here. The view is unreal. The windows start at the floor and go up to the ceiling and continue over our head. I can see Toronto's skyline and a slight view of the Island. We rest our heads back on the couch and look up at the moon and stars.

"Just beautiful," I say.

"Yes you are."

I look at him, and he's already coming towards me. I don't have time to be cautious or think. We kiss and the way his tongue moves inside my mouth astounds me. It's mesmerizing. I am weak in my knees and I feel the deepest part of my core pulsing already. That was quick.

He pulls me close, our knees touching, leaning in towards each other. He overtakes me, and I start to lie down on the couch, he lies beside me, our hips together. We're still fully clothed, so I am comfortable. He brings his hand up and cups my breast over top of my shirt and presses his hips into mine. The kissing is deeper, making our breathing erratic. He squeezes my nipple through the fabric and I quietly moan.

Charlie stops kissing me and moves onto the floor, getting up on his knees. I look at him. He unbuttons his plaid shirt and takes it off. He then takes off the white tee shirt that he is wearing underneath. He has an amazing body, hard and tanned. Ripped in the right places. He looks at me and smiles. "Your turn."

It is? I blush and start to tremble.

"Are you ok with this?"

I can do this. Think about the experience. Project Sex. I smile. "I'm fine." I sit up, with Charlie between my knees and I cross my arms, lifting the bottom of my sweater up and over my head. I put it beside me, feeling bashful about being half naked. At least I'm wearing a pretty white bra.

He stands up, bends down and takes off his shoes and socks. He flings one sock at me. I catch it and throw it back at him. He deflects it to the floor. Then he just stands there and looks at me.

"My turn?"

He nods and smiles.

I bend over, and pull off my boots and socks. That was easy. I'm smiling, feeling encouraged.

Charlie goes for the top button on his jeans. "I don't have Velcro on these pants. I wish I could rip them off for you."

I laugh timidly and watch him as he undoes the button and zipper and pulls them over his hips. They fall to the floor and he steps out of one leg and kicks the pants away with the other. He is wearing black boxer briefs and he is bulging just as much as the strippers were. He holds a hand out.

My turn again. I am attracted to him. I am here. Relax. I am fine. I take his hand and stand up. I slowly go for the button on my jeans, but he gets there first and undoes them. He unzips them and pulls them down over my hips and thighs. As my jeans fall to the floor, he holds both my hands and I step out of them, kicking them to his pile. He laughs.

Charlie takes a step back, still holding my hands and scans my body. "Wow. You are absolutely perfect," he says.

I feel uneasy, but flattered at the same time. He pulls me in close and we begin kissing, his hands roam my body. I put my hands on his shoulders and when his tongue pushes deeper into my mouth, I squeeze his neck and shoulders. I feel his hands go under my white panties and cup my bottom, pulling me higher. My hip is tender, but I quickly forget about it as his hardness pushes against my stomach. I stand on my tip toes.

He releases my bottom and attempts to unclasp my bra. Flip flop. I feel my heart start to beat faster. He is successful and I lose my breath. He pulls my bra off of my arms and I have to let him go, so he can take it off completely. I make the moment last, but succumb and he tosses my bra aside.

"Sit," he says softly.

I obey, covering my breasts. He takes my arm away as he kneels between my legs. "Please don't be shy. You have a killer body. Colleen, you are incredible." Oh. I have to get over being naked in front of a man.

Charlie kneels down in front of me and kisses me. He pulls my hips to the edge of the couch, so that my sex is against his erection. He kisses my neck briefly and then travels down to my breasts, pushing me back into the couch. I keep my eyes closed. He circles one nipple with his tongue and softly twists the other one between his fingers. He then cups my breasts, squeezing them together and pinches both nipples vigorously. I open my eyes, but let out a loud moan. He releases and repeats the process again, working gently on my nipples. It's intense. I can feel the wetness in my panties. His last pinch is the hardest yet and I arch my back, crying out, but he covers my mouth with his and kisses me deeply. I dig my hips into his, involuntarily. These sensations are unreal.

He leaves my lips again and my eyes fly open. I watch him kiss each nipple gently and then travel down my stomach, kissing and licking as he goes. He's at the edge of my panties and he looks at me. He catches me watching him and he smiles and raises his eyebrows. He slides his fingertips into the waistband and ever so slowly, he inches them down. I close my eyes. He stops. I open my eyes to see what he's doing and he starts to pull them down again. I close my eyes in embarrassment and he stops again. It's a game. I have to look at him for him to pull my panties down. Maybe I don't want them down. I look at him and he pulls them right off and throws them into our pile. Funny game. I'm completely naked. I squeeze my knees shut.

Charlie kisses my knees and hooks his arm under them and pulls me forward again, my bottom hovers on the edge of the couch. He slides a hand between my knees and gently nudges them apart. I close my eyes and smile. I'm self-conscious and I don't want to see him go there. I feel him kiss the inside of my thighs, travelling up to my sex. Then I feel his breath and a flick of his tongue on my clitoris. I shudder.

At that moment, he forces my legs apart and I feel a soft tongue firmly pressing against all of my sex. He's taking long, slow licks. His tongue delves into me each time. The flick against my clitoris makes me tremble every time, and he does it steadily, bringing me higher and higher. The rhythm is undulating. I grab onto his shoulders and squeeze hard. My feet lift off the floor and rest on his upper back. I'm pushing my hips into his tongue. I feel the exquisite sensations building up deep within me. I am almost at my peak and I moan loudly.

Charlie stops and my eyes flutter open. Why did he stop? He has pulled down his underwear and is already hovering at my entrance. He is hard and has considerable length. I want him inside me. Why is he waiting? He slaps his head and crawls to his jeans. I sit up. What is he doing? He fumbles for his wallet and pulls out a condom. He quickly rolls it on and is back between my knees. I'm glad he was thinking, because I was not. I have to be better about that.

This time he doesn't wait, he grabs my bottom and pushes into me slowly. I can feel my walls tighten around him. He kisses me hard, opening my mouth with his tongue. I grab onto his back and he thrusts faster, slapping into my inner thighs. I push my hips forward and open my legs as wide as I can, so that he can plunge deeper inside me. My legs wrap around his waist and I lie back down, my hands above my head, bracing myself against the couch. He squeezes my breasts together and I feel my insides swelling, brimming with sensation. I moan loudly and he slows down, I can feel his entire length pull out of me and back in again. It's unbelievable.

When he slides into me, he gives me an extra push against my sex and that sets me off. The next push launches me over the edge. I tense up, waiting euphorically for the peak and I explode. I moan through my breaths and feel Charlie pick up his pace. His repeated pounding prolongs my orgasm and I keep spiraling with intense pleasure. I hear Charlie groan and he plunges deep and hard a couple more times and then he is motionless.

I open my eyes and look at him. He is smiling.

"So, doc. That was wonderful for you, how was it for me?"

I burst out laughing. "You're hilarious." I cover up my breasts and he pulls out of me. I hastily find my bra and panties as he disposes of the condom. I pull my sweater on start with my jeans and he comes back.

"Where are you going so quickly?" He pulls on his underwear.

"I have an early appointment tomorrow," I say. I don't, but I learned my lesson with Dave. I need to get out of there.

"Oh." He seems sad. "I will drive you." He zips up his jeans.

"No, it's late. I'll call a taxi."

"I insist."

"No. I insist." I grab his hand and look him in the eyes. "A taxi is fine."

"Ok. I'll dial the number." He walks away and I hear him talking. "A taxi will be here in ten minutes."

"Thank you."

"Is that it?"

"What do you mean?" I know what he means. I look down and put my boots on.

"I'm not going to see you again, am I?"

"I… I have just recently separated from my husband. I am not looking to date anyone."

"Oh. Maybe we could just get together and do this again." He laughs. "I'm just kidding. I can appreciate your situation. It's not what I would have liked from you, but I'm glad I met you."

He takes the elevator downstairs with me and we wait inside the doors. He pulls his business card from his wallet out and hands it to me. *Charlie Cooper BBE BIB*. Bachelor of Business Economics and Bachelor of International Business. Interesting.
"Call me if you ever want a laugh."

"Charlie, I had an incredible time with you. Thank you."

The taxi pulls up and I run out to get inside. I don't even look back at Charlie. I can't. I realize that I didn't call Steve tonight and I hope he doesn't think that I've forgotten about him.

20.

It's Sunday and I decide to lounge in bed and try to sleep in. At eight, I give up. I am not meant to sleep in. I make a pot of tea and settle in the living room, but before I get under my blanket, I grab my Project Sex notebook. I laugh at Christine's joke.

Data Collection

Sample #2
Seek persons who understand study & are willing to express inner feelings & experiences
- *Man, aged? (in his mid-30's), entrepreneur; owned businesses. Has BBE and BIB*
- *Blonde, facial hair, muscular body*

Describe experiences of phenomenon
- *He sat beside me at the strip bar. He was funny and charming; made me relax and laugh. We had a good connection and I was attracted to him. I tried flirting and being forward. It worked. He straight out asked me if I would go home with him. I said yes. I tried to be confident. Foreplay consisted of kissing and a semi-strip tease (both of us). He performed cunnilingus on me and I almost climaxed, but he stopped just before, on purpose, I think. Then we had*

intercourse (with a condom) and I climaxed again. It all happened on his couch. I left immediately.

Direct observation

- *What is needed to be more sexual: Open communication, a common desire or goal, consent, physical attraction, commonalities in character, and <u>confidence</u>.—same!*
- *NEW: I need to feel beautiful and sexy.*
- *Cunnilingus is amazing; slow lock licks and clitoral stimulation is extremely stimulating.*
- *Future goals: fellatio*

Audio or videotape? n/a

Data analysis

Classify & rank data

- *5 out of 5 (for different reasons)*

Sense of wholeness

- *I feel strong in my convictions and believe in my research. I am doing what is right. I still want Steve back and I am learning what it takes to get him back. I want to be everything to him.*
- *I did relax a little more, but I do need to be more confident in bed, being naked and with my samples.*

Examine experiences beyond human awareness/ or cannot be communicated

- *Will I miss Sample #2? No.*
- *Guilt. I think he wanted to see me again, but he remained somewhat aloof. He laughed off his insecurities. He gave me his business card.*

- *I feel less immoral than with the Sample #1, but I do feel like I used both Samples.*
- *Do I feel guilt/bad/slutty or is it because society says I should feel this way?*
- *Remember my new moral code/ 'right' motives:*
- *I want to explore and learn about my sexuality. I believe that it is an important experience to have.*

    I drink my tea and try to envision a strip tease that I would do for Steve. I can't picture it. I can't get past taking off my shirt because I don't know if he would enjoy it. A strip tease is way beyond our usual repertoire. We never really laughed in the bedroom, so I should probably cross it off my list of ideas. But I'm learning to add spice in the bedroom. That's what all this research is about. I can't eliminate an idea based on our past sex life or because I think he won't approve. God, even my daydreams about Steve seem forced and unnatural. How am I supposed to get him back if I can't even picture the outcome? I tell my patients to visualize success and I can't even do it. Why does thinking about Steve lead me into these negative thoughts? Why does he intimidate me? He never has before.

    I get up and finish the chores that I began yesterday. I start with the vacuuming and then dust every surface of my house. I even clean each slat of the blinds on all my windows and get a ladder to attack the ceiling fan.

    Hours later, I am a sweaty mess, so I take a bubble bath. I close my eyes and listen to the radio. A song comes on that reminds me of Steve when he used to help me train for volleyball. He became engrossed in strengthening my skills and started to coach me daily. He put me through strenuous workouts and I would often cry, complaining that I couldn't do anymore because I was too tired, but he was insistent that I do more. I always felt like I failed him, but when I received the coveted Ontario University Athletics award in my last year, he never mentioned my abilities again.

    Steve would also be pretty hard on me when it came to keeping fit and being healthy. He had an amazingly toned body at that time and I didn't want to disappoint him. He would watch me during meals and would often take food out of my hand, telling me that I had had enough. I started to read about nutrition and I learned how to eat healthy on my own, so he had nothing to complain about anymore. I understand that he went about it the wrong way, but his influence had a positive outcome.

I know I have to gain more sexual experience to get him back, but now I understand why. It is another thing I have to work at to impress him. I've let him down. I've disappointed him. Now I have to work at redeeming myself. I owe him that for always helping and believing in me.

I get out of the tub, get dressed and quickly reorganize my bathroom drawers and cabinets. I always feel so satisfied and accomplished when I tidy up and arrange things. It's soothing. Just before bed, I call Steve. I listen to the message on his voicemail and melt. His voice is soothing. "I miss you," is all I say and I hang up the phone.

21.

In the morning, I lift a few weights, but the eight miles will have to wait. My hip is still pretty tender from my fall and the bruise is an ugly reddish-blue. It also hurts when I move a certain way. Luckily, the bruise is high up on my leg, so I can still wear a shorter skirt. I dress in an above the knee, gray pinstripe skirt, pink blouse and gray heels and leave for work.

I park in front of my office and walk to that same corner café for a vanilla latte. As I take it from the barista, I look around for Jack. I don't see him. I leisurely walk back to my office. The trees are almost bare and I had to pull out my warmer, wool coat, but the crisp cool air feels nice on my face.

"Good morning, Colleen. A Dr. Dave Chemello left a message on Sunday afternoon. He asks that you call him back at his office today," Margie says when I walk into the office. She holds up the yellow message, waving it.

"Good Morning, Margie." I reach for the message, but she pulls it away. I stop and look at her. She smiles.

"Who is this Dr. Chemello?" She teases and holds out the message again. She seems happy for me and I want to tell her the truth, but I think only certain people will approve of casual sex. I don't think a married woman with two kids can relate.

I grab at the message, this time snagging it. "He's just someone I met. It's not going anywhere. If he calls again, and I'm not busy with a patient, I'll take it." Forget what Christine said, I owe it to him to give him some kind of explanation. I walk into my office and close the door. I can hear Margie giggling.

That was a great start to my day.

Janie is my first patient and it's her first time in my office. She is eight and has self-esteem issues due to a learning disability. Her parents say that she doesn't seem to have close friendships; she's shy and isolates herself. She is beginning to develop sleep problems and her teachers say that she has difficulty concentrating. Those are both signs of depression. I'm going to start play therapy with her.

"Hi, Janie. This is my office and as you can see, I have a lot of toys, crafts and books for you to play with. You can choose to play with whatever you want and include me or play by yourself." I walk to the middle of my office and she follows me. "Please look around and choose something that interests you."

Janie walks over to the bookshelves filled with games and puzzles and she starts to pull out a puzzle, but then stops to look at me. "Go ahead. Take whatever you want." She takes the puzzle out and I point to the children's table. She sits down. "Can I sit with you?" She nods.

The point of play therapy is to give Janie my undivided attention for a full fifty minutes. I'll play, listen and talk to her, giving her special recognition. It's her own little break from the world, where she can relax and be herself. This will naturally raise her self-esteem and she will look forward to visits with me. Parents usually report that their children's mood improves dramatically right after a session with me.

I help her figure out the puzzle of a cat and dog and we laugh and talk about random topics. She seems content and enjoys my friendliness. The time quickly passes and I send her home with a special notebook and pencil that I keep in supply for my younger clients.

The rest of my morning sessions also involve play therapy because this type of treatment is best scheduled on Mondays. The extra attention I give them seems to make my patients' week less stressful. It's a great start to the week for me too.

I eat lunch in my office with Margie. She went out and bought us Greek salads from Sofakitis, a restaurant down the street.

"What are you cooking tonight?" Margie asks.

What? I'm confused and then realize she meant my cooking class. "Oh, right. That's tonight. I think it's sushi," I say.

"I have never had sushi," she states., scrunching her nose up in distaste.

"I never used to like it either. I only liked the simple California rolls. Those have cucumber, avocado and crab in it," I explain. "Really tame stuff. But then I went to this place called Sushi Bon and I really expanded my horizons. We'll have to try it for lunch one day, Margie."

"Maybe." She doesn't look too sure.

"Are you going to tell me about Dr. Chemello?" Then she shakes her head. "You don't have to, it's none of my business."

"I went out with him on Friday. He's nice and cute, but he's not Steve. I still want to work things out with him."

"Marriage is tough. My husband and I separated for almost two years, but we figured things out and reconciled. It was the absolute worst two years of my life, but we are now the happiest we've ever been."

"Thanks, Margie. That gives me hope."

She nods and starts cleaning up and takes my empty salad container away.

"Thank you."

The phone rings and Margie's hands are full, so I say, "I'll get it in here." I answer it on the third ring, "Hello, Dr. Cousineau speaking."

"Well, hello there, Dr. Cousineau." It's Dave.

I take a deep breath, "Hi, Dr. Chemello," I wave to Margie to shut the door. She smiles and closes it on her way out.

"You're so formal. I just wanted to find out how you are. I didn't want to wake you on Saturday, you looked so peaceful. So beautiful."

"Oh... Yes, I'm great. I had really nice time with you on Friday." I start placing the paperclips on my desk end to end.

"Nice? Uh oh," he says sadly.

"No. No. No, really. It was fun."

"Phew. You scared me. Would you like to go out again, tomorrow night?" He asks.

Here we go. "I have volleyball tomorrow night and before you ask for another night, I have to tell you something. I need to explain something to you."

"Ok."

"Do you remember how I told you that I am just recently separated?" Now I am putting the paperclips in a plastic container in my desk, separating the silver ones from the coloured ones.

"Of course."

"While the other night was great, I am not ready to be exclusive with anyone. I can't get serious with you at this time," I say, holding my breath.

There's a pause. "Colleen, your note said our night was incredible. Did I do something that turned you off or made you uncomfortable?"

"No! Not at all. Everything was perfect. You were amazing." Feed his ego. "I just don't want to string you along when I don't want a relationship."

"I realize that. I don't want a relationship either. All I'm asking for is another date. No harm in that, right?"

Is he begging? "I can't do it, Dave. You are a nice guy. Very cute and fun. I just can't invest time in you right now. I'm sorry." That was so blunt.

"No problem. I understand." He's awfully whiny. He reminds me of patient who has a tantrum when he doesn't get what he wants.

"I'm sorry, Dave."

"Goodbye, Colleen." And he hangs up.

Jeez. That was tough. Maybe Christine was right, I should have avoided his calls.

The intercom buzzes. "Your one o'clock is here," Margie says.

"Send her in, please." Back to work.

22.

I race out of the office at six. I have to be at the Culinarium for six-thirty. Driving on the Gardiner Expressway during rush hour is almost impossible and I make a mental note to leave at five-thirty next week.

Trying to locate a parking spot is equally difficult. After circling the block three times, I finally find one. Now I'm late. I rush into the building and open the door to the classroom to find that the class has already started. The chef, a skinny Japanese man, is speaking to the class.

The classroom is equipped with ten kitchen stations. Each station has a counter with a sink, a gas stove and a refrigerator stocked with whatever food is needed for the cooking class. I quietly walk to the other side of the room to the last empty station. I put my purse and coat on a stool and sit down on another one. I see that *Chef Fujimoto* is written on the board. That must be his name. He is explaining about the inside out sushi roll. His English is very broken, but I can understand him.

"It known as Uramaki. It more common in U.S.A. than in Japan and is very popular in western sushi bar. Inside out roll unique. Rice is on outside and nori is on inside. It wraps filling. That why it called inside out roll."

He holds up a nori sheet. "Nori paper like. Edible. Toasted seaweed. In most sushi I make. Nori holds sushi together."

Someone slips in to my station. From the corner of my eye, I see a man take off his coat and put it on the counter and sit down on the last available stool.

"I'm sorry," he whispers. "I couldn't find parking."

He's in his late thirties with a bit of gray in his wavy, dark hair. He's wearing a light gray button down shirt, a gray and red paisley tie, and jeans. He's very handsome.

"That's ok," I say. I'm a little irritated. I want to listen to Chef's instructions.

"Did I miss anything?"

I just shake my head, trying to listen. But when I look at him, I see that he is staring at me. He has beautiful ice blue eyes. I nervously try to smooth down my curls and then turn back to listen to the chef.

Chef Fujimoto has broken the nori down the middle and he's telling us to get the prepared rice out of the fridge. He says that it was made this morning and we could have the recipe afterwards. I stand up to get the rice, but my new cooking partner gets in the way.

"I'm Chris."

"Hi, I'm Colleen," I say. "Will you get the rice, please?" I'm here to learn, not meet men. That sounds familiar. I said that about Dave and the book club.

"Absolutely." He smiles. He has dimples. Or would it be wrong to meet a man? I really should be more open-minded.

"Get hands wet. Make ball of rice. Use handful rice," Chef says.

Again, we both start heading to the sink at the same time.

"After you," he says.

"You know what? You go ahead. I'm just going to clean the countertop." Upon inspection, it does not look the cleanest.

When I'm done, we get our hands wet, place the rice balls in the middle of the nori and start spreading the rice, pressing it down gently, until it is equally spread along the nori sheet. Chef continues with the instructions and Chris and I work quietly side by side. I'm glad, because I don't want to miss a step. It's very easy. Chef shows us how to prepare the vegetables properly, how to use tempura batter, and how to cut raw fish. Finally we are allowed to create our own sushi.

I reach for the avocado and brush fingers with Chris who wants the avocado too.

"There's enough for both of us," he says, smiling.

I reach for a paper towel and he reaches at the same time, over me, for a knife.

"This is getting ridiculous," I say, but I'm enjoying it.

He drops his knife and bends down to get it, bumping his behind into my legs. He turns around to see what he hit and places a hand on my bare legs.

"Sorry," he says. I look down at him. "Don't want to damage those beauties."

I drop my head so that my curls cover my blushing face and continue to make my sushi. First, I meet a man at a book club. Now a cooking class? Christine will not believe this.

I make my roll with tempura fried shrimp, avocado and asparagus. And I see that Chris has used raw red tuna, avocado and cucumber.

"Yours looks neater than mine," Chris says when we're done.

I look at his and it is a bit looser than my roll. "It still looks delicious," I say.

He smiles. "Wanna share?"

"For sure," I whisper. "But I think we have to wait."

I was right. Chef is now instructing us on how to make wasabi. I'm not too keen on wasabi, but I listen and make it anyway.

Chef comes around surveying our work and gives each of a glass of sake and chopsticks. "Yoku yatta," he says to me. I look at him. "Good job," he says with a smile. I smile back.

"Uh oh," Chris says. "I'm not too good with these." He is holding the chopsticks completely wrong.

I reach over him and fix the orientation of the chopsticks in his right hand. I feel his breath in my hair. I quickly sit back in my chair. "I'm sorry," I say.

"No, that's quite alright. You smell really good," he says.

I blush. He's pretty sexy. "Use the top part of your ring finger, your thumb knuckle and the connect area between your thumb and your index finger to perform like a lever." I pick up my chopsticks and show him. "Don't hold it too hard." He could be my next sample, but is it too soon? I was just with Charlie two nights ago and Dave on Friday.

He is staring at me again. I look away and pick up a piece of sushi and dip it in some soy sauce. I might as well get some practice. "Are you going to eat? I don't want to eat alone," I try to flirt.

He doesn't notice. He's too busy playing with is chopsticks. He clicks them together repeatedly. "Hey, I can do it. I'm going to try to eat with these things, but I'll probably just end up using a fork. Or my hands."

I take a bite of my sushi and it's good. I am starving.

"I missed last week's class. What did we cook?" Chris asks.

"It was Spanish night. We made seafood and beef empanadas and Spanish rice or paella." I sip the sake. It's warm, but it's not bad.

"I'll have to get here early next week to save you a spot. I like having you as my cooking partner." He smiles and picks up a piece of sushi with his fingers and pops it into his mouth. Now he's flirting.

"I think I need someone with more class," I tease.

"I'll have you know that my students think I have great class."

"Your students?" I question.

"I'm a university professor. Get it? I have class." He pokes his elbow at me a couple of times.

I groan. "Yeah, I get it. I'm just choosing to ignore it." I smile. "What do you teach?"

"I teach business. It's very boring stuff, but I have always liked to cook, so that's why I am here." He drinks the rest of his sake. "What do you do?"

"I'm a child psychologist. I do this kind of thing for fun." I shrug. "I have nothing better to do on a Monday night." Is that a flirtatious thing to say or just pathetic?

"I won't be skipping any more classes." He smiles. "I promise." He liked it.

"What's on the menu for next week?" I ask.

He pulls a piece of paper out of his pocket, scrolls down with his finger and says, "A Mexican Fiesta. I hope there will be Coronas." He laughs.

"That'll be fun." I reach over him and with my chopsticks, I steal a piece of his raw tuna sushi. I'm being playful. I am shocking myself.

He opens his mouth in mock surprise. "You took a piece of my sushi."

"We are sharing, aren't we?" I bat my eyes. It feels unnatural.

He shakes his head. "Take it all. Anything for a beautiful woman." But he then takes the rest of my sushi roll and pretends to hoard it. "Mine. All mine."

"All right. Give it up. I'm still hungry," I say, laughing.

We continue talking and finish eating the sushi. Chef comes over to our station to say goodbye. Chris and I shake hands with him and Chef bows.

"That was fun. Thanks for letting me share your station," Chris says. "And your sushi." We have our coats on and are walking towards the door.

"Thank you for making Monday night cooking class fun," I say.

"Do you want to go for a drink down the street?"

I can't do it. Even though we clicked and had a good time cooking together, it's too much, too soon. I pretend to look at the time on my cell phone. "It's late. I have an early appointment. Maybe next week?" I suggest hopefully.

"I'm looking forward to it," he says. "I'm Chris Barlotta, by the way." He extends his hand.

I smile, "I'm Colleen Cousineau." I shake his hand.

"See you next week," he says, but he doesn't let go of my hand.

"Yes, I'll see you next week," I say with a giggle.

"Oh, you want your hand back." He releases it. "Goodbye, Colleen." He smiles.

"Good bye, Chris." And we walk in opposite directions. I go to my car, laughing. This flirting stuff is getting pretty easy.

23.

The next morning, I am able to run, but only complete five miles. My hip is feeling good, even with the bruise being an ugly dark blue, almost purple. I just don't have the energy to run. I'm tired after a restless sleep. My mind would not shut off. I had thoughts of Steve, the orthodontist, the entrepreneur and now, the professor. If I was stuck on a deserted island with them, I think I would be just fine.

I dress in tailored black pants with wide legs and a fitted, baby blue shirt. My gym bag is neatly packed for volleyball later, filled with running shoes, black shorts and a white tank top. I pack a pair of leggings and a hoodie at the last minute, for after the game. I figure I'll be sweaty and I won't want to put my work clothes back on. I'm definitely not taking a shower at the university, as that would be disgusting. I shudder at the thought of athlete's foot, pubic hairs and the smell of urine. Secondly, I would have to pack toiletries, a towel, and a hairdryer. Too much work. This is already too much to carry. I put on my short wool jacket, grab my gym bag, purse and briefcase, and I leave for work.

I don't feel like a latte today, so I arrive at the office early, even before Margie, so I sit down at Margie's reception desk to call Christine.

"Hi, Ci-Ci," Christine answers.

"Hey! Are you at work yet? Am I bothering you?"

"I'm early and no, you never bother me," she says. "What's up?"

"You were right about ignoring a guy's calls," I say. Margie's desk is messy.

"I'm always right," she says with a laugh. "But why am I right this time?"

I snort. "Because it's hard to tell a man that you only used him for sex. I think I broke his heart."

"I'm sure Charlie will get over it. He seemed like a player to me."

"No, I'm talking about Dave!" Oh my god.

Christine laughs. "I can't keep track already. Ok, so you told Dave that you used him for sex."

"Well, no. I didn't actually tell him that, but it's what I really did. I told him that I didn't have time for dating. He was pretty upset." I am organizing Margie's pens by colour in her rotating pen holder.

"He'll get over it. Next time, screen your calls. Men don't need an explanation. Now what happened with Charlie?"

"Oh... um... I slept with him."

"You slept with him," she says at the same time. She laughs. "And was Charlie a good experience?"

"Definitely." I giggle.

"How did you leave him?"

"Right after sex. It was difficult to just get up and go, but I did it."

"How do you feel?"

"I'm ok. I feel a little guilty about hurting them both." And a little immoral, but I'm pushing those feelings aside.

"The guilt will go away. They're men. Know that they have probably moved on already."

I laugh. "Speaking of moving on, I met a guy in cooking class last night."

"Ci-Ci, cooking class? Really? I guess I shouldn't be surprised."

"He's pretty cute, nice blue eyes. I think we might go out after next week's class," I say.

"See how easy it is to meet men? And you were worried. You might meet a new prince charming," she jokes.

"Again, Christine, it's for experience. Not to find a new man," I scold.

"Right. Sorry. We'll have to get together and compare notes soon. I might learn something from you." She laughs.

Margie walks into the office. "I have to go. Talk to you soon." I finish putting her stationery supplies away in the proper compartments.

"Bye, Ci-Ci," Christine says.

I hang up and Margie looks at me, "Good morning. Thanks for organizing my desk." She rolls her eyes.

"You're welcome. How was your weekend?"

"I had a wonderful weekend with my husband. We stayed overnight in Buffalo and shopped and had nice, quiet dinners."

"That sounds nice." I'm jealous, but happy for her.

As soon as I put my coat away, Margie buzzes me, "Connie Baker is here for her appointment."

"Thanks, Margie. Send her in," I say.

Connie Baker is six years old, with long, brown hair and brown eyes. She walks in my office holding her mom's hand.

"Hello, Mrs. Baker."

"Hello, Dr. Cousineau," she says. "I am only here to make certain that we will be out of here early, at least ten minutes to nine. Her father keeps trying to catch us at places that he knows we will be and I want to be ahead of him."

The Bakers are separated and the situation is volatile, almost dangerous. He was abusive toward Mrs. Baker and the police records and photos of black eyes and bruises proved her case. Although the custody arrangement was a long, hard battle, that Mrs. Baker won, Mr. Baker has been ignoring and protesting the arrangement. He shows up for unscheduled visitation at her home and the hostility in front of little Connie is intolerable. Connie has been crying a lot at home, which is to be expected, but also has been acting out and crying at school in different situations.

"I will make sure that she is out the door at ten to nine," I say.

Mrs. Baker bends to kiss Connie's cheek. "I'll be in the waiting room, honey."

Connie and I go into my office and I close the door. "Get comfy, Connie." She sits down in the oversized purple bean bag chair that I have just for kids.

"How are you?" I ask.

She is holding one of the dolls from the collection of toys that I keep in my office. "Good."

"How do you like your new house?"

"It's good."

"Are you at a new school too?"

"No."

I keep asking her easy questions like these until she starts to warm up.

"Do you want to brush your doll's hair? I think there's a comb on the bookshelf."

"Why do I have to keep coming here, Dr. C?" She asks.

"Everyone wants to make sure that you're ok with the separation. Your mom and dad care about you. They want you to talk about your feelings."

"What kind of feelings?"

"They want to know if you are happy or sad, or even mad."

"I'm mad that daddy fights with mommy. Mommy always cries. I hear her in her room at night."

"You should go see your mom when she is crying and hug her. I think that would make her happy."

"Why can't they just stop fighting?" She has tears in her eyes.

"Connie, sometimes mommies and daddies just don't get along. They can't be friends anymore." I go to crouch next to her and comfort her. When she's calmer, we make three marshmallow people to represent her and her mom and dad. We use mini marshmallows and pretzel sticks to make the people. I have her act out an argument she saw between her parents. I find out in the next thirty minutes how insistent and aggressive Mr. Baker has been. The other day, he surprised Connie after school and took her to McDonald's for dinner. No one knew and when she didn't arrive home on the bus at the scheduled time, her mom became worried and called the police. Mr. Baker arrived three hours later, with no apology. And they fought loudly. Connie was extremely happy that she was able to spend time with her dad, but she was oblivious to the severity of the situation.

Connie also told me that he hurt her mom a couple of days ago. He came to their new house and when her mom wouldn't let him in, he barged the door down. He knocked her mom down onto the floor. We practice with marshmallow Connie how to go to another room when her parents are fighting and make marshmallow Connie repeat, "My parents still love me, even when they argue."

I am so thankful that I do not have children with Steve. We talked about having kids. We both want them, but the plan was that I nurture and expand my practice first. He never pressured me or talked about it much at all. He wasn't as ready to have children as much as I was. But with the way things are presently, with him not talking to me, I'm not sure the separation would be amicable if there were kids involved.

"Times up, Connie." I walk her to the door and open it to see her mom already standing and waiting. I put her marshmallow people in a zippered plastic bag for her to take home and eat later.

"We have to go, Connie. Your dad is outside." Mrs. Baker's voice is high pitched and she looks frazzled.

"I'll walk you two out." I open the door and whisper to Margie, "Call the police, just in case."

We all walk out and Mr. Baker comes up the sidewalk to meet us.

"Hi, Connie," he says and reaches for Connie, but she hides behind her mother.

"Martin, you do not have visitation right now," Mrs. Baker warns. "It's tomorrow at the courthouse."

"Fuck the courthouse!" he explodes. "I want to see my baby girl." He stands large and intimidating, blocking them from getting to their car.

"Mr. Baker, please just let them get to their car," I say carefully.

"Shut up, shrink!" He yells and comes up closely to me. He sticks his finger in my face. "This does not concern you." I smell alcohol on his breath.

"Get your hand out of my face and step back, Mr. Baker." I stand my ground, but I am terrified.

Our exchange gives Connie and her mother enough time to scoot past Mr. Baker and run to their car. Mr. Baker stumbles toward the car, but they are now safely inside. He starts banging on the windows of their car and trying the door handles, but Mrs. Baker pulls out and drives away. I can hear the police sirens getting closer.

"Mr. Baker, the police cars are for you. With the alcohol on your breath, I think you might want to get out of here," I warn.

He stumbles toward me. "You called the cops?"

"Yes. And I'm going to suggest to Mrs. Baker that she get a restraining order."

I can see the rage in his eyes, "You do that and I'll come after you," he threatens. His eyes are dark brown, almost black, and they are menacing. He hasn't been taking care of himself. He smells and probably hasn't shaved in a month. He's very tall, too, and built like a truck. He's intimidating and scary.

Margie has come to stand beside me, which makes Mr. Baker back away, but only slightly. I can see the police cars driving towards us.

Mr. Baker points at me again, still backing away, and then turns and staggers down the sidewalk quickly. The police pull up in front of us, at the curb. An officer steps out of the police car and asks, "Who called the police?" Mr. Baker turns the corner and he's gone from my view.

Another officer joins us and we quickly tell them the situation, pointing them in the direction of Mr. Baker. The first officer follows Mr. Baker and we give the second officer our statements.

When we are finished, Margie and I go back into the office.

"Are you ok?" Margie asks me.

"Yes," I say. "I'm more concerned for Connie and her mom. Please contact Mrs. Baker and tell her that I suggest that she gets a restraining order immediately. Tell her the process to get an ex parte, or an urgent motion without notice. I'm scared he's going to hurt Connie."

"Yes, Colleen."

I complete the rest of my days' appointments with an ominous feeling in the pit of my stomach.

24.

    I'm in the university locker room, getting changed for volleyball. The comforting smell of sweat and running shoes calms me, but I need to let off some steam. I'm still bent out of shape by today's events. It's another situation that I couldn't control. I should have finished the appointment earlier.

    I get out on the court and wait for more people to arrive. You never know who's going to be there, but there's always plenty willing to play. Six is the usual number of players on a side, but there has to be a minimum of three females on the court at all times. There are eight courts running and I'm guaranteed to play each game.

    However, there aren't enough females yet, and the officials won't start the game. I'm getting irritated. I dribble the ball and bump it to myself. I just try to keep my hands and mind occupied. If Steve was here, he'd be yelling at the refs to start the game.

    Finally, we're allowed to start and I'm serving first. I step forward, toss the ball up with the palm of my right hand and while the ball comes back down, I take three steps and launch forward, winding my right arm back and finally, I strike the ball with the heel of my right hand. It sails over the net to the back left corner. I get into defensive position and the ball comes back to me.

    "Mine!" I call and I dig deep, dropping on my knees and bump it to one of my teammates, who volleys it over. The other team lets it fall and I get to serve again. I hit it over and this time it lands in the middle back and is returned after two contacts. However, my team fails to send it back. Two of them watch the ball fall between them. They laugh, but I'm pissed. It was an easy hit, but they didn't call it.

    "Start calling it, guys," I yell, irritated.

    The game continues, there are a lot of bad plays being made by my team, mostly shanks, and I'm getting grumpier. Can they not hit the ball in the direction they want it to go? I don't want to lose.

Now I'm next to the setter. I tap him on the shoulder, "Make sure you set me up."

He turns to me. "Ok, Superstar." He laughs.

I look at him. What the hell was that? "Just set me up."

The other team serves and it's short. They roll the ball under the net. Our turn again. My team member serves and it's good. It gets returned and it's bumped to my setter.

"Outside, outside!" I yell.

And he gives me a gift. He volleys it and I jump up as high as I can, arching my back. I pull my right hand back to my ear and release, like I'm using a bow and arrow; I powerfully extend my arm, hitting the ball and snapping my wrist to impart a top spin on it. It goes straight down over the net. It's a mighty fine spike that the other team fails to receive.

"Nice job!" The setter says and we high five.

"You set it perfectly," I say, breathless with excitement. He's cute. He has a sandy blond brush cut, freckles and brown eyes. He is tall and extremely muscular. He doesn't have the typical build of a volleyball player. He's more like a wrestler or a football linebacker.

Our team serves again and I'm feeling better. Not so anxious or edgy. I make some great shots and we win the first game. We congratulate each other and I grab my water bottle and stand on the sidelines, waiting for the next game. The setter comes to stand beside me.

He takes a step closer to me. "You're a good player. I'll have you on my team anytime," he says.

I smile. "Thanks. You too."

"I'm Ryan." He wipes his hand on his shirt and extends it to me.

"I'm Colleen," I wipe my hand before I take his to shake.

"A good grip, too." He winks. "My kind of girl."

What's with these brave men?

"I haven't seen you here before," he says.

"I come every week. I don't miss it," I say.

"Oh," he says. "I can't believe I missed out on you." He runs his fingers over his short hair. "Follow me. We're on this court next." He starts walking and I see that he has a nice swagger to his stride.

Once you are on a team, the teammates don't change all evening. Next week I could be on a different team, but for now, I follow cocky Ryan.

The second game starts and Ryan and I really start helping each other. I set and he spikes. He bumps it to me and I tip it over. We are on fire.

Near the end of the game, we are tied 24-24. "Come on!" Ryan yells. "Let's do this!"

It's our serve and a girl on our team gets it over, barely. It's bumped twice and then I see their best player setting up for a spike. I get ready, and before he even hits it, I yell, "Mine!"

I quickly dive onto the floor, landing on my side, and before the ball hits the floor, I pop it up with my fist. Another team member sets it and Ryan spikes it over. The other team doesn't return it. We win.

My team cheers. I'm still on the floor. It seems that I have landed on my bad hip and it's throbbing.

Ryan comes over and offers his hand, "Awesome dig! Can I help you up, Superstar?"

I take his hand, and I barely feel like I'm doing any work getting up. He has me up on my feet effortlessly. He high fives me and I stumble back, wincing in pain.

"You ok?" He looks concerned.

"Not really." I pull down the waistband of my shorts and show him the bruise.

"Ouch. You got that just now?" He asks incredulously.

I shake my head and laugh, "No. This was an injury from a couple days ago and I think I just made it worse. I'm out for the last game," I say sadly. "But I want to watch the next game."

"Stay here," he says.

I pick up my water bottle and watch him go look at the schedule, then to the first aid booth.

He saunters back with an ice pack in his hand. It's the second time this week that I have my own personal emergency medical attendant. "Let's get you over to that bench." He points, puts his arm around my waist and, again, I feel like I'm flying. Is he lifting me? "We're playing on this court."

We walk past two courts and I sit down on the bench. I then, watch him pick up another bench, easily, and he places it in front of me. What is he, Superman?

He eases my leg up and passes me the ice. "Here you go."

I press it to my hip. "You'd better not lose," I tease.

"Oh, I won't," he says with a smirk. He walks across the court to get into position. Nice bum.

"I know you're checking me out," he says over his shoulder. I blush and look at my feet. The game starts and I can watch him again without being insecure. Ryan is in remarkable form. He reminds me of Steve.

Steve was a hothead in university, but rightfully so. He rocked the volleyball court. He taught me how to spike. One afternoon, we practiced our spikes over and over, for three hours at the park by the school.

"I can't do another one," I had huffed, putting my hands on my knees.

"Do five more and then you can stop." I had managed to complete the five and had taken a drink of water. He had put his volleyball under one arm and had taken me by the hand. We had walked under the trees and he had stopped me suddenly, and kissed me. I had melted. "You are everything that I want in a girl. Smart, funny, sporty and beautiful."

I had giggled. "You're embarrassing me." I had put my arms around his neck.

"Get used to it, Colleen. I am putting you on a pedestal, and you're never coming down." He had touched my face tenderly. "I love you," he had whispered.

"I love you, too."

We had gone home and made love and cuddled all night. I remember that so vividly. When did that stop? We had a sexual connection. I want to get that back.

"Heads up!" Ryan yells. And a ball soars over my head. Someone from another court throws it back to him. "Keep your eye on the ball, Superstar!" he kids.

I watch the rest of the game, focusing on Ryan. He has a good eye and receives the ball with confidence. He has an amazing body. I can see the strength in his every movement. His muscles flex and bulge in all the right places. Steve used to be strong, but not like this. Ryan is almost Herculean.

Finally, the game is over and my team has won. He comes over and high fives me. "Good game," I say, standing up, trying to stretch out my hip.

"It would've been a better game if you were playing. I liked to watch you dive and bend in your black shorts." He winks. He puts his arm around me and we start walking toward the locker room doors.

I shake my head. "Are you always this bold?" I ask.

"Only when I see something I like," he says seductively.

I get out of his grasp, "I am going to get some clothes on." I feel like I'm on display.

"Come on, I'm just kidding." He laughs. "Meet me in front, by the snack bar, when you're done. I have a suggestion. An invitation, if you will."

"Ok." I giggle. I am giddy like a school girl. What is with me? Ok, so I'm very attracted to him. That's a good thing.

25.

I open my locker and get out my gym bag. I take my shorts off and put my leggings and hoodie on. My work clothes need a hanger, but I stuff them in my gym bag anyways, along with my coat. They're just going to the cleaners.

In the bathroom area, I wash my hands and face. What to do with my hair? I take the elastic out of my hair, releasing my curly pony tail and run my fingers carefully through my mane. It'll have to do. I put on some mascara and lip gloss and look at myself. I am excited to hear about his invitation. It's probably just to go out for a drink. I can handle that. I obviously can't go home with him. I'm all sweaty and gross.

He would be a great sample, if I did go home with him. The chemistry is definitely good between us. He's fun and has an amazing body. Really? I'm already thinking about being with another man? What's the mandatory time frame that I should allow between having sex with different men? Wow. Who the hell am I? I shouldn't be thinking like this.

Relax. It's just a drink. There should be no pressure to go home with him. Besides, it's is a week night. A Tuesday night. I mean, the weekend was different. It's meant for playing and being free to do what I please. I won't stay out late because I have to work in the morning. I shake my head and try to calm myself. My nerves have me feeling a little scatterbrained.

I limp slightly out of the locker room, but catch myself and walk as best as I can towards the snack bar. Ryan is already there, waiting, wearing black workout pants and a blue University of Toronto hoodie. He looks like he should be attending the university. Young and hot. I wonder how old he is. If he's too young, I could say goodbye a lot easier.

"You clean up real nice," he says approvingly.

I look down at myself, "This is not cleaned up. This is the best that I can do."

"I beg to differ. I see that you are still hobbling." He takes my gym bag from me and flings it over his shoulder and his other arm comes around my waist again.

"You are coming with me for a beer," he says.

"I hope it's not to some place fancy." I reach for my hair. "And you said it was a suggestion or an invitation. That was a demand." I'm trying to buy time to think. I need experience. Going out with Ryan will give me experience. Trust myself.

"You are adorable. And I have your bag and I have you, so you are coming with me." He laughs.

"Where are we going?" I ask. We start walking down the corridor.

"I was going to suggest the campus bar, but two things are wrong with that idea. One, it's quite a walk on the other side of the campus and although I'm sure I can carry you the entire way, I'd rather not expend my energy in that respect." He winks.

What does that mean? Is he saying he wants to expend it another way? With me? Flip flop.

"And two," he continues, "I don't want to mingle with twenty-something year olds."

"Aren't you twenty-something?" I joke.

"Superstar, you cut me to the quick." He gasps dramatically. "I am not a student. I was a student here once. I played volleyball, too. But that was many years ago. I have a real job now, as a lawyer."

"You're joking," I say surprised. "You can't be a lawyer." And played volleyball at my university? I'll ask about that later.

"Why not?" He asks. He leads me outside to the parking lot.

I have no reason to say or think that and I admit it, "You just didn't peg me for a lawyer. A bartender, maybe." He makes me feel at ease, flirting is easy with Ryan.

"And you agreed to go out with me?" He questions playfully and squeezes me tighter. "You are too easy."

"Hey, you've abducted me. I have no choice. Remember?" I whine.

He shakes his head. "I'm stuck on this bartender thing. I wouldn't peg you for a bartender type of woman. Now a lawyer, that's more your style."

I laugh. He's funny. Cocky, but funny.

"Now, I know we just met, but I really want to take you out for a drink, if you'll let me." He stops. "This is my car." He point to his silver Audi.

I cock my head to the side. "Can I trust you?" I know I can. And it is just a drink. For now.

"Listen, text a friend. Tell them my name, Ryan Page. My office is on College Street."

"It's ok. I believe you and I trust you," I say.

He smiles and opens the passenger door to his Audi. "Get in, Superstar."

I climb in and get out my cell phone and start texting Christine. I thought I could finish the text before Ryan got in because he was putting my gym bag in the trunk with his, but I don't.

"Caught you!" He laughs. "Text her my office address. 539 College Street."

"A girl can't be too careful," I say, laughing with him. "Where are we going?"

"Hoops on Yonge."

He starts the car and I finish texting Christine. "I do have to work at nine tomorrow, so I can't be out too late," I warn.

"One or two drinks only, I promise," he says. "First, what is your last name? You have me at an advantage."

"Cousineau."

"Colleen Cousineau," he says sounding it out. "Now let me guess what you do for a living." He looks at her and drives a few seconds in silence. "You are an athletic wear spokesmodel." He smirks.

"Ha ha ha."

"I'm kidding. I would love to see you on a runway dressed only in knee pads and holding a volleyball, though." He lifts his eyebrows. "Seriously, you are a teacher or some sort of psychologist."

I'm impressed. "You're good. I am a child psychologist."

"I know how to read people," he says. "How did you get that nasty bruise?"

I tell him the story and we arrive at Hoops. The bar has a multitude of flat screen TV's, some on the walls and others in the private booths. There's a massive plasma screen, too. All TV's are broadcasting some type of sporting event. We find a booth in the corner and a petite, brunette waitress comes over immediately, as it's a Tuesday night and not very busy. She smiles flirtatiously at Ryan, but he doesn't seem to notice. We pick out two very different types of draft beer from their extensive large draft menu and she takes the menus back, brushing her hand on his.

"You are sporty and smart. I like that. Did you play volleyball in university?" He asks.

"Yes, I did. And I wanted to ask you about that. I went to the University of Toronto, too."

"What years were you at the school?" He asks. We figure out that we were at school together only for his last year.

"And I never passed by you on campus. That's so disappointing. You could have been Mrs. Ryan Page." He frowns, but his crinkly brown eyes are anything but sad.

I wonder if he knows Steve, but I wasn't about to ask. I don't need to bring up my miseries. The waitress comes back with our beer.

Ryan takes his beer without even looking at her and raises it in the air, "To meeting the Superstar."

"Why do you keep calling me that?" I poke the orange slice that is floating in my beer.

He drops his arm. "We are in a co-ed volleyball league. I almost didn't join thinking it was going to be all out of shape, moms and dads who just want to get out of the house." He rolls his eyes. "I found out that I was right and I probably wasn't going to come back next week, until you showed up. You are an amazing player. A worthy adversary." He bows slightly. He's so cute. "Now don't leave me hanging!" He lifts his glass again.

I clink my glass against his. "I've been coming for quite a while. You're right. It's not the best volleyball in the world. I get so mad when they miss the easy ones, but it gets me out of the house." I take a sip of my beer, it's orangey.

"How are you still single?"

"Well, I haven't been, up until a month ago." I look down. "Separated," I say quietly.

He grabs my hand. "You seem ok, are you?"

I look up immediately. "Absolutely." I fake a smile.

"That is so not a real smile." He laughs. "But you are out with me, so you're not too shy to meet people. I think you're on the right track."

"Yes I am," I say and I hold up my glass. "Cheers to you, Ryan Page. Fellow Superstar." I'm getting bold.

"You say the sweetest things." He clinks his glass against mine.

Talking to Ryan is easy. We have a lot of things in common and he is very witty and energetic. I don't feel like I have to be fake or flirt with him. We order a second beer and talk about university volleyball. He tells me about his last year at school and having to deal with this first year kid who thought he was a god on the court.

"He would show up late for practices, never complete the warm-up, but he complained like a bitch when he didn't start a game," Ryan continues. "He would criticize the other players, but his only value was that he could spike the ball, pretty much every single round. He was good, but not that good." He takes a sip of is beer. "This guy's arrogance was unrelenting off the court, too. In the locker rooms, at the bars… Everywhere. I tried to avoid him."

"It's hard when you don't get along with a teammate. You can't trust them," I say.

"Talk about trusting! This guy had a girlfriend and from what I hear, beautiful. Legs up to here," He points to his chest. I laugh. "Kind of like yours, Superstar." He touches my hand. I could feel my face heat up.

"Anyway, she played volleyball, too. I hear she was also extremely smart. A dream come true for most men. And he cheated on her all the time. She had no idea."

I snort. "What a jerk. Do you remember his name?"

"Hmmm... I cannot remember. I'm usually amazing at remembering names, too. Maybe I'm just blocking that arrogant prick from my mind. I'll remember his name tomorrow when I'm in court. It always happens that way. Now I deal with pricks on a day to day basis at work," he says.

I laugh. "You must like your job."

"Of course I do." Ryan's eyes light up. "I couldn't be happier. Well, I could be happier if you came home with me."

Flip flop. Oh my. Should I? I take a long drink from my beer and try to avoid his eyes. Maybe we could go out another night instead.

"What do you say, Superstar? Want to come back to my apartment and enjoy my hot tub? It'll be good for your hip."

I pause, and take another long drink. He is fun and I feel good talking to him. But a hot tub? That makes me nervous. My beer is now gone. He laughs.

"Do you like me?" He asks and takes my hands in his.

I nod and stare at our hands, unable to talk. I'm confident he'll be able to give me experience. And I do want to see him shirtless.

"I just don't want this night to end. We can continue our conversation at my apartment. I will make sure that you are home for work, whether it be tonight or after breakfast tomorrow." He tilts his head and grins.

He is smooth. "I don't have a bathing suit," is all that I can manage. I found my third sample.

His eyes flash and he laughs, "Don't worry about that." He signals the waitress.

Don't worry about that? Am I going in naked? Wow, he really is confident. I admire him.

Without a word, he helps me out of the restaurant and into his car.

I am a little scared this time because I don't know him. I am going to his apartment. What if he's an ax murderer? What if there isn't any real chemistry? He's hot and I want to touch his body, but what if it fizzles from there?

Ryan starts the car and looks at me. "You look like a deer caught in headlights. We don't have to go to my house." He puts his hand on my thigh.

He's not an ax murderer. I relax and smile.

"There's a smile." He leans over and kisses me softly on the lips. Flip flop. It feels warm and gentle. I kiss him back, touching the side of his face. I can verify that we have chemistry.

He pulls back about an inch, "Let's go," he breathes.

26.

It is a surprisingly short drive to his apartment. It's crazy how close Ryan lives to me. I guess I can make a quick getaway, if necessary. We pull into the underground parking, and even before I can unbuckle my seatbelt, Ryan has the car door open for me. He also puts his arm around me to help me walk. Such a gentleman.

"I'm pretty sure that I can walk, Ryan," I say.

"Is that your way of saying, 'quit touching me'?"

I shake my head. "No, not at all. I just don't want you to think I'm feeble and weak."

"I would never think that. You're just the opposite." His roam my body, "Now let me watch you walk, Superstar." He leans against the trunk of his car, arms and ankles crossed.

"Really? You're going to watch me walk?" I'm feeling shy.

"Yes. I have to make sure that my client is capable of walking or I will have to begin litigation with the University of Toronto."

I roll my eyes. I start walking on the black asphalt toward the elevator. My hip aches, but I keep it steady. "See? I'm fine."

Ryan whistles. "Oh, yes you are." He jogs over and swats my behind and keeps jogging to press the button for the elevator. He's so energetic and playful. I love it.

As soon as I reach him, the elevator door opens and we step in. He presses 21 and stands back on the other side of the elevator. Arms and ankles crossed again, eyeing me.

"You really aren't making me feel comfortable," I say, squirming under his gaze.

"I'm sorry. If I stand closer to you, I might lose control. I'm trying to be a nice guy, I really am. But you are adorable in your cute hoodie and your curly hair." He comes to stand beside me and takes my hand. "Here we are," he says.

He leads me out to the hallway and I only see two doors on the floor. He unlocks the door closest to us and I walk through. It's a gorgeous condo, decorated in black and white, with splashes of neutrals. It's open concept with the living room leading into the dining room and the kitchen. Most of the walls are a soft black, except for the kitchen, which is white with black lacquered cabinets and black marble countertops.

"Nice condo, Ryan. But I figured you for a framed sports memorabilia and pool table kind of guy," I joke.

"That's over here," he says, laughing. And he leads me over to a billiards room off the dining room.

"I knew I could read you a little bit." Signed and framed hockey jerseys hang on the wall with other sports banners and some trophies. There are also foosball and air hockey tables in the corner and a traditional Brunswick billiards table in the centre of the room. I do a double take when I see his university volleyball team pictures and wonder if I would recognize anyone. I'm walking towards it when Ryan calls to me.

"The hot tub is on my balcony, outside these sliding glass doors. Would you like to join me?" He waves two bottles of beer that he has taken out of a stainless steel fridge that sits in a bar area of the room.

The picture can wait. I look down at myself and then back up at him. I shrug, pointing out the obvious.

"In the bathroom over there," he points to a door beside the bar. "There are an assortment of bathing suits, wraps, and towels. Take your pick."

I smile and shoot him a thumbs up.

The bathroom is massive, about as big as my kitchen, and the bathtub fits about four people. I'm overwhelmed by his house, the situation, and by Ryan himself. I sit on the side of the tub to collect myself, but my vibrating phone disturbs me.

I see that I have three texts and two voicemails from Christine. The texts have many exclamation marks, smiley face emoticons and she has written, *GO FOR IT!* I listen to one of the messages and she is screeching excitedly, something about how Ryan Page is a hot bachelor and one of the wealthiest lawyers in Toronto. *Oh my god, Ci-Ci! Do him!* I don't think I need to listen to the other message.

I do text her back to let her know that I'm with him at his apartment on Gerrard and that I'll call her tomorrow. I put my phone in my purse and it buzzes instantly, probably with her response, but I ignore it.

I look around and easily find the basket of bathing suits on a shelf. Where did these come from? Are they left over from the multitude of women he has brought over for the same purpose? I shake my head. No reason to be jealous, but as I look through them, I don't think I can wear any of them. The bathing suits are all made by high end designers, but how am I going to wear another woman's suit? Were any of these washed? I don't want to smell them. Yuck. Who knows what is crawling around in them?

I could wear my own panties and sports bra, but would he think it's weird? I start to panic and turn in a circle with my fists clenched. Then I see a black and white striped bikini hanging on the back of the bathroom door. I inspect it and it has a price tag still on it. It even has that hygiene sticker on the lining of the bikini bottom. I look at the size. It'll fit! What luck! Why is a brand new bathing suit in the bathroom? Did he buy it? Whatever. I'm wearing it. I rip off the sticker and the price tag and bury them in the garbage can under the sink.

The bandeau top fits perfectly and the side ties on the black bottom are adjustable. It's not what I would have chosen for myself, but it'll have to do. I fold my clothes neatly and put them in a different basket on the shelf. I put my hair back up in a high ponytail, and pause to look at myself.

"You've come this far. You can't quit now. He's a sweet guy, smart and very sexy. You could do worse. Do it for the experience." It's like I'm pumping myself up before a big game.

Before I head out the door, I grab a gauzy white robe that is hanging on the back of the door. I need to cover myself up a little.

I step out on to the balcony and it's a chilly night. I pull the robe tighter around me. The sky is dark, I can't see the moon, but millions of windows are lit up in the buildings around us. They look like stars. The traffic buzzes down below.

Ryan is already in the hot tub and I stand above him, looking down. I can't see his upper body very well, just the top of his bulging chest and the rips in his deltoids. Yummy. I can't believe how much I adore his body.

"Coming in?" He asks.

I turn around and undo the robe, slipping it off and place it onto a small chair. Without looking at him, I quickly step into the hot, bubbling water. It's a perfect temperature.

He hands me a beer. "That suit is perfect on you. You look great," he says and he moves closer to me.

"Can I inquire how you have accumulated such a collection of bathing suits?" I ask as I take a swig.

"You might not believe me, but I have three sisters. They all go to the university and come over all the time," he says rolling his eyes.

"Really?" I'm surprised.

"Really. I'd like to tell you that I have had a harem of women over, but honestly, Superstar, you've been the only one in a very long time." He touches his beer bottle to her shoulder.

"I'm not sure if I believe you. You are cocky and forward and very flirty."

"I meet women all the time, but they seem fake and are interested in me for the wrong reasons. Unfortunately, it's part of the profession. I can't trust a lot of women."

"Look how easy it was for you to bring me home."

"Believe me, I am questioning that myself. But when you yelled at me on the court to set you up, I knew you were worth talking to."

I blush. "I was having a bad day."

Ryan moves closer to me. Our thighs are touching under the water. "Is your day getting better?"

I nod.

Then he kisses me. Flip flop. The kiss is not gentle. It's searching and forceful. I can feel his desire. Maybe it has been a long time since he's been with a woman. His tongue slows down its rhythm and he bites my bottom lip softly. That spikes my arousal and I lose my breath. He knows what he's doing. He breaks away for a second to take my beer bottle from me and places it on the table beside the hot tub.

We start kissing again and I feel him lift me up to sit me sideways on his lap. I let him. The water level is just below my breasts, but the cool air on my wet skin doesn't bother me. Ryan's head is tipped up and I bring my hands onto the back of his neck, supporting his head. His one hand slides up to my neck and down my back to my bikini bottom. I feel his fingers dip between the fabric and my skin, but his hand slides right back up. He repeats this over and over. His front hand is also moving in no particular direction, it's just rubbing my shins, knees, thighs and up to my outside hip, playing with my bikini strings.

I let my hand fall to Ryan's shoulder and down his arm, feeling the indentation of his triceps and the swelling of his biceps. My hand travels back up his arm to feel his pectoral muscles and then down under his arm, along his stomach. I'm excited. I can't see them yet, but I know they're there. I can feel every muscle of his abdominal area. I can't wait to take a peek.

Ryan's front hand starts to climb up, away from my lower body. He's touching my stomach, sliding his hand back and forth along the edge of my bikini bottom. Then it rises again, and slides along the bottom of bandeau top at my rib cage. Uh oh. Further up it goes, and I hold my breath. Should I stop him? Tell him to go slower? He cups one of my breasts in his hand and pinches my nipple through the fabric with his fingers. That feels good. I moan. I'll let him do it some more.

He starts kissing down my neck and he has pulled away from me slightly, his other hand comes to the front of my body. He has both of my breasts in his hands, squeezing them together, biting at them through the fabric. I give into the pleasure, tilt my head up, arch my back and let the sensations overwhelm me.

All of sudden, Ryan has one arm under my legs and he is standing with me scooped up in his arms. He must stop picking me up. I almost complain, but as soon as he steps out of the hot tub, he places me on the floor. He grabs a towel from a basket, bends over and starts patting my feet and legs dry. He then takes the towel behind me, holding the top two corners on either side of me and pulls me in close to him and he kisses me gently. He wraps me up, tucking the corners into to the top of my bandeau. He's sweet.

Ryan grabs another towel and starts the same process on him. When he gets the towel around him and he's rubbing the towel back and forth across his back, I get my chance. I can see every ripple and motion of his six-pack. He wraps the towel around his waist and walks toward me. All abs. I lick my lips instinctively.

"You keep that up and I'm going to take you here, outside, on this chair." He outlines my lips with his thumb and gently tugs at my bottom lip. He takes a step closer to me, reaches up and very gently takes the elastic out of my hair. My curls fall around the top of my bandeau top.

"Wow. You are beautiful," he whispers. Flip flop. He takes my face in his hands and starts kissing me hard, pushing his tongue in my mouth. I don't mind this. I step closer to him and press my hips against his. Through the towel, I can feel his hardness against my stomach. I reach up and rest my hands on his shoulders, pulling him closer. I quiver with anticipation.

Ryan slides his hands down to my waist, to my lower back and down my behind. He reaches really low on my bum, almost to my thighs. What is he doing? Without any struggle, he has me in the air, my legs straddling his waist. *Ryan!* I want to screech. But I don't say anything.

I stop kissing him and clutch his shoulders, panicked, but as he starts to walk into the condo he says, "Don't worry. You're a little bird in my arms," I squeeze my legs tightly around him. He smiles and walks a little further. When I feel him lowering me down, I release my grip. I expect to touch the floor, but I end up sitting on the edge of the pool table.

Ryan takes off his towel and lets it fall to the floor. He undoes my towel, looking into my eyes, and it drops onto the pool table. My wet bottom is still on top of the towel.. We start kissing again. I'm still between his legs and he slides me right to him, pressing his hardness into the flimsy bathing suit that barely covers my sex. I can feel a surge of electricity between my legs. I am very turned on. I feel him playing with the strings on the sides of my bikini.

Ryan stops kissing me. "You ok?"

I nod.

He smiles and says, "Good. I'll be right back."

I shiver with nervousness and excitement. Where is he going? Another beer, maybe? But we didn't even finish the first ones.

Within a minute, he is back and I still don't know why he left. He puts his hands on my waist and starts kissing me again. I like kissing him. I could do it all night. But then I feel him untie one side of my bikini bottom. Uh oh. A second later, the other strings are undone. Yikes! My bottom is bare.

He inches back from me, we are nose to nose. "Did I overstep my boundaries?"

"I'm not sure."

"Do you like kissing me?"

"Yes."

"Let's keep kissing and if I do something that makes you uncomfortable, you tell me.

"Ok."

"Colleen. You are beautiful and you turn me on. I want to please you, but I have to know that you want this."

"Yes, I want this."

We start kissing again and his hands caress my naked behind and slide up my back and back down to my behind. I feel his thumbs press on the front of my hips and closer down the crease of my leg to my heat. Then they slide up my stomach and over my breasts, tweaking both nipples. I try to close my legs, to stop the throbbing, but he just comes closer to me. I can feel the hardness of him. I can't believe how much I want him inside of me. I moan softly.

Now his hands are behind my back and he's fiddling with something else, and it takes me a second to figure out what it is. I glance down and see him putting on the condom. I look away quickly. I'm too shy. When did he take his bathing suit off? I can't stop this now. I don't want to stop this. I'm ready.

Ryan grabs my bottom and I feel the tip of his throbbing manliness hovering at the entrance of my sex. Then, I feel him. Large and penetrating. I moan loudly. He enters slowly, letting me adjust to his size. He has substantial girth and length. Wow. It doesn't hurt, it just fills me.

He takes his lips off me and his eyes are dark and he looks concerned. Something carnal takes control of me. I don't answer. I grab his hips, put my legs around the back of his thighs and pull him deeper into me. He groans. He slowly pulls out of me and when he pushes into me again, he lifts me up by my behind off the pool table. It feels so deep this way. This position is so good. He takes control and moves my whole body into his. I dig my fingers into the back of his arms. I am not thinking anymore, just feeling.

Ryan keeps the slow pace and tilts me back onto the pool table. My bottom is back on the edge of the table again. He really likes to throw me around. As I think that, he takes my legs and brings them straight up, my ankles in his hands. This is very creative. I feel so completely full. My walls are bursting with him. I'm glad I still have my bandeau top on, I feel exposed here on my back. He pumps once, watching me. He pulls out slowly and pumps again. The sensation is incredible. I put my arms over my head. He does it again. Deliberately slow, hard thrusts.

"Please," I beg. Did I say that?

His eyebrows lift and he smiles, but his pace doesn't change. He opens my legs wider; my legs are a wide vee. It's a different feeling. I close my eyes and accept the intrusive thrusting and the forceful pressure on my clitoris. It's animalistic. He thrusts again hard and retracts slowly. He brings my feet together again, repeating his slow pleasurable torture and starts kissing my toes. It tickles and adds a different intensity to my pleasure. I can feel the pressure building up deep inside me. I can feel every inch of him inside me. I'm almost there.

"Faster. Please," I plead. I am beside myself.

He smiles again and withdraws completely. What? My eyes flutter open. He pulls me up by my hands and has me in his arms quickly. I'm not touching the floor. Does he have adult attention deficit disorder? I was really liking that.

Ryan doesn't go far, he places my feet on the floor and my back against a wall. I look down and glance at his erection. I'm stunned. That was inside of me? He is very well-endowed. I'm surprised that it can fit inside me. It arouses me greatly. He leans down and kisses me, his breath is ragged.

He kisses my neck and shoulder, and I realize that he's slowly turning me, so that I'm facing the wall. What position is he putting me in now? He kisses every inch of my back and runs his hands down my arms. He takes my hands, and places them on the wall, at shoulder height. He gently slides down my bandeau top to my waist, releasing my breasts. He presses his chest into my back and grabs my breasts from behind, cupping them, squeezing them together, tugging at my nipples. The pleasure shoots through my body, pulsing between my legs. I feel his hardness pushing against my bum. He seems very turned on, too.

Ryan releases my breasts and I feel kisses on my lower back, he must be on his knees. This man is hyperactive. He stretches the bandeau top down over my hips and lets it fall to the floor. His lips kiss my behind, his hands feeling every curve. He pulls my hips back towards him, my hands almost come off the wall and I feel a tongue at my apex. He's going to lick me this way? I almost stand up to stop him, but his knee pushes my feet apart and he pulls me back. His tongue plunges into my wetness. My hands drop even lower on the wall. I'm at a ninety degree angle, looking down at the floor. His tongue is swirling from my sex to the back of me. I didn't know that spot was so erotic. I'm moaning loudly and breathing hard. He's grabbing my behind with both hands and I feel his thumbs dip into me. The rhythm of his tongue increases, dipping into my wetness and back into the new erotic zone, and his thumbs plunge into me at different times. It sets me over the edge. I let go and stop thinking. I come hard and fast, crying out. I am all sensation. My knees start to give out, but he is on his feet holding me up.

"That's my Superstar. But I'm not done with you yet."

Ryan has me back up, hands high on the wall, and I feel his hardness, drive into me. He is taking me from behind. I've barely regained my senses from my climax, but the feeling of him is wonderful and I welcome it. He thrusts into me hard and fast, his one hand on my sex, fingering my clitoris, his other hand higher up than mine on the wall. I push my hips back into his. I want to feel all of him inside me. He groans.

"Not yet." Ryan pulls out and lifts me up, carrying me to another room. He is voracious. He pushes open the door and puts me down on what I assume is his bed, I can't see anything.

Ryan turns on a bedside lamp and I look around. We are definitely in his bedroom. The walls are black, his headboard is dark walnut and his bed is covered in dark gray bedding and pillows. He pulls back the duvet, jumps onto the bed with me and says, "Get on top."

I don't argue. This, I can do. I crawl over to him and straddle him. He's seems larger than before, and I take him in my hands. He's bigger than both my hands, hard and smooth. It's probably the size of three of my fists put together, maybe four. I lift up and place him at my entrance and slowly take all of him in me. Oh my.

I automatically start moving my hips up and down, back and forth and he's pushing his hips up so I can feel every inch of him. I lean over him and put my hands on his headboard, continuing my rocking rhythm. Ryan starts fondling my breasts with his hands and tongue, squeezing my nipples, sucking them. I'm groaning and I can't believe that the delicious sensations are building up inside me again.

He suddenly turns me on my side. I'm facing him, chest to chest. My top leg is over his hip and he's still inside me, thrusting. He takes my top leg and raises it up in the crook of his elbow. Thankfully I am flexible.

Ryan raises his eyebrows and smiles. He takes it further and my leg is now stretched, so that my calf is now resting on his shoulder. I'm doing side splits on his body and he's fucking me fiercely now. The feeling is incredible. He thrusts hard and fast and over and over. I am all feeling and sensation. It's wonderful. I come again, exploding, moaning loudly.

Ryan is right behind me. His breath quickens and he lets out a loud groan, stiffening and releasing and stiffening again. And then he is calm, only his heavy breathing can be heard.

I am spent. He rag dolled me and I loved every minute of it. But I can't move. I feel him pull out and I am a little sore. I'm afraid to put my legs together. I roll over on my back, with one of my arms above my head, my eyes closed. And I feel him lie next to me and brush a curl away from my eyes.

"Sleep," he says. "I'll make sure we're up early."

I'm momentarily concerned with how I'm going to handle the next morning, but I don't argue. Maybe he'll leave me alone in his house like Dave did. I fall asleep instantly.

27.

     I open my eyes and stare at the strange alarm clock on the bedside table. 5:53 am. I quickly realize where I am and carefully look beside me. Ryan is still here, asleep. Dammit. I carefully get out of the bed, trying not to disturb him. I want to get my clothes on quickly. I have the feeling that he is insatiable and I don't think I can handle another acrobatic workout.

     My bruised hip is only a minor problem, as I feel I am tender everywhere. My muscles and joints are screaming at me. Probably from all the positions he put me in. Oh, and as I walk, I can feel that my girly parts are inflamed and sensitive. Wow.

     Surprisingly, his condo is like a maze. I can't find the bathroom where I stored my clothes. And then I hear voices. Female voices. I freeze. I'm naked in the middle of a strange house. I try to get my bearings, but the laughter seems to be coming closer. I turn a corner and I see the bathroom door. I look in both directions first, and then run into the bathroom, locking the door. I don't think anyone saw me.

     I take a shower, keeping my hair dry, and dress in my volleyball clothes. I pinch my cheeks and run my fingers through my curls, trying to scrunch up the messy pieces. It's hopeless. I have sex hair.

     Rummaging through the vanity drawers, I find a toothbrush and toothpaste. The toothbrush doesn't look too used, but I run hot water over it and scrub it with my thumb, until I'm satisfied. I brush my teeth and gargle with mouthwash too. Deodorant and vanilla body spray are also in the drawers, so I take advantage of them. He can't be lying about his sisters, there are even a couple of boxes of tampons.

     Now what? I fold up my towel, place it on the counter. I rub it around the counter to dry up my splashes. I look around. There is nothing else to tidy up. I just sit on the edge of the tub and wait. I'd love to leave, but what do I say to the women that are out there. Is it his sisters? Or his harem?

I hear Ryan's voice and the girls' voices again. And then there's a knock at the door. "Superstar?" Are you in there?"

"Yes," I say quietly and open the door.

"Good morning, beautiful. Are you all ready to go?" He is already dressed in gray dress pants, a white shirt, and a pale purple tie. He looks gorgeous. I don't know how he finds shirts to fit him. His biceps are threatening to rip his sleeves open.

"I'm ready whenever you are," I say, looking around.

"Unfortunately, we have company. My sisters came over for breakfast," he grumbles. "I really have to change my locks."

"Oh," I mumble. I am underdressed for meeting his sisters.

He takes my hand. "You'll be fine. Let's get you a cup of coffee and we'll get out of here."

We walk into the dining area and there are three girls sitting around the black lacquered dining table, eating bagels with cream cheese and fruit. They are jabbering away, but they stop when they see me.

"Girls, this is Colleen. Colleen, these are my sisters." He points, "Gabby, Belinda, and Kate."

I wave shyly. "Hi."

At the same time, they all say, "Hi."

Ryan takes my hand again and leads me into the kitchen. I feel their eyes burning into me. He pours coffee into a large to-go cup and shows me the sugar and creamers. I pour one creamer into it and take a sip of the coffee. It's delicious.

"Are you ready?" He asks and places a lid on my cup. It seems like he's rushing me.

"Yes."

Once more, he takes my hand and we step into the dining room. "We both have to be at work, so lock up when you're done. I'll see you later," he tells his sisters.

"It was nice meeting all of you," I say.

The girls smile and wave.

As he leads me out the front door, I remember that the bikini I was wearing is still in the games room. The bottoms are on the pool table and the top, on the floor. I blush profusely and start walking faster. Ryan closes the door, but we still hear the girls burst out laughing.

Ryan grits his teeth. "I'm going to kill them." He's walking fast towards the elevator and I follow staying quiet. "Listen, I didn't want you to have to endure an inquisition by them. They are tough girls. They like to take care of me. Oh, I'm never going to hear the end of it later." He presses the elevator button and I hear him curse.

I don't say anything.

"Hey, Superstar. What's wrong?"

The elevator doors open and we step inside. Ryan presses the button for the garage.

"Nothing. I'm not a morning person," I try to smile. I don't know why I'm quiet. I do feel awkward and I'm actually starting to feel guilty. Not for what Ryan I did, but because I am going to have to tell him that I have no intention of ever seeing him again.

"You're a bad liar." We walk into the parking garage to his car and he opens the passenger door. But before I get in, he takes my coffee, puts it on the roof of his car and takes me in his arms for a gentle, warm hug.

He releases me slightly and steps back. "I had a fantastic time with you last night. I'm sorry if it felt like I was kicking you out. You are an intelligent and beautiful woman. I would love to get you know you better." He smiles softly.

Uh oh. I look down. "I didn't expect this to happen at all yesterday. You are also a great guy and last night was… wonderful." I blush. "But I am not ready to date and commit to anyone. This was a…"

"A one night stand?" He says incredulously.

That's the term I was looking for. I nod.

He cocks his head, "Really? I guess I understand. I can't say I'm not disappointed." He allows me to get into the car and then passes me my coffee, before closing the door,.

He gets in and starts the car. We are both quiet. It does not get easier each time I do it. Taking the feelings out of casual sex is difficult.

We don't say anything during the drive to the university's parking lot. He pulls up beside my car and I almost expect him to throw me out.

He takes my hand and looks me in the eyes, "I have never met anyone like you, Superstar. I know I just met you, and it may sound crazy, but I can read people and I know you are someone that I can see myself with." He ducks his head shyly, "I can honestly say that I have never said that. Life has been mainly about my career, never women.

He is baring his soul. I feel awful. I shake my head, "Ryan, it's not the right time. I need to find myself."

"I understand," he says again. He opens up the car console and pulls out a card. "This is my card. You have my number. Use it if you need legal assistance or if you want to join me in my hot tub again. Either way, I'm yours." He smiles sadly.

I take his card, "Thanks Ryan." I want to say something to make him feel better, but I can't find the words. I just used him for sex.

He's ever the gentleman and gets out of the car to open my door. He hugs me. "Take care, Colleen," he whispers in my ear.

"You too."

He gets my gym bag from the trunk and I take it to my car, without looking back. I notice that he waits until I'm in my car, with it started, before he drives away.

That was hard. I feel bad for Ryan. He'll have to explain his one-night stand to his three, meddlesome sisters. How awkward would that be? I fondle my wedding band that is still attached to my key ring. It was another amazing experience and Ryan is one of a kind. How can I get that same type of honesty and openness and passion with Steve? Is it possible? Or is it too late?

28.

I rush home to wash my sex hair and get ready for work. I put on snug, cream coloured pants, a hip-length, white sweater and tan riding boots. I did have enough time this morning to run, but I didn't bother. My body feels too beat up. Thinking about how Ryan got me into all of those positions gives me goose bumps. Would I ever have enough nerve to suggest things like that to Steve?

My brain is scattered with thoughts that I can't seem to calm down. I don't need a latte, but I need something to distract me and even, comfort me, so I decide to get a steeped black tea.

The café is as busy as my mind this morning, so I pick up a stray newspaper and read it in line patiently. I am pleasantly surprised to find an article about one of Ryan Page's lawsuits and I devour it while I wait for my tea.

"We have to stop meeting like this," a voice says.

It's Jack again. "Good morning. Why is it that we keep running into each other here? Where is your clinic again?"

"On Isabella. Just a block away," he says and takes a sip of his coffee.

My name is called and pick up my large tea. "Small world." I smile.

"How's your hip?"

"Oh, it's much better. Just a tiny bit of a bruise. I've been taking care of it." The hot tub might have aided in its progress.

We walk out of the café. "I'm glad to hear it. And by the way, you look beautiful this morning, Colleen. "

"Thanks Jack." I blush.

"Have a good day," he says and turns to walk down the block.

The flattery warms me. *Hold on!* I am not supposed to like attention from Jack. It's Jack. Jack is taboo. I roll my eyes. He's just a friend. *Calm down, Colleen.*

Margie is running late, I notice, as I unlock the door. I glance at the schedule briefly and head to my office.

"It's a busy one today!" I hear Margie shout after she slams the door.

No time for chit chat. My first patient arrives and I don't stop until after lunch. During my mid-afternoon break, Margie tells me that Christine has called three times. I look at my phone and she has blown that up, too. I call her immediately.

"Ci-Ci! What the hell?" Christine explodes.

"I'm sorry. I've been super busy today and I haven't had time to call," I apologize.

I tell her about my evening with Ryan, not in great detail, but enough that she knows we had sex. She congratulates me.

"Are you going to see him again?"

"Do you ever listen to me?" I scold.

"I know. I know. You want Steve back. But this is Ryan Page. Ryan Page!" She emphasizes. "Not only is he rich and powerful but you saw him naked. You fucked him."

"All right. Enough! He is pretty sexy and his body is rock hard," I say thoughtfully.

"How's his package?" Christine asks crudely.

But I laugh. "Nice. Very nice."

"I bet!" She laughs. "Project sex is coming along nicely, I assume?"

"Ha ha." I pick the fuzz off my sweater. "I felt guilty today."

"Oh Ci-Ci. Why? You hooked up with a legend."

"I don't think he dates very often and he told me that he could see himself with me. He was very disappointed that I didn't want another date."

"You must have made an incredible impression, but it's not your fault that he fell for you. Did you suggest that you were looking for a relationship?"

"Not at all. I assumed we both wanted casual sex."

"Do not feel guilty. Did you enjoy your experience?"

"Definitely."

"Focus on that. You did nothing wrong. Hey, can you meet me for dinner later?"

"No, I can't. I have my art class at six." I wince, waiting for the sarcasm.

"You and your crazy clubs." She sighs. "Listen, I am working through the weekend, but I am taking you to Sangria on Sunday night."

I wince again. I'm scared to ask, "What is Sangria?"

"It's a Latin club with Salsa dancing." She's excited.

Eek. "I don't know, Christine." I'll feel like a fool.

"Ci-Ci, they give you a lesson first and if you don't like it, you can just dance your normal style. You're a good dancer," she urges.

I do like to dance. "Ok. I'll go."

"Perfect. We'll talk later. I have to go," Christine says.

"Good bye, Christine."

29.

The rest of the day goes by quickly and I leave at five to get to the Art Barn School. I remembered the stressfulness of rush hour traffic the other day, so I left an hour early. Now, I can calmly eat my protein bar on the way and actually score a great parking spot.

I'm excited to take another crack at my watercolour painting. I tend to pay attention to detail, and the instructor has been very attentive and helpful in this respect.

Students are already gathering in the studio, some are seated at their easels and others are filling their water dishes. I hurry to find an empty easel, take off my coat and put on my smock. I try to pick out our instructor Shawn Lauzon, because he has our paintings. He lets them dry in the studio overnight and then takes care of them until our next class. I see him at the front of the room, handing out watercolour paint tubes.

"Hi, Shawn," I say.

Shawn looks up and smiles, "Hi, Colleen. How are you?" He has longer, wavy brown hair that curls around his ears and bright, brown eyes. He's wearing blue plaid long-sleeved shirt over a simple white t-shirt and baggy jeans. He looks like an artist. Laid back and easy going.

"I'm great. Looking forward to getting started." I smile back.

He pulls out my forty-eight inch square painting from behind the counter. "You are doing such great work. I'll make sure I come around to help you." He smiles again and turns away to help another student.

I get comfortable at my easel, and take out my own set of watercolour paint tubes. I splurged and bought the best, plus I don't like to share. The instructor's tubes get paint all over them and the students don't close them properly and they dry out. I take care of mine.

I squeeze out some yellow, ochre and brown paint on my pallet and start mixing a bit of everything together with water. Shawn explained to me last week that as sun light is coming from above, the top of the grass will be lighter than the part close to the ground. I started with a pale yellow, so now I'm taking a darker yellow to paint the stalks.

I'm completely involved in my painting, but after a while, I feel someone at my side. I look up. It's Shawn.

"I didn't want to scare you." He smiles. "It looks good."

"Thanks," I say.

"Can I show you something?"

I nod and hand him my brush. I try to get out of his way, but his thigh is between my legs. I'm stuck.

"You want to try for a natural effect, so you want to make sure the lines are not all parallel but cross each other and go in different directions." He paints so fluidly. "You see what I mean?"

I nod enthusiastically. "You're so good."

"You have a lot of potential," he says. He hands me back my brush and our fingers touch.

"What else can I do to make it better?" I'm eager to learn.

"In term of brushes, you can use a pointed round brush to add fine details once the initial washes of colour are dry. For now, you can use the tip of the brush handle to drag the colour and draw some grass blades." He dips the end of my brush in the ochre paint and shows me quickly.

"And an old and distressed flat brush with uneven hair," he picks up another one of my brushes, "like this one, is a good tool to suggest the texture of grass in the middle ground. Watch." This time I watch him, rather than what he is doing. He has very full lips and his tongue actually sticks out a little while he concentrates. He's pretty cute.

Shawn steps back and I quickly focus on my painting. "Thank you so much," I say.

"Anytime, Colleen." He lingers a bit staring at me, but then quickly turns and walks away.

I watch him leave and see him run his fingers through his hair. His shirts lift up and I can see his some bare skin. He looks lean and fit. I shake my head. I am in awe of him, not attracted to him. He has so much talent, there's so much he can do with his hands. There's that double entendre again. I just mean that I'd love to see his work.

Near the end of the class, Shawn makes his way back to me. "How are you doing?"

I sit back and we look at the canvas together. "I don't know."

"I like how you did the wheat grass here, but here," he points, "it looks a little choppy."

"Yes, I noticed that, too." I frown. "I want to throw it out and start again."

"No!" He looks at me. "We can fix it, I promise."

135

He squeezes a bit of gold paint onto the pallet, takes my brush and says, "The foreground can be painted with stronger colours and with more details, although there is no need to paint every single blade of grass."

He's working a miracle. "Amazing," I say.

"Simple," he says, "You just need to know the right techniques."

Reminds me of my research. "Do you have any of your own work here? I would love to see it."

He drops his head and rubs his scalp with his fingers. He's thinking. "I don't normally invite my students but," he lowers his voice and leans in. "I'm having an exhibition this Friday night at Gallery 123 in York."

"Congratulations. That's amazing," I gush.

"If you are interested, it starts at eight. Don't feel pressured. You're probably a busy woman," he says.

"I am completely interested. I will be there," I say excitedly.

He tilts his head and smiles. "Now I'm nervous."

"Why?" I'm confused.

"Never mind," he says, shaking his head. "I would love to have you there."

"Thank you. I'm excited to go."

I see some of the students packing up their belongings. "Time's up!" Shawn says loudly. "Keep your paintings on your easels and I will collect them tomorrow morning." He turns and looks at me, "Thank you for coming."

I smile and start packing up my brushes and close my pallet. I can use the same paint next week. It dries out, but I can rework it again with water. I put on my coat and Shawn meets me at the door.

"Have a good night, Colleen," he says.

"You too," I say and I walk out into the crisp evening air. Shawn stays behind in the studio. I know that I am somewhat inexperienced with men and perhaps I can't read all of their signs, but I think he's interested in me. Or I could be over thinking it. He did meet me at the door to say goodbye, but he's nice like that with everyone. Isn't he? I shake my head. It doesn't matter. I'm looking forward to Friday night. I just want to see his work.

I get home and put my painting supplies away and complete the usual recordings for work while eating a salad. I'm about to call it a night and I see my Project Sex notebook. I open it up and update the data.

Data Collection

Sample #3

Seek persons who understand study & are willing to express inner feelings & experiences
- Man, aged? (in his early 30's), lawyer, volleyball enthusiast (played in university)
- Sandy blonde brush cut, brown eyes, freckles, extremely muscular, sexy, and attractive.

Describe experiences of phenomenon
- I was attracted to his hard body and his appearance; well-endowed. He was intelligent, funny, playful, and energetic. Foreplay consisted of kissing, and breast manipulation in the hot tub; heavy petting on the pool table.
- Different positions!
- The Clasp (in the air, holding my behind, my legs wrapped around his waist).
- The Mermaid (he was standing; I was lying on my back, my legs straight up in the air.
- The Eagle (he was standing; I was lying on my back, my legs in a vee).
- The Column (both of us standing, my hands against the wall).
- The Lustful Leg (Side splits, lying down). I climaxed in this position. He allowed me to climax.
- Some positions needed strength and agility; he delivered. He performed cunnilingus on me, from behind/kneeling, while I was bent over holding onto the wall, holding onto the wall. I climaxed.

Direct observation
- What is needed to be more sexual: Same qualities as with Sample #1, plus sexual freedom or creativity.
- Cunnilingus with anal stimulation is surprisingly erotic.
- Climax denial is intense.

Audio or videotape? n/a

Data analysis

Classify & rank data
- *5 out of 5. (especially in girth and length!)*
- *He surpassed Sample #1 in sexual prowess and 'acrobatics'.*
- *I was more attracted to Sample #3, than Sample #1 or Sample #2*
- *But there was more anticipation with Sample #1. Sample #3 was more in the moment.*

Sense of wholeness
- *I am still trying to achieve my goal; I visualize myself with Steve doing these sexual acts.*
- *I need to let my mind go, erase negative thoughts and go with the flow during sex; stop holding back or questioning motives and sexual exploration and trust how I am feeling at the time.*

Examine experiences beyond human awareness/ or cannot be communicated
- *Sample #3 is a better match for me; intellectually, similar interests, and has an amazing, charming personality.*
- *Sample #3 needed the release; no dating or sexual contact. He was eager to please.*
- *Guilt. Telling Sample #3 that I wasn't interested in another date.*
- *We both fulfilled a need, without any regrets—am I telling myself this? How can I speak for Sample #3?*

    I had to research Kamasutra sex positions on the internet to find out what they were called. I shuffled through one hundred different positions to find the right ones. I didn't know that there were so many sexual positions. No wonder Steve strayed. I didn't know I was so uneducated about sex. I still have a lot of work to do.

Perhaps my art teacher will be my next sample, or my cooking partner, Chris.

I am exhausted. I still have the notebook on my lap when I fall asleep.

30.

At work the next day, I realize that it is Thursday and I have nothing to do in the evening. Thursdays used to be book club night, but I can't face going to that ever again. It would be too awkward if Dave is there. It's too bad. I liked the people. Oh, and so much for taking over the club from Maryanne. I swear under my breath. She really needed a break.

I scan my agenda and see that on my To Do list I have written, 'Call the local airport/flight school'. I click on the internet icon on my laptop home screen and google 'aviation lessons in Toronto'. I find a company that is located right in the downtown core on Toronto Island.

Just as I was about to dial the phone number of the academy, Margie buzzes me. "Jack Fraser is on line one. Would you like to take the call?"

"Yes, I'll take it Margie. Thank you." I pick up the phone. "Hi, Jack."

"Hi, Colleen. I hope I'm not bothering you." He has such a deep, manly voice.

"Not at all." I look at my laptop screen at the flight academy contact information. It'll have to wait. "What can I do for you?"

"How's your hip?"

"It's good. I did fall on it again at volleyball the other night, but it's fine." I think Ryan stretched it out for me.

"Oh. Well, I don't want to push, but I'm wondering if you wanted to go for a run on Saturday."

I smile. "I'm always up for a run. Can you handle eight in the morning?"

"Absolutely. I can be at your house for seven forty-five. Is that ok?"

"Sounds great."

There's a pause. "I'm looking forward to it." Jack says. "I'll see you then."

As soon as I hang up, Margie buzzes me again, "Andrew, your next appointment, is here."

"Send him in, please."

I close my laptop. Flying will have to wait again.

At the end of the day, I decide to go to the aviation facility on Toronto Island and check it out. I think it's strange that they don't close until eleven, but I figure people fly planes when it's dark too. I have so much to learn.

I leave my car at my office and take the streetcar to the ferry terminal. The ferry is extremely dirty, so I don't bother to sit down. Is this thing ever cleaned? I know that in the summer, over thirty thousand people take the ferry every day. That's a lot of children and germs. Thankfully, the ride is over quickly before I start really stressing about it..

The ferry took me right over to the airfield. The actual airport is to the right, but I see a sign for Island Air pointing to the left. I find the facility's office, or hangar, between two large buildings. The main hangar door where airplanes enter is closed, so I enter through the civilian door.

The entire hangar is metal and there are only a few two-seater airplanes inside, but about twelve could fit inside the glorified garage. The floor is white cement and it is pristine. I don't know how they keep it so clean.

The only person I see is a bleach blonde haired man at a desk. He is the stereotypical pilot, if he is one. He is tanned, with a square jaw and perfect, white teeth. He just needs some of those wings attached to his shirt and a pilot's cap. He is too involved in paperwork to notice me.

"Excuse me," I say softly.

He looks up and smiles. "Hi. How can I help you?"

"I think I would like to get my pilot's license."

"Do you want a recreational pilot permit or private pilot license?" He studies me.

"I am not sure. That's why I am here. I need some more information. Do you have time?" I ask.

He looks down at his desk and then back up to me, "Give me a few minutes to finish up this paperwork and I'll take you on a tour and go over the programs and prices with you."

"No problem." I look around the office and there's nowhere to sit, so I head back outside. The smell of jet fuel pervades the air, and more than a dozen little two-seater planes are parked around the tarmac.

Two men come out of the building beside the hangar and walk to one of the small planes. The one man stands at the nose with a clipboard and a pen and says, "You can begin anytime, Zach."

The other man, who must be Zach, starts walking around one of the small planes. He pulls the nose, wing and tail covers off and places them to the side. I then see him inspecting the wings and tail. He bends under the one wing, fiddles with something, and then I see a clear blue fluid leaking out from the plane. The flow of liquid stops and he comes back out and reaches on top of the wing to do something else.

The man with the clipboard is writing things down and watching Zach carefully. It looks like he is testing Zach.

"You ready?" Zach says to the other man. He nods and gets into the plane as Zach pulls the chalks from under the tires and throws them off to the side, far away from the plane.

Zach gets into the plane and after a few moments, starts the engine. It is loud and the propeller starts turning quickly. Then it's a blur. They slowly taxi to the runway.

As I'm watching, the bleach blonde man from the office comes up behind me and asks, "Are you ready for a tour?"

"Yes please."

"I'm Jarvis, the hangar manager," he says.

"I'm Colleen. Nice to meet you."

Jarvis shows me around the hangar and explains that all the pilots clean the hangar floors and do all of the maintenance in the hangar. If you are a member of the club, you must do your part. He shows me the kitchen and lounge. There are laptops, suitcases and backpacks scattered everywhere. He says that the building is safe and everyone respects each other's property. A conference room is upstairs and he explains that it is the classroom where ground school is held.

"There are ten to twelve people registered for the next recreational licensing class. Two-thirds of the participants are usually retired and one-third of the class usually wants a career in aviation. You may be the only female." He looks at me.

I shrug my shoulders. That doesn't bother me. "Are you a pilot?"

"Yes, I've been flying for two years. I just have my recreational license. It allows for some awesome date nights with my wife," he smiles proudly. "I've flown around the city and even to Niagara Falls."

We get back to the hangar and I lean over the desk as Jarvis explains about the different licenses. The private pilot license consists of forty-eight hours of ground school and forty-five hours of flight instruction; seventeen hours dual and twelve hours solo. Then there is a written exam and the final practical flight test. The recreational pilot permit is less intense, but as the name suggests, it is for personal enjoyment only. It is only twenty-five hours; fifteen hours dual and five hours solo and the same two tests. I would be flying a Cessna, one of those two-seaters that are outside.

"I think that I would like to start with the recreational pilot permit." I'm not necessarily looking for a career change. "When do I begin?"

"Awesome! Let's fill out this paperwork and the next school begins three weeks from today," Jarvis says.

Just then, a man bursts through the door. "I did it, Jarvis! I'm a pilot." It's Zach and he's grinning from ear to ear. He has brown, curly hair and blue eyes. I think he's in his early forties. He places a couple of headsets on the counter.

"Congratulations, Zach!" They shake hands and slap each other on the back.

Zach gives me the once over. "New recruit?" he asks Jarvis.

"Yes, she just signed up for the recreational permit. Colleen, this is Zach," Jarvis says.

Zach offers his hand, "I'm Zach Brown."

I shake his hand, "Nice to meet you. I'm Colleen Cousineau." He's very good looking. What's with all these hot pilots?

"Let's get this paperwork done, Colleen," Jarvis says.

Zach is still holding onto my hand. He looks at me, cocks his head and then releases it. Does he want something? I turn to Jarvis and Zach leaves the hangar. I guess not.

Jarvis and I fill out my information, I write him a cheque for the full amount and he tells me to expect an email about the class schedule. The first class will be *Getting To Know Your Plane*. We shake hands and I leave the hangar.

"Hey!" I hear someone shout. I turn around and I see Zach waving at me from underneath a Cessna. He's putting the chalks back under the tires. I wave back.

"Can you help me?"

I walk over just as he pulls down the tail of the plane.

"Throw that tail cover over the tail."

I point to some mesh on the ground.

"Yes, that's the cover."

I open it up and he tells me to turn it a certain way and I drape it over the tail. He releases the plane and he comes beside me and starts buckling the cover together to keep it in place.

"You are going to love flying," he gushes. "I've wanted to fly since I was a kid. I love the challenge of piloting a small plane, and I even use a computer flight simulator at home to practice."

"I've always been interested and curious," I say. I'm not sure if I'm the hard-core simulator type, but the challenge intrigues me.

"It's neat that not many people do it, and it's great to be up in the air, seeing things from a different perspective."

"I can't wait." I have goose bumps.

"I can take you up sometime, now that I am a qualified VFR pilot." He winks.

"What does VFR mean?"

"A visual flight rules pilot. It just means that I can only fly in weather conditions that are clear enough to see where I am going." He tugs on the cover to make sure it's secure. "I'm serious about taking you up. You'll get a taste of how a small plane works. It's not like a Boeing 737."

I hesitate. "I just met you." It's like getting into a strange man's car. But I just did that the other day with Ryan after volleyball.

"Well, we take off from here and we return to the same spot. I promise you a safe flight, return home and my hands will be too busy to touch you the entire time." He laughs.

I still don't know what to stay.

Zach digs into his pocket, "Here's my business card," he hands it to me. "I usually go up on Thursdays around this time. If you want to meet up, just give me a call."

I look at his card. *Zachary Brown, Bank of Canada CEO*. "Thank you. I'll think about it."

"I hope you do." He smiles.

"Nice meeting you." I smile back. I start walking toward the ferry terminal. The ferry comes every fifteen minutes and I don't see one yet, so I have a seat on a bench.

I am excited to learn to fly. Before my dad died, he would take me up in his two-seater every Sunday. My mom would never come with us though, she was too scared. I do remember the feeling of the lift off, there's nothing like it. I've been on domestic and international flights, like the Boeing series of airplanes, but you're safe and protected in those. In the small airplane, you feel every gust of wind, every dip in the flight and you do feel like you are falling.

I think I will go flying with Zach before flight school begins. Maybe he can teach me a few things, so that I'm ahead of the game.

31.

    The next morning, I am up an hour early and I run ten miles on my treadmill. I slept very well and I have a great deal of nervous energy. Perhaps it's the thought of flying or maybe it is because of the art opening tonight. The running helped release some of the energy, but I still think I'm going to skip my morning latte. I dress for the day with my evening plans in mind. I have on a short, black dress and a pair of heels. It's not the most appropriate attire for the office, but I am not doing any play activities today. I'll either be in a chair or behind my desk. I quickly grab a business jacket as an afterthought.

    When I step outside, I see that Steve is waiting on my porch. I immediately get butterflies in my stomach. That's a good sign. I still want to be with him. But I am apprehensive about why he stopped by . Why is he here? Does he want me back? He looks handsome in his suit and tie, but he looks older. Stress maybe?

    "Hi, Colleen," he says, barely looking at me.

    I touch his arm. "Hi, Steve." I look up through my lashes, like Christine does. "I've missed you." I have to try what I've learned.

    He doesn't even notice. "Look, I have these papers you need to sign." He holds them out to me.

    I know that the papers are a separation agreement. I feel sick and my heart beats faster. This is not what I want. I press on anyway. I ignore the papers and touch his hand, "Do you want to come inside and talk about it?" I try my best sexy voice.

    "Are you sick?" He asks.

    Dammit. I try to laugh and throw my head back.

    "What's wrong with you?"

    Why isn't this working? I step closer to him and gently touch his arm. "I just thought you could come in and we could sit down and talk about us." I step even closer to him and reach for his face.

    Steve steps back. "I just want those papers signed."

I take another step forward and push his hands down and put my hands on his shoulders. "We can talk later." I start to lean in.

"Colleen! What are you doing?" He looks at me outraged.

"I'm just trying… I haven't seen you. We need to talk," I blurt out.

"I don't want to talk! Just sign the fucking papers!"

I tear the papers out of his hands and throw them off of the porch. He just stares at me. I storm back into the house. I don't want him to see me cry. I look through the crack of the curtains and watch him pick up the papers and stare at the front door. He doesn't know what to do. He finally turns and leaves down the walkway. Our walkway.

I drop to the floor and start sobbing. What did I do wrong? I touched him. I was sexy. Why doesn't he want me?

I sit on the floor for a while letting the tears fall. Why am I doing Project Sex? Why did I change my moral code for him? Why do I need experience if he doesn't even want me? I don't know how long I sit there, but I slowly start to pick myself up, find some tissues and look at myself in the hallway mirror.

I shake my head. I'm stronger than this. I wasn't ready for him. The situation wasn't right. There wasn't enough time. I need more experience. I blow my nose and wipe the mascara that has run down my face and leave for work. I'll plan for another time and place and Steve will see that I am enough woman for him. I am more determined than ever.

32.

     I work late and finish my recordings, so I don't have to do them on the weekend. I am tired, but because I am extremely motivated by today's events with Steve, I don't dare cancel my plans. If I was correct on my instincts, I think Shawn is interested and I may have a chance to gain more experience. I'm going to try to be sexy. I need my sexuality to come naturally. Being with Ryan really opened my eyes, but I still held back and questioned my limits. What can I do differently tonight? I think I have to attempt my first seduction. That makes me very nervous. I can do it. Right? Yes, I can. I have to be determined.

     When I arrive at Gallery 123, it's just after nine. Through the large front window, I see several people drinking wine and mingling. There are more people than I thought. I didn't think there would be a large turnout. How renowned of an artist is Shawn Lauzon? I feel insecure all of a sudden. I might be out of my league.

     I look to see if the taxi I took is still here. It's gone. I have to stay. I have to go through with this. Why I am so afraid? Ok, forget about the Sex Project and go in for the experience and culture. That's it. My heart slows down a little.

     With my head up high, I walk through the door and an attendant takes my coat and a server offers me a glass of red wine on a tray. I take it and gulp it down nervously. Liquid courage.

     I scan the room. I do not recognize anyone and I can't see Shawn yet. Everyone is talking quietly and pointing at the different artwork. I try to blend in and look around. The gallery is a large white room with hardwood floors and high ceilings, vaulted with large slabs of wood. In the centre of the room is another room. It's strange. It's about five feet by five feet, with one single door. I'm not sure what could be inside such a small room, but I think its main purpose is to use its walls to display more artwork. Track lighting highlights each piece of artwork individually. I am curious to see Shawn's pieces up close.

Just as I get to the first piece, a man comes up to me, extending his hand. "Welcome to Gallery 123 and the Shawn Lauzon exhibit." He is a handsome African American man, wearing a fitted, pale blue shirt, red and black striped tie and tight blue pants down to the ankle.

I reach for his hand and there's barely a squeeze before he takes his hand back, "Thank you," I say.

"I am Dale, the gallery owner. Please peruse at your leisure." And he's gone.

It's too bad. I thought I had some company. I walk to my right and stop at a smaller oil canvas, depicting a lake. I believe it's impressionistic. It's very bright and vibrant, using a lot of colour and light effects. The second piece is abstract. It somehow reminds me of the first lake painting. I check out both titles: the first one is *Lake*, the second one is *My Lake*. The second is also an oil painting and incorporates the same colours as *Lake*, but there is a different flow; each brushstroke has a curve to it, some are thick some are thin. There is more depth to *My Lake*. I like it. Maybe it's the way he feels when he views the lake.

I'd love to talk to him as a therapist. Get him on my couch. I giggle to myself and grab another glass of wine as it cruises by me. Get him in my bed.

As I examine the rest of Shawn's work, I notice the same theme with every two paintings. One is impressionistic and one is abstract, but he uses different mediums. I wonder which painting style he likes more. I'd love to paint abstract. It would allow for more creative freedom, but I wouldn't know where to start.

Images of Steve pop into my head and I remember how I embarrassed myself this morning. I tried my best to do what I learned from my experiences lately, but I've really only had three new encounters with men, that's four in my entire life. I shouldn't be so hard on myself. What I need is more exposure and practice to flirting with men. And I should learn how to come-on to a man. I make a mental note to observe Christine in action. I should have watched her before tonight. I need more confidence. I don't know if I can seduce Shawn tonight. I'm not ready. I begin to panic again.

I quickly decide that I need to go home. I scramble for a place to put down my wine glass, but suddenly feel a hand on my arm. It's Shawn. He doesn't look like much of an artist tonight. He's wearing a gray fitted button down shirt and gray dress pants. I think he got a haircut too, because the curls around his ears are gone. He looks very handsome. He takes the empty wine glass out of my hand and replaces it with a full one.

"Hi, Colleen. I'm surprised to see you here," Shawn says. I notice that his eyes are hazel, with flecks of gold.

"I though you said it was ok that I could come," I say timidly. "You invited me, didn't you?"

"Yes. Of course. I am very glad you came. I'm just surprised. I figured you would have something better to do on a Friday night." He's very cute. I wonder how old he is. Perhaps in his late twenties? He looks so young.

"This is amazing. I am very happy to be here. You are a wonderful artist. Um, not that I didn't think you were before, this just validates it," I gush. The wine is going to my head.

"Thank you." Shawn smiles. "Come sit down with me." He leads me to a small bistro table by the door and pulls out a tall chair. I sit down and he sits down beside me.

"Don't you have to mingle? I don't want to monopolize your time."

"Colleen, I don't know any of these people. The gallery owner set it up." He points to Dale.

I nod. "I met Dale. Briefly."

"He's a social butterfly. Please stay and talk to me," He asks.

"Ok." I play with my wine glass. "Your work is incredible. I wanted to ask you about the theme." We continue to talk about painting styles and mediums and our own lives. He went to school at Sheridan College in Toronto and he is only a year younger than me. He works at the Art Barn School in the evenings and is a high school art teacher during the day. Shawn is quiet, but full of passion and enthusiasm for art and life, in general. I connect with him on a different level that I've never experienced with another man.

"I have always thought that people who are creative with their hands have a great deal of physical energy," I say.

He laughs. "Why do you think that?"

"I'm not saying that you are hyperactive. You probably have a lot of energy for art, but focus that energy when you need it. For instance, when you're working on a new painting, you most likely paint for hours and days at a time."

"You're right. When I am at my easel, I feel whole, like life could not get any better. My art makes me complete." He has such long, graceful fingers and I watch his hands as he talks. "Does that sound strange to you?"

"Absolutely not. I have dealt with all kinds of people in my profession and I've had to analyze different personalities. I find that creative people, when in their creative zone, live life more fully."

"Scientists in a lab are just as creative. You probably work long hours and with great concentration, but still have the same enthusiasm for your job at the end of the day."

"Now you're right. I never thought of my job as creative."

"You just do something that has a different meaning for you."

"Perhaps it's not that different than yours. When I am doing my job, I am absolutely fulfilled. I rarely have that feeling anywhere else in my life. I'm sure you can relate to that."

"Yes, I can."

His long fingers slide down the stem of his wine glass. I want his hands on me. I take a long, slow sip of wine.

I take it a step further. "I've also read in my studies that creative people have a strong dose of Eros." He cocks his head to the side and looks at me. I continue, "The desire to be creative or feel creative correlates with the urge to have sex."

"You read that?" He asks softly.

Flip flop. I feel a pulsing deep down. I clench my knees together. "Yes. How do you feel about that?" We stare into each other's eyes.

"I'm sorry to interrupt." Dale puts his head between us. "Mr. and Mrs. Gagnon are leaving. Shawn, you must say good bye to them."

Shawn looks at me, touches my hand, and says, "I'm sorry." He leaves with Dale.

It is pretty late and the Gagnon's started a procession. Everyone decides to leave at the same time and Shawn is busy shaking hands and kissing cheeks. I stand up and walk over to the paintings to give him space.

I overhear one woman in a fur wrap, "Shawn, darling. Wonderful work. Just exquisite. You must come over and meet my other friends." I see her kiss each of his cheeks. Shawn just smiles and opens the door for them.

I don't want to leave yet. I am interested in what Shawn may have to offer me. I hope he doesn't usher me out too.

I hear the door close and the room is suddenly quiet. I turn around and only Shawn remains. We are alone. It's funny how my confidence can quickly turn to uneasiness.

"You did very well tonight," I say, pointing to the sold stickers on the wall beside the paintings.

"Those stuffed shirts just want a piece of art for their office or oversized mansion'" he scoffs. "They don't care about the artist. They just care that the artist is popular and by acquiring a piece, they become trendy."

"Don't say that. The artist is the creative genius. Without you, there would be no art," I say. He laughs. "Was that cheesy?" I blush. I have had too much to drink.

"Don't apologize. It was cute." He takes my hand. "Come upstairs."

33.

"Ok." I say. Why not? I take my wine glass with me. This is what I wanted.

We walk upstairs to a very long and narrow apartment. The living room, dining room and kitchen are all laid out in front of me, and beside me is another small flight of stairs, that lead to a loft bedroom. It's clever how the bedroom juts out and overlooks the main floor. It is very modern, with white walls and furniture, and extremely high ceilings. Glossy black tile covers the floor and windows comprise an entire wall, from floor to ceiling.

"This is stunning," I say, walking over to the window. "Is this your apartment?"

"Yes. I rent it from Dale." He sits down on the arm of a white, suede couch. "Would you like more wine?"

"Yes, please." I've had enough, but it's helping me to be brave. He walks to the kitchen, which seems really far away, and takes a bottle off the counter. I sit down to compose myself.

He comes back and pours wine into my glass. I take a small sip and place the glass on the table in front of me. What do I do now? He sits down beside me. How do I begin a seduction?

"I have never been to an opening and I'm glad that my first experience was at yours," I say, placing my hand on his knee. That's a good move.

"I'm happy that you came." His eyes are beautiful.

I place my other hand on his thigh and lean in slightly. "I hope you mean that," I try my sexy whisper.

His eyes darken. "I mean it. You're my favourite student. Now what were you saying about creative people and sex?"

I blush, but stay strong. "I believe that our creative motivations are based on our most primal passions, such as happiness, fear, hate, love… and lust."

He closes the gap between us slowly.

"Creativity is ultimately sexual," I finish and he kisses me. It works!

Shawn lips are smooth and full, his tongue is soft and lingering. He has moved closer to me and his arms are around me, his hand sliding up and down my back. My hands are on his thighs. I rub slowly up his leg and I feel his hardness. He's hard already?

Shawn puts his hand on mine, stopping me. I pull back and look at him. What's wrong? Oh no. I'm not good at this.

"I don't want to ruin our relationship at the school," he says.

Oh. That's all? "It's ok. Really." I start kissing him again. If I don't ever go back to art class, I'd be fine with it. I'd rather have sex with him than paint.

He stops me again. "Do you want to go upstairs? It's more comfortable than this horrid couch."

I nod repeatedly and smile. This is easy. Almost too easy.

He leads me by the hand, up the stairs, and I am a taken aback by the unprotected view of Toronto.

"Can people see us?" I ask shyly.

"If they really wanted to look," he replies and begins kissing my neck. I forget about any potential voyeurism.

The bedroom is surrounded, not by walls, but by short panels of glass. He is leaning against the barrier and I am pushing my hips into his hardness. I can feel my panties getting moist. I've been ready all night. Our lips find each other again and I devour him. My hands find the buttons on his shirt and I undo each one, down to his pants, and untuck his shirt. I fiddle with the button on his pants, undo it, and unzip his fly. I take a deep breath and start kissing his neck, then his chest. He has nice abdominal muscles too. I bend down and kiss each one of those.

I am on my knees now, licking his lower stomach, just above his underwear. I look up at him. He's looking down at me. Waiting. Flip Flop. I guess I've started something that I have to finish.

I pull his pants down over his hips and feel the hardness of him over his underwear. I kiss him that way and breathe my hot breath onto his length. I pull the edge of his underwear away from his skin and I lick the tip of him. It's very soft and there's no taste. I can do this. I hear his breathing change, it's raspier. I think he likes it. This convinces me that I'm doing something right. I swirl my tongue around the tip over and over. I pull his underwear down around his ankles and he steps out of them. I look at his *it*.

He is big, but not overwhelming. This isn't so scary. I kick off my shoes and take him in both hands and rub up and down the length of him. He likes that. I put my mouth over the tip of him. It's so hard and smooth. Slowly, I put more of him in my mouth, circling my tongue. He moans. That gives me the confidence that I need. I put the entire length of him in my mouth and release slowly, sucking hard. I repeat this process over and over. I flutter my tongue at his tip and when he's deep inside my mouth. He's moaning very loudly and his breathing is erratic. He is losing control. I am making him lose control. I like this power.

Shawn is holding onto the glass barrier with both hands and I can see him watching me. Every so often he flips his head back. And then I hear him whisper, "Colleen, I'm going to come."

A warm, flow of liquid hits the back of my throat. It's not a pleasant taste, but I swallow and keep manoeuvering him in my throat. He's bucking his hips and moaning loudly. I'm delighted that I can pleasure him in this way. I know that I can do this for Steve, too.

When he stops, he beckons me up and he kisses me. "Your turn." I'm feeling very relaxed and receptive to whatever he has in store for me.

Shawn turns me around, so I face the bed, and unzips my dress. He gently takes it off of my shoulders and it falls to the ground. I step out of it.

"You have beautiful skin," he whispers. He kisses my shoulder while unhooking my bra and takes the straps off my shoulders. I let it fall to the floor. I feel him slip his fingers under the elastic of my thong and pull it down over my hips. He lets my panties drop to the floor. I step out of them.

He walks around me and takes me by the hand and persuades me onto the bed. He doesn't get on the bed with me. Instead, he opens his night stand drawer, pulls out a condom, and places it on the bed beside me. He crawls on top of me and we start kissing again. I can feel his erection below my stomach. Wow. He is recharged already, but he doesn't take me right away. He takes his time and slowly kisses down my body, biting at my breasts. All of his body weight is on me, with his chest on my hips and my legs wide, on either side of him. He works my breasts, squeezing them together, pinching and licking my nipples.

I push my hips up, bucking him, trying to relieve the pressure that is accumulating between my legs. He kisses lower down my body, down my stomach and then I feel his hot breath at my apex. His tongue dips in and out slowly and he swirls it around my clitoris. It feels incredible. I feel him put a finger slowly into me and my hips rise up to meet the pleasure.

"You are ready," he whispers.

And then he's up. My legs are in the crooks of his arms, and he lifts my bottom off the bed. He slides his legs under mine and sits facing me, with the bottom of my thighs overtop of his thighs. He tears open the condom wrapper and rolls it on. His erection is at the entrance of my wetness. He enters me slowly.

I close my eyes and lift my arms over my head onto the bed, I melt into the mattress. I want to feel and savour every inch of him inside me. My core pulses with eagerness.

He pulls my hips down onto him, so that he fills me completely. He keeps his hands on my hips and slowly rotates his own. It's a gentle pressure, but because he is so deep inside me, it feels amazing.

Then his hands are on my stomach and he's tapping it. I look at him and he gestures for me to give him my hands. I do, and he pulls me up to a sitting position. He releases my hands and grabs my behind and starts pulling my hips into his, plunging into me hard. I quickly put my hands on the bed behind me to hold myself steady. I start to respond to the building ache inside me. I dig my heels into the bed and lift my behind up so that he can pull me easier. I meet every thrust. I am moaning and I can feel my orgasm coming.

Shawn brings his arms up, encircling my back and my arms wrap around his body. He is lifting me up and down onto him hard and fast. I can feel his entire length drive into me. Every ounce of pleasure I feel overwhelms me and it takes my breath away. I succumb to it. I can hear Shawn moaning loudly.

"Come for me," he grunts.

We both explode together. He shudders and I dissolve into his arms, savouring the feeling. He kisses my cheek and helps me to lie back down. He pulls out of me and covers both of us up with a blanket, he lies on his back beside me.

After a few minutes, I realize that I want to go home. I don't want to sleep in Shawn's bed. I listen for a few seconds and I hear deep breathing. Maybe he's sleeping. I don't even care. I can tell him that I don't want to stay. I slowly slip out from under the blanket and find my bra and panties, and put them on. I put my dress back on and pick up my heels. I look at Shawn one more time and he hasn't stirred, so I walk downstairs and out the apartment door.

Downstairs, I find my coat and call a taxi. Even though it's three in the morning, it doesn't take long for it to arrive.

I pull my coat tightly around me and sigh loudly. I did it. I seduced a man. I was eager and I initiated everything. Wow. I travel home with a smile on my face.

34.

I wake up the next morning to a knock on the door. I look at the clock. It's seven forty-five. Who the hell is here?

I stumble out of bed, pull on my robe and go to the front door. I look through the crack of the curtain and I see Jack standing on my porch. I shake my head. I forgot that we were going for a run today. How did I forget? What do I do? I am not awake yet. I take a few steps back to my bedroom and then back to the door. I can't think. Crap. I open the door.

"Good morn-." He stops. "Did you forget?" He looks down at my robe.

I shake my head, squinting at the bright sun. "Come in. I will be ready in ten minutes." I run to my bedroom. I hear him laughing.

I pull on running tights and a long spandex shirt. In the bathroom, I brush my teeth, put my hair up and wash my face. I go to the front door. "See? I'm ready."

He points to my feet. Dammit. I run back to my room to get my running shoes. I go back out the hallway and sit on the floor to put my shoes on.

"Rough night? He's smiling like the Cheshire cat.

"No. Not at all. Morning just came too quick." I grab my Garmin watch from out of my purse and put it on.

"Do those things work?"

"Yes, it tracks your pace, distance and heart rate," I say. "Give me one minute." I run, one more time, to my bedroom and come back out handing Jack my other Garmin watch. "Try it." I show him how to set it.

He puts it on. "Thanks. I'll give it back."

"I know you will." I smile. "Let's go. I'm ready."

We leave and head toward the water. It's a cold day, and I probably would not have gone for a run. I would have slept in. But now, feeling the fresh air on my face, I'm in the mood. I'm surprised I'm not hungover. I drank a lot of wine.

There aren't a lot of people on the trails to avoid yet, so it's easy to think while I run. I run through my experience with Shawn and I can't wait to document it. I am very proud of myself.

"What are you thinking about?" Jack asks. "You're smiling."

I blush. "I just love to run. Even after not getting enough sleep. Thanks for waking me up."

We talk about work and his new physiotherapy clinic. He starts to slow down about forty-five minutes into the run. I slow my pace to match his.

"You're supposed to keep your pace and not slow down," he says. "I'm not going to get better."

"Ok, you asked for it." And I take off. I'm not sprinting, but I'm at a very comfortable quick pace, probably a six minute mile. I can usually hold this for fifteen to twenty minutes, and then I'm dead.

Jack keeps up, but not for very long. I hear him slow down and I look back and see him stop, rest his hands on his knees, and pant heavily.

I jog up beside him, kicking my heels into my bottom, like I have all the energy in the world. "Need a rest?" I tease, circling him.

"I don't want to hold you back. You keep going and I'll just...," he gasps, "...die here."

I laugh at him. "That's ok. I'll take a break. We still have to run all the way back."

He groans and makes his way to a bench. We're right in front of the lake now at Harbour Square Park, which is close to the ferry terminal. There are hundreds of people gathering to go over to Toronto Island, probably trying to enjoy one last ride at the amusement park before it closes for the season. I buy two bottles of water from a vendor and sit beside Jack.

"I was on the ferry the other day," I say, handing him the water.

"What for?"

"I signed up for flight school. I start in three weeks." I am proud of this and bragging a little. If he sees Steve, he could tell him that little tidbit.

He laughs. "You never cease to amaze me. Is there anything you haven't tried?"

"I could give you a whole list." Lately, I've crossed a few things off of my sexual experience repertoire, but I won't tell him that.

"You will have to fly me somewhere one day." His smile is so charismatic. It's too bad he was Steve's friend. I can't cross over that imaginary line. Maybe I could hook him up with Christine.

"I'll see what I can do." I smile.

"I'm sorry, Captain Colleen, am I not good enough to fly with?"

I scrunch up my nose and shake my head. "Well, for one I will not be navigating an Airbus or a Boeing, so you can call me pilot, not captain. And yes, I do have standards." He's so easy to joke with.

He reaches for me, but I'm too fast. I get up and start running backwards away from him. "You'll have to catch me."

"Colleen! Stop!" He tries to warn me.

Too late. I fall backward over a little dog that someone has on a leash. I catch myself, but still land on my hands.

Jack rushes up beside me. "You ok?"

"Yes, I'm fine. Just my ego is damaged. You must really think I'm a spaz." I am embarrassed. I quickly get up and brush myself off. I apologize to the dog owner. The little Shih Tzu is fine. I start rubbing my wrists. The impact hurt them. We move off the pathway and onto the grass.

"Spaz does not come to mind when I think about you. I might think clumsy and awkward, but not spaz. Your injuries could definitely give me a lot of business though. First your hip and now your wrists. I should give you my card." He smirks, but takes one of my hands and brushes the dirt off of it. He does the same with my other hand.

I laugh. "That's real nice. Make fun of the spaz. Is that what you do with all of your clients? Taunt them into making their appointments." I pull my hand away and elbow him in the ribs. "Or maybe you go for runs with them and push them into oncoming traffic. You'll always get a repeat client that way."

He swats my elbow away. "I just push them into little dogs and children. If you continue to have these minor accidents, you may have to be my client."

"I'm sure you have a lot of clients who need you more than me." I playfully push his chest.

He catches my hands and holds them there, on his chest. "Trust me. I need you." He's looking at me so carefully. I don't think he's joking anymore. His face looks serious. I feel uncomfortable.

"Colleen?" I turn around and I see Dave, the orthodontist. My stomach twists in a knot.

"Uh. Hi, Dave," I stammer and quickly pull my hands out from under Jack's and step between them. "What are you doing here?"

Dave and Jack are staring at each other. Uh oh. Dave pulls his eyes away and looks at me. "I was going for a little jog. What are you up to today?"

Jack steps around me. "We were running." He holds his hand out to Dave. "I'm Jack." Oh lord.

Dave briefly shakes it. "Dave, this is Jack, a very good friend of mine. And Jack, this is Dave." I don't know how to introduce Dave. The-guy-I-had-a-one-night-stand-with doesn't seem appropriate.

Jack looks at me strangely.

I don't know what to say. It's all very awkward. "Oh. Well, it was nice to see you. Call me if you want to get together again," Dave says, scowling at Jack.

He had to say *again*. "Yes, it was nice to see you, too. Have a good day."

Dave smiles at me briefly and then resumes glaring at Jack.

Jack doesn't back down. He keeps his eyes locked on Dave. Dave eventually turns and walks away.

I start walking the opposite way down the path. That was very uncomfortable. How could I have avoided it? Not be at the waterfront? That's not very realistic.

"Who was that?"

"Dave? I met him earlier this week."

"You're dating?" He asks incredulously.

"No, I'm not dating. I'm not going to see him again." Why is he so surprised?

"You slept with him?"

How did he know that? "That's none of your business." I keep walking. Jack doesn't need to know about my sex life.

Jack pulls my arm and stops me in my tracks. "I know you're hurting about your separation, but having sex with a stranger isn't the smartest thing to do."

"Thanks for the advice, but I'm a big girl, Jack. Please, I don't want to talk about this with you. Don't worry about me." I put my hand on his arm. "Can we run back home now?"

Jack pauses and takes a deep breath. "You're not going to see him again?"

"No. I am not interested in seeing him again."

"Ok. Let's run. Just let me clear the path of little dogs or children in your path. I don't want you tripping." He stands in front of me, unsmiling, but raises one hand in the air, waiting. "Don't leave me hanging."

I cautiously slap his hand. "I don't know how you get any clients with your attitude." I take off running, but he catches up and easily meets my pace.

"You don't know me very well at all." He's said that before.

There are more people on the trails now and we have to dodge them, so talking to each other is pretty difficult. I hope we don't run into

Dave again. Or Ryan. Or even, Shawn. Do I have to hide in my house? I didn't think about those kinds of consequences.

Jack acted like a jealous boyfriend at first. I know he cares about me, but that was too much. Good thing he calmed down. He's like a protective big brother. I smile. He is such a good friend and a great running partner. He doesn't hold me back, I don't feel that I have to wait for him, and he is fun to talk to. I wouldn't mind running with him again.

We slow down and walk the last block to his car. I can hear that Jack is a little winded, so I don't talk to him. I could run another five miles. Maybe ten.

After a few minutes, he says, "That was great, Colleen. You really pushed me. It's what I needed."

"Anytime. And I mean that." I have never found a running partner that I have clicked with or who could keep up with me. "Call me," I say.

"Maybe we could set up a schedule. I'll call you this week. I'd say, let's do this again tomorrow, but I think I may need a day off."

I bend forward, touching my toes. And he does the same.

"Would you want to do something together tomorrow? Not running, but maybe have dinner?"

I hug my legs tighter and bury my face in my knees. What? I guess friends go out for dinner, too. It's not wrong. "Oh, I have plans tomorrow night. I am going to some sort of Latin nightclub with Christine." I slowly stand up and reach back to grab my foot, to stretch out my quadriceps muscles. I could see us sitting at a sports bar, drinking a few beers. That'd be fun.

"Colleen, I would really like to take you out on a date. What do you think about that?"

Oh. Crap. He wants to date me. I thought we were establishing a good friendship. Why a date? I switch feet, hold the stretch and take a deep breath. "Are you sure that's appropriate?"

"Absolutely. I have no ties to Steve, if that's what you mean?"

The imaginary line. He wants to cross it. All he really wants is another conquest. He wants to add me to the roster of his girlfriends. No thank you. "I like you and I value our friendship, but I still want to see if Steve and I can reconcile." I let go of my foot and put my hands on my hips.

"But you dated that loser at the harbor?"

Loser? That was uncalled for. "Jack, I went out with him one time. It was an experiment." I can't tell him that I am participating in casual sex for research purposes.

"Experiment? What does that even mean?"

"It doesn't matter. The point is that I still love Steve."

"Are you kidding me? Colleen, he has moved in with his secretary!"

I feel like the wind has been knocked out of me. "I don't believe you." I shake my head, looking down.

"Trust me," he softens his voice. "He told me the other day when he came to my clinic. He strained his back while moving her stuff into his apartment."

I bend over, hands on my knees. I'm shaking my head and I feel like I'm going to vomit. I take long, deep breaths.

I feel his hand on my back. "God dammit. I'm sorry. I don't mean to keep hurting you, but you are so fucking blind when it comes to him. He has moved on. You need to move on too."

"No!" I stand up and back away. "I still have a chance." I turn around and start walking to my house.

"Colleen, I am so sorry. Please talk to me."

Jack is wrong. I can get Steve back. I will seduce him and show him how much I have changed. I'm getting so much experience. Steve will love the new me. That woman means nothing. It doesn't change a thing. Steve will love the new me. Steve loves me and we just lost our way. I try to erase Jack's words from my head.

I walk into my house and don't even look back at Jack. I head straight for the shower and let the hot water soothe my body and mind.

35.

After a long nap, I eat lunch and relax in front of the television. I brought my research notebook with me to the couch to complete last night's findings.

Data Collection

Sample #4
Seek persons who understand study & are willing to express inner feelings & experiences
- *Man, aged 31, artist, high school art teacher.*
- *Wavy brown hair, hazel eyes, slender, fit.*

Describe experiences of phenomenon
- *I was attracted to his mind and creative genius first. He is intelligent, laid-back, and relaxed. I initiated foreplay: kissing and fondling over his jeans. In his bedroom, I performed fellatio and he ejaculated in my mouth; I swallowed. Immediately had intercourse. Spider position: Both seated on the bed, my legs over his, face-to-face. We both climaxed again.*

Direct observation
- *What is needed to be more sexual:*

- *Confidence, the desire or motivation to experiment sexually, a connection with sample*

<u>*Audio or videotape?*</u> *n/a (will that every be completed?)*

Data analysis

<u>*Classify & rank data*</u>
- *5 out of 5. For different reasons.*
- *I was not attracted sexually to Sample #4; I wanted the experience, so it became sexual.*

<u>*Sense of wholeness*</u>
- *I am still trying to achieve my goal; I visualize myself with Steve doing these sexual acts.*
- *Negative thoughts have vanished; I did not withhold or question.*
- *It was a great experience.*

<u>*Examine experiences beyond human awareness/ or cannot be communicated*</u>
- *Sample #4 would challenge me creatively, but not mentally or physically.*
- *I'm not sure if Sample #4, thought about me sexually or not. It was my conquest.*
- *I felt powerful; I instigated foreplay and fellatio.*
- *No guilt, except that I can't go to art class anymore.*

I'm proud of myself. I really came out of my shell with Shawn. The wine helped to lower my inhibitions or maybe it was an aphrodisiac. Whatever it was, I shouldn't depend on it. And I think I need to work on suggesting and being comfortable with new sexual positions. I've heard that dirty talk is quite erotic, too. Although, I think talking about sex during sex would be difficult, I'm not sure that I would be good at it. Please put your thing in my thing. I don't think so.

It is only mid-afternoon and I don't have any plans. Christine said she was busy tonight, so I can't call her. I decide to get dressed in jeans and a sweater and walk downtown alone.

Saturdays afternoons in Toronto are busy. Tour buses are running, markets are open, and the number of museums in the city, plus the CN Tower, draws travelers from all over the world. I love the hustle and bustle of Toronto. I just want to people-watch and maybe grab dinner.

I walk to Yonge Street and head toward Dundas Square. Sometimes that area holds mini concerts or other events on the weekend. As I get closer, I see that the square is blanketed with people. I see a large banner that reads, *Poutine Cook-Off* and in the park are vendors and booths devoted to the fattening potato concoction. I'm not too keen on poutine, but walk through the vendors slowly. People are walking around, sampling different varieties and I see a voting station to pick the best recipe.

Looking through the crowd, I think I see Steve up ahead. I think I might be imagining it. I do a double take. Yes, it is him. He looks handsome. But my heart plummets. He's with a woman and they're holding hands. I step out of the line of traffic, so they can't see me and I peek through some hanging *I Love Poutine* tee shirts that are being sold.

The woman he is with has dirty blonde hair, and she's wearing jeans, a thick sweater and high heeled boots. I can't see her face because her hair is in the way. I creep up closer to the next booth and I pretend to look at the ugly brown and yellow baseball caps. I stand on my tiptoes to try and catch a glimpse. I still can't see what the bitch looks like.

The next booth has more hanging tee shirts and as I move them to the side, to peek through them, a whole rack falls down. I bend down to pick them up and apologize to the vendor. When I look up, I can't see them anywhere.

"Colleen?" Oh no. I slowly turn around and breathe a huge sigh of relief. It's only Jack.

"Hi, Jack."

"I thought it was you. I mean, only you could knock down an entire rack of tee shirts. Did you get hurt in the process?"

"Ha. Ha. I'm fine." I look over his shoulders to see if I can see Steve.

"Are you looking for someone?" He looks in the same direction..

"Um... No." I give up. I'm not going to see what the woman looks like. "What are you doing here?" It seems like he has forgiven me for my outburst this morning.

"I came for the poutine. What else? I'm surprised that you're here. You don't strike me as the cheese curds and gravy type."

I turn up my nose, "You're right. I don't like it. I was bored and went for a walk. I ended up here." I take one more quick look for Steve, but can't see him anywhere. "You came to Dundas Square just for the poutine? You knew there was a whole cook off going on?"

"Yes. It's my favourite day of the year. It's even better than Christmas."

"You're kidding me, right?"

"Nope. Hold on. I want to buy a bowl. Or are you leaving?" He raises his eyebrows.

"No, I'll wait for you."

"Good." He smiles and walks to the next vendor. He returns with a large paper bowl overflowing with fries, white cheese and gravy.

"Are those jalapenos?" I ask.

"Yes they are." He smiles and licks his lips. "Spicy and delicious."

"You know that you are eating all those calories that we burned off today."

"I brought you a fork." He laughs.

"No thank you," I say. "I am hungry though." I look around and see food vendor trucks down the street. "Grab a bench and I'll be right back."

I look at all the greasy food choices and settle on a falafel pita with tzatziki sauce. I also buy two plastic cups of draft beer and head back toward Jack. I give him a beer.

"Beer? Nice. Thank you." He takes a sip. "What are you eating?" I tell him and this time he turns up his nose.

"It's chickpeas," I defend myself. "It's really good."

"You'll eat that, but you won't eat Canada's national food dish?"

"It's not Canada's--"

He cuts me off. "Shhh!"

I laugh. "It originated in Quebec!" I say quickly.

"Eat your fucking awful."

"Falafel," I correct him.

"Whatever."

We eat and watch the craziness of downtown Toronto. A live band has started to play and more people crowd into the square. Our view is blocked off, but I don't mind because the music is pretty good.

"I need another beer," Jack says. "Would you like one?"

"Yes, please. I'll stay here and guard your spot."

He takes our garbage with him and disappears in the crowd and I watch couples, families with young children, teenagers and the elderly walk by me. It's such a wide variety of people.

Jack comes back carrying four plastic cups of beer. "Two for you and two for me."

"Thank you. I'm happy that I ran into you. I was starting to have an unpleasant night."

"Why?"

Do I tell him? We already had that heated discussion this morning. I don't want a repeat.

"You can tell me anything, Colleen," he urges.

"Just before I saw you, I saw Steve and his new girlfriend."

"Oh," he says plainly, barely looking at me.

That's all I get? "I didn't talk to them or run into them. I just saw them from afar. I wasn't able to see what she looked like."

"Is that what you were looking for when I first saw you? Are you curious to see what she looks like?"

"Well, yes. I'm very curious. He left me for this bitch. I want to see what she's got that I don't."

"Ok." I think he rolled his eyes.

That's not fair. He said that I can tell him anything. Perhaps it's better that I don't argue with him. I decide to let it drop. "Anyway, I'm happy to see you."

He frowns at me, "I'm glad that I am just a distraction for you." He chugs the rest of his beer and puts the empty cup under his other full one.

Why is he upset? "Jack? I didn't mean it that way. I enjoy being with you."

"Forget it," he mumbles. "Want to get closer to the band?" He stands up.

He's avoiding something, but I don't want to fight with him anymore, especially if it's about Steve. And I surely don't want to talk about a date with him. "Do you think we can get through the crowd?"

"Finish one of your cups of beer first." I do as he says and he takes my cup and puts it under his own. The he takes my hand and leads me carefully to the front of the stage.

Side by side, we start dancing to the music, but it's really confined. I'm enjoying myself, but a woman keeps pushing into me from behind. At first I think it's an accidental bump, so ignore it, but by the third time I stop dancing and turn around. A very large woman is dancing vigorously with a beer in her hand. The beer is splashing everywhere and she's oblivious to that, and to the fact that she's knocking into everyone around her. I return to my groove, but by the fifth shove and beer on my boots, I turn around and glare at her. I'm ready to knock her off of her feet or throw the rest of my beer at her.

Jack is suddenly behind me, his front to my back, and he yells into my ear, "She's not worth it. I'll dance behind you. She won't be able to bother you."

I start dancing again and I can feel him move against me. He bumps into me lightly and says, "Sorry. It's the lady again." I notice he leaves one hand on the side of my hip. I can feel his hips rub against me as he casually dances and I brush it off. I don't mind. I'd rather it be him, than some stranger.

I finish my beer and Jack takes our empty cups, squashes them and drops them onto the ground. We continue dancing and when I feel a bump again, his hand reaches a little further and takes a hold of my waist. He's holding me close. Protecting me.

A slow song comes on and we dance at the slower pace, echoing each other's movements. Both of his arms are around me now, his thumbs hooked in the belt loops of my jeans, under my sweater. I fiddle with my hands, not knowing what to do with them and end up resting them on his hands. I relax completely against him and my head rests just under his chin.

I told Jack that I don't want to date him, he knows how I still feel about Steve, and yet, I am dancing so affectionately with him. I am probably giving him the wrong signals. It just feels so comforting, I don't want to let go. And he doesn't seem to want to release me either. I'm so starved for this type of affection. I didn't know that I needed it. I thought I was tougher than this. I'm not being fair to Jack.

The song ends and the band's set is over. They thank the crowd for coming and exit the stage. I break away from Jack, afraid to look at him. I am confused. I feel guilty for leading him on, but I also like his company. He quickly finds and picks up our squashed beer cups, grabs my hand, and we walk with the dispersing crowd to the street. He drops the cups into a garbage can.

"Can I walk you home?" He asks.

"Sure." I don't let go of his hand.

We walk in silence. I can't read him. I'm not sure if it's awkward for him or if he's enjoying our time together. I remain quiet and hope for the best.

When we are almost at my house I ask, "Do you live close to me, too?"

"No, my car is back at Dundas Square."

"Oh Jack. You didn't have to walk me home." I feel very guilty now.

He stops and faces me. "Colleen, if you haven't figured it out, I like you. I would do anything for you."

Here we go again. He likes me or just wants to sleep with me. Either way, it's not going to happen. "Jack," I start.

"Stop. I know. You want to reconcile with your husband. I get it. I actually adore you for your conviction and pity you at the same time." He takes my other hand. "I will be your friend, and I will always be here for you, but I don't know how long I can wait for you to figure out that I can be the man you so desperately want and need."

Before I can respond, he bends down and kisses me tenderly. I let my eyes close and appreciate the softness of his lips. He pulls away suddenly and my eyes flutter open.

"Good night, Colleen."

I watch him walk away and I want to run to him and apologize, but I know that's not what he wants to hear. I didn't know he felt that strongly about me. He's a great friend and a very sweet man, but Steve still has my heart.

Inside my house, I call Steve, and this time I leave a message, "We need to talk. Please call me back." I hope he does. This needs to be resolved.

36.

I wake up tired. I didn't sleep very well. I shuffle to the kitchen to make a cup of tea and toast and return to the comfort of my bed.

Being alone sucks. I miss waking up beside Steve. I miss the coziness of sharing the house. I have always been independent and I enjoy throwing myself into my work, but I miss companionship and the love of my husband.

In the midst of my pity party, the phone rings. Maybe it's Steve.
"Hello?"
"Hey Ci-Ci. Ready for tonight?"
"Yes."
"Ok, what's wrong?"
"Can we have a girl's day?"
"I'll be right over."

I should have called her earlier. I take a shower and get ready for the comfort of my best friend.

Within an hour, Christine knocks on my door and I grab her arm and we head out to walk downtown. I think that some shopping therapy will do wonders.

"How often do you take a new man home?" I ask, looking through dresses at the Bay.

"It's just like you to get straight to the point." She giggles. "I don't have a set schedule. If I meet a man I like, then it happens."

"Do you spread them out? Do you take breaks?"

She steps closer to me. "Where is this going?"

I sigh. "I just want to know what is right. Is there a morally right answer to how often someone should have casual sex? I feel like I'm out of control."

"You are overthinking again. If it feels right to be with someone and you can enjoy it without guilt, then there is no maximum limit." She looks me straight in the eyes. "You also have been faithful to only one man in your entire life. You deserve this break of character."

"How much out of character can I go? I had sex with my art teacher this week. That makes four men in one week," I say sheepishly.

"I can easily top that without regret. But this is about you. Do you regret it? Feel guilty? Or are you ashamed?"

"I feel both regret and guilt. I wish that I was having sex with my husband, not random men." I want to do those things with Steve.

Christine thinks for a second. "I get it. You miss your husband, but are you having sex with these men because you want to get back at him or do you want to hurt these men because you are hurt?"

"Neither. I'm doing this to explore my sexuality."

"I just wanted to make sure you still had the same motive."

"If you're not ashamed, then you have absolutely nothing to worry about." She hugs me.

I relax a little. "Do you think I'm an idiot for wanting Steve back?"

"Ci-Ci, you are a very intelligent woman. You work hard to get what you want. If you think that you can work things out with Steve and live a happy life with him, then I don't think you're an idiot. You seemed happy when you were with him, but I don't know his side of the story."

"A friend told me that he moved in with a woman already and I actually saw him holding hands with a woman last night," I admit.

"I see. That's why you needed a girl's day. Wow. He moved on quick. Asshole," she mutters. She hooks her arm through mine and we walk out of the store, into the second level of the mall.

"We haven't even talked since he left! He showed up on my doorstep with separation papers, but left immediately after I threw them on the ground. I've called him every day, begged him to meet me…" I stop and lean on the railing overlooking the first level. I'm on the verge of tears.

"Stop doing that!" She snaps. "Ignore him for a while, and then the next message you leave, you tell him that you realize your mistakes and that you took him for granted. Repeat anything that he has told you about why he left and own up to it."

I stand up straight and stare at her dumbfounded, "But I don't know why he said all those things. How can I own up to something if I don't believe in it or understand it?" I don't want to tell him that I am a robot.

"Admitting that you have faults shows a better side of you. You are telling him that he is right. Who doesn't want to hear that?"

"I guess. Isn't that luring him under false pretenses?"

"Sure, but you'll have him in the same room with you. You'll be able to talk and perhaps show him the new things you have learned."

"Can't I call him now?" I want to try this immediately.

"No! Ci-Ci, give him a break from your phone calls. Give it two weeks."

That's a long time, but Christine's advice sounds solid. Two weeks will give me a chance to get some more experience, too.

"You really would make a great therapist." I smile.

"You can buy me lunch to repay me for my fountain of knowledge."

We both laugh and hook arms. I'm so happy that I can talk to her about anything. I never knew that I could. We continue to gossip and shop all afternoon. We also find sexy, new outfits for our night out at Sangria. After a late lunch we finalize our plans for meeting up later and go our separate ways.

When I get home, I feel better about everything and I'm looking forward to more girl time with Christine. I just need a quick nap to recharge for this evening.

37.

At ten o'clock, Christine and I walk past the long line of people who are waiting on College Street to get into Sangria. All Christine does is smile at the bouncers and they let us in. I can hear the whines and groans in the line, but follow Christine in. I had a long nap and I am ready to dance and feel the energy of this place. I'm disappointed to find that the music is quiet and club is not full yet, but I notice that the dance lesson has already started.

"We're late!" Christine pulls me to the front of the room, right by the instructor. That's Christine for you. I would have stood in the back. I see a large sign that reads, *Welcome! Tonight's salsa instructor: Bonita.*

Bonita, a beautiful woman in a flamboyant, red and yellow ruffled costume, has the couples in a closed dance position and they are doing a basic salsa step. Christine and I copy everyone else. Christine wants to lead, so she takes my right hand with her left and places her right hand on my left shoulder blade.

Bonita yells, "Feel the music. Move your hips." She comes up behind another couple and puts her hands on the woman's hips. "Keep your hips loose and don't be afraid to sway your hips."

Everyone knows the steps. We must have missed the beginning instructions, so I focus on another couple's feet and try to figure it out. I step backward with my right foot, and then my feet come together. Pause. Then I step forward with my left foot, and then my feet come together. Pause. It's pretty easy.

Christine laughs at me. She tries to force my hips to move more than they can. I am wearing a gray skirt, long in the back, short in the front, and it's really swishy. It moves well with the music. Christine's outfit is glued to her body; she's wearing a strapless, silver top and tight black skirt. She's got the mambo down already and every curve is accentuated while she dances. She looks seductive. I feel stupid.

"The lead should guide the follower by giving claves. Claves are tugs or pushes on the hip or shoulder that let the follower know when to turn, hesitate or dip."

I become more confident with the basic steps and Christine encourages me. She then claves me; she tugs my right hip and leads me to the right. And then she dips me! I laugh and my head tilts all the way back. I see a man smiling down at me and I quickly stand up. I look at him and he winks. He is cute, but I quickly look away. I am dancing with a woman. Actually, I'm dancing horribly with a woman. I'm embarrassed.

"Excellent." Bonita praises us.

Christine turns me in the other direction and we keep dancing. I look back to see if he was still watching me, but I can't see him in the growing crowd.

The instructor teaches us how to pivot and to turn with a partner and Christine and I are laughing and having a great time. I have missed her.

Christine took Steve and I to a dance club once and I had a great time. Steve isn't very coordinated, so he was happy standing at the bar, drinking beer and watching us. I saw him talking to a beautiful shooter girl and he bought us all 'sex on the beach' shooters. The shooter girl kept coming back to Steve and at one point, they seemed to be deep in conversation. I tried to ignore it, but her hair was in his face and he was the one to push it back behind her ear. He did that to me all the time. It bothered me, but I kept dancing.

Near the end of the night, they were talking again and they both looked at their watches. It looked like they were saying goodbye. About five minutes later, he looked at me and mouthed, "Be right back." He returned thirty minutes later. He said that he had to take a call from work because there was a problem. I didn't question him, but thought it was strange to have an important call at two in the morning. I'm questioning the whole thing now.

Suddenly, the music starts booming. The instructor waves to us, takes her sign, and walks away. I guess the salsa lesson is over. The song that is playing is a Latin remix of a top forty song. It's upbeat and I'm ready to let loose. We dance for a while and then Christine grabs my hand and leads me to the bar.

"What do you want?" She yells over the music.

"Doesn't matter," I yell back.

Christine easily gets the attention of a handsome bartender. She holds two fingers up to him, but I can't hear what she orders.

I watch the crowd of people dancing and I want to get back out there. I have been so concerned with my separation and reconciling with Steve for too long. This feels wonderful to forget and enjoy myself.

Christine nudges me. She's holding two shot glasses and two limes. I scrunch up my nose. She smiles. I squeeze in at the bar, get the salt ready and we do our tequila shots. She bought me a Corona, too, so I chase the horrible taste down my throat with the beer. She urges me to finish the entire beer. We both drink quickly and we're back on the dance floor in minutes.

Two men start dancing beside us and I recognize the one from before. He is much cuter up close. He is in his mid-twenties, with dark brown hair and brown eyes. He looks Spanish. He's wearing a dress shirt, with the top button undone and dress pants. He's a good dancer.

Christine catches my attention and gives me a thumbs up. I give her one back. The guy dancing with me gets closer, but it could be because the crowd is getting thick. I don't mind. An authentic Latin song begins, and I start to walk towards the bar, but the Latin guy grabs my hand and stops me. I look at him and he smiles. Ok, I'll dance.

He definitely knows what he is doing. His hips sway in all the right ways. He spins me around and catches me perfectly. His hands are on my hips, the small of my back, everywhere, with such grace and gentleness. I am mesmerized by this style of dancing.

Christine brings me another tequila shot and a beer. We do the shot and go back to dancing with our men. We dance song after song. Some are faster than others, but I feel light on my feet. Maybe it's the tequila, but I feel sexy and alive. He is a great dance partner.

His smile is soft and he keeps his eyes on mine, each dance. I'm the one who breaks free of his gaze from time to time, but I'm always drawn back to his eyes.

A slow song comes on and he takes me in his arms. I can feel his hips sway against mine. He's holding one of my hands, close to his shoulder and the other rests on my lower back, closer to my behind. He smells nice and he has a hard body. I am enjoying our closeness.

The music picks up pace and we start dancing the way we were before, but this time, when he spins me away from him, he pulls me so that my back is against his chest. He puts his hands on my hips and persuades me to shake my hips more. I do and I put my hands in the air.

His hands slide up my body and his fingertips graze my breasts. Flip flop. I quickly look around. The dance floor is too packed for anyone to see. When his hands come back down, he lightly brushes my nipples and cups my breasts in both hands for a split second. It's so sensual and risky. I blindly drop my hands to his head, briefly caress his neck and then bring them down beside me, putting my thumbs in his pockets. His hands rest on my hips and we grind to the music. I am very turned on. He nuzzles my neck and I feel his lips on my ear.

He spins me around to face him and one of his feet ends up between mine. His upper thigh is rubbing against my heat as I move my hips to the beat. He pulls my hips forwards and my back arches slightly. I put my arms around his neck. My tank top has pulled down slightly because of the friction and the tops of my breasts have emerged slightly. I am not wearing a bra. He pulls me close with his hands at my ribcage, under my arms, and I feel his thumbs at my breasts. First, they are on top of my shirt and then, on my skin. He presses his thumbs downward, underneath the material, and he finds my nipples. I look around again. No one is watching. I close my eyes and moan. The loud beat of the music, the flashing lights, and the risk of getting caught is intoxicating.

Suddenly, he takes my hand and leads me off the dance floor and past the washrooms. He opens the door to the right and we are in a small office. It has only a desk, with mounds of paperwork on it and a phone. I hear him lock the door.

He pushes me against the door and kisses me with such force that the back of my head hits the door. His tongue pushes into my mouth and I respond with equal passion, grasping the back of his neck and shoulders. I don't have time to think.

His hands travel up my body and he pulls down the front of my tank top, releasing my naked breasts. He takes them both into his hands and squeezes the nipples hard. He bends down to suck each one loudly. He pushes them together and his tongue flicks at them. I feel his teeth biting. Then he comes back up to kiss me. He pushes his hips into mine and I push back. His erection is solid and pushes into my thigh. His hands go to my waist and then slip behind my back and then down to squeeze my bottom. My back arches as he pulls my hips forward. I let him, but question if I'm going to let this happen here, with this stranger.

I get my answer quickly. He starts pulling up my skirt and I open my eyes, panicking, but close them quickly and focus on his soft mouth. This is in the moment and completely unexpected. The spontaneity is exciting. This is the exact experience I need. I try to relax.

My dress is bunched up around my waist and is hands are on the lacy waistband of my thong underwear, his fingers glide over and under them. He follows the line of the thong down my backside, pulls it away from me and lets it snap back in place He's teasing me and I can feel the wetness in my panties. He brings his hands to the front of my panties and puts a thumb on either side, under the edge of lace. His thumbs dip lower and press into my clitoris, they massage it and I squeeze my legs together to ease the pressure.

One of his hands leaves my apex and he lifts it to his face, stopping our kissing. He puts his thumb into his mouth and closes his eyes. "Mmmmm," he murmurs. He puts that hand behind my head and starts kissing me again. I feel his other hand dive into my panties and his fingers plunge into me. It takes my breath away. I moan.

I run my hands from his chest down to his pants and I undo the top button and unzip him. His kissing becomes more heated and his breathing quickens. I can do this. I let go of his pants and they drop. I reach for his hardness with both hands and he moans. It's large in my hands. I'm excited by its size.

He kisses my neck and ear. I pull his underwear away from his skin and feel his hardness in both hands. I run my hands up and down the length of him. I stroke him to the rhythm that he is making as he fingers me.

He takes his hands and places them on my chest, pushing me away. He holds his forefinger up, telling me to wait, and he opens the top drawer of the desk, pulling out a condom. He rips it open and I watch him roll it onto his erection. I'll contemplate how he knows about the supply of condoms later. Right now I just want him badly.

When he comes back to me, he pulls my dress up quickly and rips my panties off of my body. He throws them to the floor. I momentarily remember how expensive they were, but am distracted quickly when he uses his knee to open my legs wider.

He puts one hand on my bottom and I feel his tip at my entrance. He forces himself inside of me. "God you are so wet," he says. He thrusts upwards and I feel myself go on tiptoes with every plunge.

It's so primal, so raw. His hands cup my behind and he pulls me into him. My one leg rises and wraps around the back of his thigh. I can feel him inside me better. I'm standing on one leg, but he holds me solidly in place.

My back bangs into the wall as he begins to pump fiercely. His breath is ragged. I can feel my insides tightening up and my core pulsating. I gasp with every thrust. It is so deep and stimulating. I feel myself rising to the top. I'm at the brink. He lifts me off my feet. My legs wrap around his waist and I come hard and fast. My orgasm lasts long and I try to catch my breath. He moans loudly and his hard rhythm ceases, pumping rigidly once or twice more and then I hear him release his breath.

He lets me down and he walks to the desk. I smooth down my skirt and pick up my panties. I scrunch them up in my hand. He turns back to me, smiles, takes my hand and we are out on the dance floor again. We start dancing and I nonchalantly drop my panties onto the crowded floor.

Christine grabs my hand. "Where did you go?" She yells.

I shake my head and smile.

"You had sex! Oh my god!" She laughs. "Come on, let's dance!"

We dance until three in the morning and leave the club, looking for a taxi. I see my mystery guy and he winks at me. I have no interest in talking to him. It was an amazing experience, and I just want to go home.

Christine and I share a taxi, but I get out first.

"Call me tomorrow, Ci-Ci. You are crazy!"

"Good night, Christine."

38.

    I can't move when my alarm rings the next morning. My head aches, probably from the tequila, and I'm exhausted. There's no way that I can tolerate my morning appointments without vomiting or falling asleep.

    I call Margie on her cell. She doesn't pick up, so I leave a message, "I won't be able to make it in until one. Please reschedule my appointments with my apologies." She will be shocked again. I fall back asleep quickly.

    Four hours later, I wake again feeling better. I still have a few hours before I have to get to work, so I go to the kitchen and make a cup of tea. Before I head for my bedroom, I grab a pen and my Project Sex notebook. I prop myself up in bed and start writing.

Data Collection

Sample #5
Seek persons who understand study & are willing to express inner feelings & experiences

- *Man, aged ? (early 20s?), Latin, good dancer—Mystery Man*
- *Brown hair, brown eyes, toned, fit.*

Describe experiences of phenomenon

- *I was attracted to his dancing, the way he moved. The eye contact was intense. Dancing was a type of foreplay. It happened fast. It was intense and erotic. Intercourse happened while standing up. It lasted maybe ten minutes.*

Direct observation
- *What is needed to be more sexual:*
- *Confidence, desire, a connection with sample*

Audio or videotape? n/a - shocking!

Data analysis

Classify & rank data
- *5 out of 5. For different reasons. This has not changed.*

Sense of wholeness
- *I am still trying to achieve my goal: I visualize myself with Steve doing these sexual acts. This has not changed.*
- *Negative thoughts have vanished: I did not withhold or question. Only one question: how did he know the condoms were in the desk drawer?*
- *It was a great experience: I was spontaneous, willing and did not hesitate.*

Examine experiences beyond human awareness/ or cannot be communicated
- *Alcohol may have played a part (tequila shots).*
- *I didn't know his name, didn't know his profession, we did not speak, yet there was an intense connection.*
- *Movement of our bodies together, rhythm of the music must have attributed to the passion.*

My inhibitions have decreased incredibly, but I still would like to experiment when I have not been drinking. I know this is an important factor as to why I am so receptive to a new experience. But something else is missing and I can't put my finger on it. It was an intense and pleasurable experience, but I think I need to do more or add more. I'm not sure what it is I'm lacking.

I have a leisurely shower and put on a navy, wraparound dress. I eat a bagel with another cup of tea and then take my time driving to work. I get to my office at noon.

"Hi, Margie," I say when I walk through the door.

"Who are you and what have you done with Colleen?" She smiles. "Are you ok?"

"I'm fine. I did not feel well when I woke up. The extra couple of hours sleep did wonders," I explain. "Is everything under control?"

"I'm glad you're feeling better. There is a slight problem. Connie had an appointment this morning and I rebooked it for tomorrow, there were no other available time slots that fit her schedule. The issue is that we moved it to today in order to mislead her husband."

"Right. Her husband knows that she always has Tuesday appointments. Did you at least put it at a different time?"

"Of course. I changed it to the last appointment of the day, rather than the first."

"That's all we can do, I guess. Thank you." I start to walk into my office. "Go take your lunch or take the afternoon off, if you want it. You deserve it." I smile.

"Seriously, are you feeling alright? First, you take an entire morning off and now you want me to ditch work?"

I start laughing. "Life's too short."

"I'm out of here before you change your mind."

"Go!" I command.

My afternoon drains me. My patients seem more upset and stressed than usual. I try breathing techniques with most of them. It's hard for preschoolers to understand how to breathe in through their nose and slowly out through their mouth. We pretend to blow up a balloon inside our tummies and then blow the air out through our mouths. When that doesn't work, I pull out the bottle of bubbles and we blow them in my office. It actually helps me too.

At five, my last appointment leaves and I lay down on my couch. The phone rings not too soon after and I growl, and crawl over to my desk to pick it up.

"Colleen Cousineau."

"Hey Ci-Ci. How you feeling?"

"I took the morning off. What does that tell you?"

"You? You took the morning off? You must have been feeling pretty shitty."

"Just tired. I'm better now. How are you?"

"I'm good. Just seeing what your plans are for this evening. I want to hear all about your Latin lover." She giggles.

"What day is it again?"

"Wow Ci-Ci, you are out of it. It's Monday."

Monday. Cooking class. "It's Mexican night at the Culinarium." I look at my watch. "What the-! It's six?" I must have fallen asleep on the couch.

"What's wrong?"

"I have to leave. I'm going to be late. I'll call you later." I hang up and scramble for my belongings.

39.

Just like last week, I am stuck in traffic, but this time I am going to be at least 20 minutes late for class. I can feel anxiety in my chest and the traffic is stressing me out. I want to flip off the silver sports car that is trying to inch its way in front of me. I wish I had my bottle of bubbles.

I take some deep calming breaths and fiddle with my wedding band on my key chain. I didn't call Steve last night. That's the first time since he moved out. I hope he doesn't think I've given up. This adds to my anxiousness. Christine's plan had better work.

I find a parking spot after circling the block four times, but I have to wait for the lady to continue getting into her car, put her purse down, put her seatbelt on, and every other step that I could do much faster than her. Really? You need to adjust your rearview mirror too?

I notice that I'm gripping the steering wheel with both hands and clenching my teeth. I loosen my grip and take some more breaths. Why am I so stressed? I guess I'm overtired. Late nights are not good for me. I should have gone out for a nice, quiet dinner with Christine. I prepaid for the cooking class, but it was only $20. I should have bailed.

I yawn and finally pull into the parking spot. Well, I'm here now. I walk slowly to the school. I know I should hurry, but I'd rather not break an ankle running in my heels.

I do try to sneak in, but Chris, my partner from last week, waves me over to the back of the room.

"I saved you a spot," he says, smiling. His dimples are adorable. He takes my coat from me and places it over his on a chair. He's wearing a tee shirt that is too snug for his ample biceps. It gives me a pretty good idea of how fit he is. He's even better looking than last week. He doesn't look like a business professor at all.

"Thank you. I almost didn't make it."

"You haven't missed much. Chef Facundo is retelling the complete history of tamales." He fakes a yawn.

"Tamales? Come on, let's get on with this." I'm irritated.

"You look very pretty today," he says, touching my arm.

"Thank you." I smile and lighten up a little.

Tonight's chef is a short, very robust Hispanic man. He smiles as he talks and giggles at the end of every sentence. I think he's nervous.

"The tamale has changed in size, colour, shape, and filling, depending on the location and the resources available." He giggles. "The wrappings varied from cornhusks, to soft tree bark, to edible leaves, such as avocados and bananas." He giggles again.

Chef opens his fridge and takes out a rectangular glass dish and a large bowl. "Please take out your soaking corn husks and your masa."

I stay seated and yawn again. Chris stands up to get it. He is wearing jeans. Nice bum. He puts the food on the counter in front of us. He pokes at the doughy stuff, which I assume is masa. I watch him, but then he slaps my hand.

"What did I do?"

"You yawned. That's like the sixth one. Are you tired today?"

"Yes. Very."

"Busy day or long weekend?"

"Both. But more so, I went to Sangria last night and stayed out way too late."

Chef begins to instruct us further. Chris whispers, "Is that the Latin nightclub?"

I nod.

"You know how to salsa dance? I'd love to see that." He smiles and raises his eyebrows.

He is very cute. I whisper back, "It takes a good partner to dance like that." I think about my Latin man's hands on me. Flip flop. He had the moves. "I had fun. Did you do anything this weekend?"

"Nothing cool like that. I should start hanging around with you. You seem to live an exciting life."

"Not really. I like to try new things, but that was the first time I've ever been there." And probably the last, too. I don't want to make a habit of having sex at a bar. What was I thinking? That was pretty insane.

"New things? I'm a new thing. Wanna try me?"

I laugh. I just realize that he's been flirting with me all along. I missed it. "That would be new. Let me think about it." I am getting better at flirting.

We ignore Chef and continue whispering about our hobbies and interests. Chris likes to rollerblade along the harbor front and plays hockey on a house league team. He also likes to experiment with food at home. He was a chef when he was younger. Our interaction is like salsa dancing. He offers information and flirts, touching me, and then I reciprocate. It goes back and forth and we get closer to each other. The flirting is extremely obvious.

"Am I boring you?"

"I am so sorry. Was I yawning again? I don't mean to be." I touch his thigh. "You're anything, but boring." I look around. "I need to get up."

"You're leaving?"

"No, I was just going to walk around the kitchen, but leaving sounds like a better idea."

"Oh." He looks sad.

"Do you want to go for a walk with me?" I want to keep our conversation alive, but I also wonder how his lips would feel. I know he's interested. How far do I want to take this today? I feel awake all of a sudden.

His eyes brighten. "We have missed quite a lot of steps anyway. I don't even know what we're making anymore." He grabs our coats. "Let's go."

I'm excited that he decided to come with me. We quickly and quietly leave the kitchen and put our coats on outside.

"I don't mind missing Mexican night, but next week is Lebanese food. Spinach pie, hummus and falafels."

"Mmmm. Sounds delicious." I'm not thinking of food right now. I want to feel Chris' strong biceps. I stick my arm in his and he doesn't seem to mind. "I'm trying to keep warm," I say. He's solid.

"I like it. And if it gets too cold, I live down this way."

That is convenient. "How far down?"

"Five blocks."

"Let's head there then. Going for a walk might not have been the best idea. I don't think I can take the cold much longer." It's actually not that cold. I'm being quite the temptress.

40.

Chris holds my arm a little tighter and we quicken our pace. What a change of direction I just had. I'm going home with him. Is he thinking of going in the same direction that I am? I wonder if he'll be gentle or if he'll teach me something new. I am excited to go home with him, but he hasn't said a word though. That worries me.

"This is my apartment," he says. "Let's get you warm."

We walk inside and the lobby concierge nods to us as we walk to the elevators. Chris pushes the button and he turns to me. "I feel awkward telling you this, but I'm very nervous about you coming to my apartment. My wife and I separated less than a month ago and I have not even looked at another woman in twenty years. For you to come up to my new apartment is unimaginable and yet, here you are."

"I don't have to. I can walk back to my car." I'm disappointed, but I was in that same position not too long ago.

"No. Please. I want you to come up. I just moved in, so please excuse the mess." The elevator opens and he ushers me in.

"Just for a little bit," I say. I still have a chance. I think he needs an ego boost anyway. "You can show me your kitchen."

He smiles. "That's a little boring."

We step out of the elevator and walk down to the end of the hall, past a few apartment doors. He opens his door and I realize that he wasn't kidding. He just moved in. There are still boxes everywhere.

"Again, I apologize for the mess. I work all day and then don't feel like unpacking. If you can see past the boxes, it is a nice place."

It really is charming. One entire wall is exposed brick with a grand bookcase filled to the brim with books. A little further, on the same wall is a cozy fireplace in the living room. It has a high ceiling, but it slopes downward from the brick wall to the kitchen on the other side of the room. The counters and cabinets are made of reclaimed wood. It reminds me of a cottage.

"I feel silly apologizing all the time, but all I have to sit on are these two folding chairs or…" He points past the boxes. "The mattress on the floor."

I laugh. "I'll take the mattress. You take the chair," I joke. I take my coat off, look around, and place it on a box. He smiles. I take off my shoes and do sit on his bed. I prop myself up on a few pillows, so that I'm not lying down. I don't want to seem too obvious.

He takes me literally and sets up the folding chair beside the bed.

"Chris. It's ok. Come sit next to me."

He is completely nervous. He looks at me for a few seconds, folds the chair up, puts it back where he got it from and sits next to me. I prop the remaining pillows up for him behind his back, but he is sitting stiffly.

"You seemed really confident at the school, Chris. What happened?"

"You happened. It was easy to flirt when you think nothing is going to transpire, but now you're here. It changes everything."

I laugh. "I'm harmless. Why don't we go cook something?" I figure he needs to do something he enjoys to relieve his stress.

He jumps up. "What do you want me to cook?" He's excited like a little boy.

"Can you bake? How about chocolate chip cookies?"

"We didn't even have dinner."

I give him my best puppy dog eyes.

He laughs. "Oh, ok. I'll see what I've got."

We go into the kitchen and he pats the counter. "Sit here." I jump up and he starts rifling through his cupboards, pulling out random food. Instant pudding, vanilla wafers and icing sugar. He opens the fridge and pulls out egg, cream, milk and raspberries. "It's not chocolate chip cookies, but it'll do."

As he starts spooning stuff into bowls, he rambles on about how he found his apartment and how it was a great deal. He stands in front of me and kind of looks where my legs are, and goes to reach, but drops his hand.

"Do you need to get in here?" I ask softly and move my legs partially over.

"Yes," he says and tries to open the drawer, but he has to touch my legs to move them over a bit more.

"Sorry."

He smiles shyly at me and goes back to stirring and creating. I hop down and lean over with my elbows on the counter beside him. He gives me a quick look and turns to grab an ingredient.

"What are you making me?"

"A trifle."

"I don't think I've ever had one."

"It has layers of cookies, whipped cream, fruit and pudding."

"Sounds delicious."

He gets out his little hand mixer and starts beating a mixture. "Is that whipped cream? I used to lick the beaters when I was a kid."

"I'll be done in a minute." He beats the mixture until soft peaks form and he hands me a beater.

I stare at him and take long licks. "It's delicious. Want to try some?" I put some on my finger and raise it close to his lips.

It seems like a full minute for him to think about it, but he leans in close and encircles my finger with his mouth. I can feel the tip of his tongue slightly and then he releases. I open my mouth slightly and keep my eyes on his the entire time.

My same finger goes back in the bowl of whipped cream and I step closer to him. "Want some more?"

He nods, leans in to take it again, but I put my finger in my own mouth.

He watches me and tries to dip his finger in. He almost misses the bowl. He looks away to make sure he has more whipped cream on his finger and offers it to me. I take it, but I don't let go of his finger. I bite it gently, grab his hand, and take more of his finger in my mouth. Past the second knuckle. I swirl my tongue around his finger and then slowly pull it out of my mouth.

I figured he would continue from there, but he turns back to his mixing bowl. He still needs some encouragement. I pull the belt at my waist, the bow unties, and my dress falls open. He does a double take. I am wearing a navy, lace bra and matching panties. I dip my finger into the whipped cream again and bring it in front of his mouth. He goes for it, but I dab it on my collarbone and put the rest in my mouth.

Chris' eyes travel over my body and he takes a step closer. He slowly bends down and I feel his tongue lick the whipped cream. His lips kiss up my neck and find my mouth. Good boy.

His kisses are soft at first, even hesitant. His tongue is gentle and massages mine. I put my hands on his chest and I can feel his solidness through his tee shirt. I wring the tee shirt with my fingers and pull it away from his body. He is a great kisser.

He puts his hands on my back and his kisses get deeper. I hear his breath deepen and his hands reach lower and rest at the top of my behind.

I take a step closer so that my breasts are touching his chest and I arch my back and lean into him. I make sure that our hips have gentle pressure against each other. I am assertive because he is so shy.

He opens up my dress, grabs my lacy bottom with his hands and pulls my hips into his. I can feel his hardness against my hips. He pushes a little too hard and I stumble back into the counter.

"I'm sorry," he says, backing off.

I grab him and start kissing him again, but this time I'm too aggressive and I knock him off balance. This is no good. I take his hand and start leading him to the mattress. I stop halfway there, and run back to get the bowl of whipped cream. When he sees it in my hands, he starts to laugh. We both walk to the mattress and I put the bowl on the floor.

He looks at me, "I don't know what to do."

I smile and slowly slip out of my dress. I let it fall to the floor. "Does this give you an idea?" I say softly.

Chris walks toward me and I lie down on the bed. I dip my finger into the whip cream and wipe it on my stomach. He kneels onto the bed, bends over me and licks it off. I get some more on two fingers and walk my fingers up my stomach to the middle of my breasts. He licks everywhere my fingers have been. I get up on my elbows, unhook the front closure on my bra, but don't take it off. It falls open loosely, barely covering my erect nipples. He just stares at me for a minute. He dips his fingers in the whipped cream, flips open one side of my bra and dabs some on my nipple. He does the same with my other nipple. He bends close and licks it off both my nipples. He is so tentative and gentle. It feels unbelievable.

I sit up suddenly and he sits back onto his heels. I let my bra slide off and I kneel in front of him. I untuck his shirt and pull it up and over his head. He has a great body. I kiss his chest softly and put my hands on his hips. I squeeze his thighs and kiss his stomach, my breasts rubbing against his legs. I feel his hands lightly touching my back. I go for his belt and sit up again, unbuckling it. I peek up at him and he's watching my hands. I start to undo the button on his pants, but he stops me by placing his hands on mine. I look at him.

He sits up off of his heels and grabs my face, he kisses me deeply. He is still so tender and uncertain. I bring my hands to his waist again and go for his pants again. I undo the button this time and unzip them. I very carefully put my hand on his hardness. He moans immediately. Oh, how I want to make him feel good.

"Lie down," I say. He does and I try to pull down his pants. I look at him, requesting his permission, and he lifts his hips to oblige. I pull them right off of his legs and put them at the end of the mattress. I crawl up his legs and straddle him, my breasts resting on his chest. We start kissing again and he grabs my breasts, fingering my nipples. I get up on my hands, breaking lip contact and I rub my sex slowly over his hardness. I arch my back and push my breasts into his face. He squeezes and bites at them, breathing heavily.

I move down his body, kissing his neck, chest and hard stomach. I lick the top of his underwear and I take the waistband in my hands, ready to pull them down, but he gets up and pushes me onto my back. He again, just looks at me. It's like he's scared or really doesn't know what to do.

He needs a little assistance. I reach behind him and dip my fingers into the whipped cream once again. This time I open my legs and dab it onto my panties, over top of my clitoris. He stares at me. I lick the rest of the cream off of my fingers and finger my own nipple. I am being extremely seductive.

Chris slowly crawls over to me, between my legs. He puts his hands on the mattress between my legs and opens my legs wider. He dips his head down and I can feel pressure and his hot breath on my sex. I dig my fingers into his hair and lightly push his head down. The pressure increases and then I feel his fingers, pulling my panties over and his tongue pries into me. I moan loudly. There you go!

He pushes his tongue deep inside me over and over. I am breathing heavily. It feels incredible. The pressure on my clitoris is overwhelming. He has pushed my legs apart and my calves are resting on his shoulders. His fingers are under my bottom and his thumbs are also plunging into me. It's putting me over the edge. I don't want to come yet. I push his head away and try to close my legs. He moves out of the way, sitting on his knees again and looks at me blankly.

I reach over and start pulling his underwear down. He straightens his legs and lets me. I throw them over my shoulder and smile. I push him down and lower my head towards his erection. He is quite large. I position myself between his legs and put the tip in my mouth. His girth is unbelievable. I can't put him in my mouth. I do the best that I can, licking the tip and sucking hard on what I can put in my mouth. His breathing is erratic and I can see him clutching the sheets on the mattress. I suddenly feel his hands on my shoulders. He's pushing me away.

I look at him and he's shaking his head. "You're going to make me explode and I don't want to do it that way." He opens a brown leather box on the floor beside him and he pulls out a condom. It had better be extra-large. He rolls it on with little difficulty.

I lie down on my back again and he looks me in the eyes as he pulls my panties down. He tosses my panties and spreads my legs when he comes to kneel between them. He places his tip at my entrance and I actually brace myself. I can feel him enter me and it fills me instantly. But I know that he has more to give me. I lift my hips and he pushes a little deeper. I think I might climax immediately. My inner core pulses with extreme pleasure. I push again, wanting more. He plunges once more and

I yell, "Faster, please!" He starts pumping faster and I feel like my insides are going to burst open, but I come hard and fast. I moan loudly. I can feel my walls vibrating against his hardness and then I am numb.

When I calm, he pulls out and rolls me over, my cheek on the mattress. I feel him push my legs together and then he straddles me. I'm a little concerned when I feel him at my bottom. I feel his length dip down between my legs and then his tip at my entrance again. He pushes into me and I feel like I have to open my legs to receive him, but I can't because his legs are keeping mine closed. It feels so tight and full. I can feel the length of him slowly drive into me and then slowly pull out again. It's a breathtaking sensation.

I lift my hips, so he can take me more easily. He puts a pillow under my hips and that helps considerably. He starts to move faster, thrusting into me with more force. I can feel another orgasm stirring inside. I grab his sheets tightly. His breathing changes dramatically. With every thrust he exhales and his pace increases.

My insides tense further, the buildup is incredible. I moan in ecstasy. With one more hard thrust, I finally get to the brink, the tension escalates and then releases fiercely. I feel the explosion wash over me. Chris is right there after me. I hear him moan loudly, thrust quickly and then still. He collapses on me to catch his breath and then he pulls out and comes to lie beside me.

"That was unbelievable," he whispers.

I smile. Yes it was. But I immediately feel like something is missing. It's a pang of... I'm not sure what. I do know that I want to leave, but I don't want to be rude. We lie side by side, without a word, for at least ten minutes. I look at Chris and he's just staring at the ceiling.

"Are you ok?" I ask.

"Yes. I just can't believe what happened actually happened."

"It was great."

"It sure was."

"Um. I have to work in the morning. I should probably leave."

"Oh. Ok." He's not upset, but he is not ok either. He gets up and starts finding his clothes.

I do the same. After I put my shoes and coat on, I grab my purse and head toward the door. "I can just walk to my car. It's just down the street."

"I'm not going to let you walk alone. I'll take you there." He grabs his coat and his keys. "Let's go."

We walk in silence down the street. There are only a couple of people in a pizza parlour that I can see, and no one on the street. It's very quiet. And very awkward. I wonder how it can go from experiencing every inch of each other's body to feeling like strangers so quickly. It's unfortunate that it has to be this way. I'm really going to miss the Lebanese food next week. I can't go to cooking class ever again. Mmmm. Falafels. Jack called them fucking awfuls. I smile, but put my head down quickly. I wonder what Chris is thinking.

"This is my car," I say.

"Oh." He stops and avoids my eyes.

"Thank you for this evening." I walk closer to him. "I didn't expect any of it to happen. You are an amazing lover."

He looks at me and blushes. "I've only been with one other woman besides you and that was my wife."

"You were incredible." I kiss his cheek.

"Thank you. You were pretty incredible, too. Would you like to go out again this week?"

Here we go again. "I have a very busy week."

"I understand. Will I see you at cooking class next week?"

"I think so." Probably not. I turn and unlock my car door. Chris opens the door for me. "Good night, Chris."

"Good night, Colleen."

I drive away, pleased with my accomplishments. I seduced a man and pretty much controlled the outcome of my sexual experience. I was extremely confident, but he was insecure and apprehensive. We balanced in that sense. Would the result have been the same had we both been aggressive?

I get home quickly and get ready for bed. Lying in bed, I wonder how it will work between Steve and me. He has a lot of experience, but I want to show him my new abilities. How am I going to seduce him?

41.

The alarm wakes me and I just lie there. I don't feel like running again today. I turn over into fetal position, and with my legs together I realize that my girly parts are sore. No wonder. Chris was enormous. I smile.

I get up, lift a few weights and stretch instead. I might look into trying a yoga class. I need to do something different. I dress in tan pants and a pale pink sweater, and try to tame my curls into a low bun.

By not running, I have more time for breakfast, so I make an omelette and toast. I sit and enjoy it with my favourite tea. I see my research notebook poking out of my purse, so I pull it out.

Data Collection

Sample #6
Seek persons who understand study & are willing to express inner feelings & experiences
- *Man, aged 40, professor.*
- *Brown hair, brown eyes, toned, fit.*

Describe experiences of phenomenon
- *I met him twice in cooking class. He was fun and playful in class, very flirtatious. Outside of cooking class, he was insecure and hesitant. I seduced him. I took the lead and controlled the situation. We used whipped cream and he licked off me. He performed cunnilingus, but I stopped him before I*

had an orgasm; I wanted it to last. I performed fellatio; His girth was incredible. I could not put the entire thing in my mouth. He stopped me before he had an orgasm. We had sex in the missionary position and I climaxed immediately; his size was pleasurable. He turned me over and we spooned, my legs closed, his over mine, closing them. I climaxed again. He climaxed, too.

<u>Direct observation</u>
- What is needed to be more sexual:
- Confidence, arousal, desire, a connection with sample, this one was me teaching him, almost like a trial run for when I seduce Steve.

<u>Audio or videotape?</u> n/a – I should just omit this every time.

<u>Data analysis</u>

<u>Classify & rank data</u>
- 5 out of 5. For different reasons. This has not changed.

<u>Sense of wholeness</u>
- I am still trying to achieve my goal; I visualize myself with Steve doing these sexual acts. This has not changed.
- Negative thoughts have vanished; I did not withhold or question.
- It was a great experience; I was in control for once. I felt sexy and seductive.

<u>Examine experiences beyond human awareness/ or cannot be communicated</u>
- No alcohol!
- I feel like I might be ready to seduce Steve, but I need some direct observations between Christine and her samples.

- *I have this feeling that I am forgetting something or that it was not a perfect experience. I do not feel complete or whole when the encounter is over.*

What is this feeling that I am missing? I feel sexually satisfied, but it doesn't seem to make me feel complete. It's like a feeling or an emotion is omitted. I'm happy and confident. What else could there be? I don't want to attempt anything with Steve until I can figure it out.

I pack my things and leave for work. I decide to stop in at the cafe for a latte and order one for Margie too. I look around the cafe, take my time grabbing extra sugar for Margie and slowly walk out the door. I don't know why I'm hoping to see Jack. I do want to see if everything is copacetic between us. I don't want us to feel uncomfortable around each other and I think I would miss him if he decided he couldn't be friends with me. I don't see him, so I walk to work. I look back one more time to make sure I don't miss him.

"Good morning, Margie," I say, placing her latte in front of her, with the extra packets of sugar.

"Good morning, Colleen. What a nice surprise. Thank you."

"You're welcome. Did you have a nice afternoon off?"

"Yes. I got a mani and a pedi." She waggles her fingers for me to see."

"Beautiful."

"Ready for a long day?"

"Oh right. We rescheduled everybody. What do you think about ordering sushi for lunch today?

Margie scrunches her nose. "I guess we could try it."

"I'll order it during a break and have it delivered." I smile. "Don't worry. I promise it tastes good." I walk into my office. "Send the first patient in when he arrives."

All of my patients arrive on time during the morning and my last patient before lunch is fourteen-year old Kayla, who has been caught shoplifting on numerous occasions. She comes from a wealthy family and can afford the items she steals, so there has to be an underlying reason for the misdemeanors.

Her parents sent her in a taxi to my office and she seems uneasy. I start to ask questions about her family and home life and I can see her getting more tense and upset.

"What do your parents do that make you upset?"

"They don't do anything," she grumbles.

"Come on. They don't do anything to make you upset?"

"No. They don't do anything. They don't ask how I am and they don't talk to me. They work."

Poor Kayla. That's tough. But to act out to get attention isn't the right way to go about it. "How do you feel after you've stolen something?"

"When I do it, it's exciting, but afterwards I feel empty. And I feel like I have to do it again to feel normal. Does that sound weird?"

"That is perfectly normal." It hits home a little because I've been aware of being unfulfilled lately. But she has a feeling or a need to feel whole because she is missing something in her life, the love and attention of her parents. Is that what I need too? I make a mental note to look into my own feelings of dissatisfaction.

We talk a little more and try some relaxation therapy. We practice deep breathing techniques and I also advise repeating a mantra that she can create. I suggest *stealing this will not make me feel better or normal*. I explain that she can substitute these techniques for the urge to steal. I tell her that she also needs to communicate with her parents. I make a note to call her parents and explain the situation. They need to help her through this before it becomes a serious addiction.

"Our time is up, Kayla. Do you need me to call a taxi?"

"No. My brother is picking me up."

"Ok. Have a great week. You are doing awesome." I pat her back.

Kayla turns to me and hugs me. I'm caught by surprise, but I hug her back.

She releases and ducks her head, avoiding my eyes. "Bye."

All that girl needs is some love.

As I watch her walk out of the office, Margie says, "Jack called fifteen minutes ago. He would like you to call him back."

"Thanks. Lunch should be here soon. I've already paid for it." I close my office door and dial Jack's number. He answers after the second ring.

"Hi, Colleen."

"Hi, Jack. How are you?"

"I'm great. Sorry for bothering you at work, but I was going to drop off your Garmin watch after work today. I forgot to give it back to you on Saturday. Will you still be at your office at six?"

"Jack, you can still use it. I don't mind."

"No, I'd like to drop it off before I forget."

"Oh. I'll be leaving here at six. I'll wait for you."

"Maybe we could go out for dinner? That is, if you don't have plans."

This again? I don't know if we can be friends if he keeps asking me out. I could tell him that I have volleyball tonight. It really is volleyball night, but I want to wait another week or two before I go back. That's one activity that I can't give up. Ryan said that he didn't like the house league team, so I'm hoping he quits when he doesn't see me there.

"As friends," Jack interrupts my thoughts.

That's better. "Sure. That would be great. I was going to say that I didn't want to argue with you again about dating, but we can definitely go out as friends."

"Why do you have to overthink things? I just want to hang out with you." I can hear anger in his voice. "Listen, maybe I made a mistake. I'll drop off the watch in your mailbox. Have a good day, Colleen."

"Jack?" He hung up.

"Lunch is here," Margie calls from the front.

What is wrong with Jack? I don't need this aggravation.

I go out and help Margie with the take out bags. We bring it to my office and I set it out on the table in front of the couch. I try to shake off the phone call.

"Those are California rolls," I point. "Start with one of those and if you handle it, then we will move on to tastier ones." I smile and dig into a sunshine roll that has mango, unagi, tempura, cream cheese and smoked salmon.

I watch her bite into her sushi, chew, and contemplate. "I like it."

"Woohoo!" I clap my hands. I explain the other types of sushi to her and we eat and chat.

"How are you, Colleen?"

I look at her and smile. "I'm great." I know that she's referring to my separation, so I open up a little more. "I was a mess at first, but I feel better now."

"You'd never know that you were a mess. You seem the same to me, overly perfect even." She shrugs. "I guess we all cope in different ways. I cried all day when my husband and I were separated."

I only cried once. It was that morning I failed to seduce Steve on my porch. "I have a handle on things, I guess."

"You sure do. You even seem more relaxed than I have ever seen you."

"Is that good?"

"It's great." Margie laughs. "You aren't tidying up my desk as much anymore."

I roll my eyes. "Yes, I can be a little organized."

"I'll say. You're even a little mechanical at times."

There's that word again. I guess everyone sees that in me, not just Steve. My brows furrow and I clench my teeth.

"I'm sorry, Colleen. I didn't mean anything by it. I admire your work ethic and self-discipline. But honestly, you seem calmer and happier."

"Thanks, Margie. I feel that I'm in a really good place." I unclench my teeth.

"Does that mean you're going to put yourself out there? Maybe see that Dr. Chemello again? You have so much to offer someone. Steve was such a fool."

"Oh no, Margie. I'm going to get Steve back." I start to clean up our plates.

"Why? How can you want him back? He's with someone else?"

I stop in my tracks. "How do *you* know that?"

She is hesitant. "You know that he is with someone?" I nod my head. "Well, last night, I saw Steve and some woman at a restaurant, holding hands."

"A blonde?"

"No, she was definitely a redhead. A big, bushy redhead. When she leaned over the table to kiss Steve, I thought the candle was going to light her hair on fire."

I'm confused. I saw him with a blonde on Saturday and two days later he's with a redhead. That's so strange. He can't be serious about the woman he supposedly moved in with. And which woman did he move in with? The blonde or the redhead? Maybe he didn't even move in with her.

"I'm sorry, Colleen. I didn't mean to upset you."

"I'm fine, Margie. Really I am. Thanks for telling me." I'm excited about the news. It gives me hope.

"See? There's that calmness about you again. You should be screaming and throwing things. It's kind of eerie."

I just shrug and smile. I can't tell her about Project Sex. We finish cleaning up our plates and throw out the trash.

"Thank you for the sushi," Margie says. "I really enjoyed it. I'll have to introduce my husband to Sushi Bon."

"You're welcome. And thanks for having lunch with me today. I appreciate the company."

Margie smiles at me and walks back to her desk.

42.

The rest of the afternoon flies by and the last patient of the day is Connie Baker.

"I'll wait out here, Connie," Mrs. Baker says.

"We'll be done a bit early again, so you can be on your way."

Mrs. Baker smiles at me and nods. Before I close the door, I notice how rigid and tense she is, while she bites her thumbnail.

"Margie, please get Mrs. Baker a tea."

Margie nods and Mrs. Baker smiles at me. "Thank you," she says.

"Get comfortable, Connie." I close the door and watch her choose a pink chair at the children's table. She immediately grabs a red crayon to colour on a blank piece of paper. I sit down beside her and take a blue crayon and a blank sheet also. I start drawing a rainbow. "What are you drawing?" I ask.

"A flower."

"Mine is a rainbow."

She looks at my page and then looks back down at hers.

Like our last visit, I start with easy questions to put her at ease. I ask her about her friends at school and her new bedroom, but she's really into her colouring and I can't seem to break her away from it. "Do you want to play a game?"

Connie looks up at me. "What kind of game?"

"It's a card game. I've played it with other kids and they really enjoyed it."

"Ok."

"Great." I get up from my chair. "I left it in the reception area. I'll be right back."

As soon as I step out the door I am pushed hard and I fall to the floor. It surprises me and I lose my breath.

"Don't say a word," a voice hisses.

I look up and I see Mr. Baker standing over me, holding a knife. He closes my office door. I quickly scan the room and I see Margie and Mrs. Baker on the floor, their mouths taped and their arms behind their back. Their hands are probably taped up too. Their eyes are wild. My heart is racing.

"Get up slowly," he orders. He looks maniacal. His dark eyes are wide and he is sneering at me.

I carefully stand up and say, "Mr. Baker-."

"Shut up! Go sit on the chair." He says through gritted teeth and he points, with the knife, to Margie's chair. I move towards the chair and he follows me. He lifts up the knife and comes right beside me. I start to panic and fall back into the chair, but he takes the phone cable and slices it in two. "Stay there and don't move."

He walks over to the two women and forces them to their feet. As they struggle to get up, I see that their hands really are taped behind their backs. They make muffled cries behind their taped mouths. He holds onto their arms and pushes them toward the single bathroom in the reception area. "Get in."

They stagger slowly towards the bathroom and I cringe as Margie hits the side of her body on the door frame when they both try to enter at the same time.

"Dummies," he says under his breath and closes the door. He grabs a chair and wedges it under the handle.

While he is occupied, I look on Margie's desk for something. A weapon. Anything. I find a letter opener and quickly grab it. I stare at it in my hand for a second. Where am I going to put it? My pants don't have pockets. I stick it in my waistband. It's cold and very uncomfortable, but I leave it there.

Mr. Baker turns to me. "We are going to go for a ride with Connie."

"A ride? Where?" My voice squeaks.

"That doesn't matter." He stands really close to me and I can smell alcohol. "You do exactly as I say and you won't get hurt." He slaps the flat end of the knife blade against his hand.

"I-I have more patients… They are coming soon… If I'm not here they will know something is wrong." He starts walking towards me as I try to convince him of my lies, but his demeanour frightens me to the core. I stop talking and push the rolling chair back, but it hits the wall. I can't escape him.

Mr. Baker looms over me and snarls, "You don't have any more patients today. I called to make sure. Your receptionist sure gave me a lot of information over the phone. She thought I was a parent of one of your patients." He laughs callously. "You are going to go back into your office and get Connie. You are going to pretend that nothing is wrong. Can you do that?"

"Y-y-yes," I stammer. What am I going to do? Do I pull out the mail opener now? I don't think I can do that. We're just going in his car. It's just a ride. If the situation gets volatile, then I'll use the opener.

"Go. Now." His voice scares me and I jump off the chair.

I open the door of my office and Connie is still colouring.

"Hi, Connie. I'm back."

"Where's the card game?" She asks.

"Oh right." I forgot about that.

"Hi, Connie," Mr. Baker says softly. "It's so nice to see you."

Connie drops her crayon and just stares at him. "Mommy?!" She yells.

"It's ok, honey. Daddy's here." He pushes me towards Connie. "Make her feel better," he whispers to me.

I stumble towards Connie. "Your daddy just wants to see you. It's ok." I hold out a hand. "Come on. Let's go." She takes my hand. She trusts me.

"Where's mommy?"

I turn to Mr. Baker for an answer. "Mommy asked me to pick you up. She had to go grocery shopping."

"We went grocery shopping yesterday." Smart girl.

"She forgot a few things. Dr. Cousineau, please get the keys to your car."

I look at him. My car? I walk to my desk, still holding Connie's hand, and open my purse. I see my cell phone. I'll take my whole purse. I start to put it on my shoulder.

"Just your car keys." His eyes are black and menacing. They send jolts of fear up my spine.

Dammit. I get my keys and put my purse down. Connie and I walk out of the office with Mr. Baker in tow. I look towards the secured bathroom and cringe. He didn't turn the light on for them. There's not even a window in there. I'm sure they can break their way out. They'll be fine. They have to be fine.

We get to the front door and Mr. Baker puts his hand on my shoulder. It feels like a brick. He tightens his grip and I wince in pain.

"I'll get the door." He bends close to me and whispers, "If you do anything stupid, I'll cut Connie." I can see the knife out of the corner of my eye.

Would he cut her? Could he actually kill me? Oh my god. This is crazy. He loves this little girl and yet, he could be a cold-blooded killer. It doesn't make sense.

He opens the door and my eyes scour the street, hoping that someone will see me. A car drives by and I try to make eye contact with the driver. It doesn't work. There is no one else on the street. We walk down the pathway and stop at the sidewalk. Does he know that the car in front of him is mine? Another car drives by, but Mr. Baker takes the keys from me and distracts me. He pushes the button on my keychain, and I can hear my locks disengage. He looks down at my car and smiles. "Isn't this convenient?"

Mr. Baker opens the back door and turns to Connie. "Get in, honey." She climbs in, unaware as to what is actually happening.

He firmly grabs my arm and leads me to the driver's side. He opens the door and when I'm just about to get in, he grabs me by my waist to turn me around. "Don't do anything stupid," he hisses. Then his expression suddenly changes. He looks quizzically at me and then his black eyes open wide. He's angry. His hand is on my opener in my waistband. I reach for it, but he already has it in his hands. "Stupid shrink." He pushes me down onto the seat and slams the door.

I'm so stupid. I had the opportunity to fight back and I blew it. But, really? Could I have stabbed him with the letter opener? Probably not. But now, I have the chance to open the door again and run down the street, but I can't leave poor Connie. I look back at her and she is looking out the window. She doesn't seem concerned at all. He loves her. He wouldn't hurt her, would he?

It's too late to do anything. Mr. Baker gets into the car and puts my keys into the ignition. "Drive," he orders.

I look at him. I don't know where I'm going, but I don't say anything. I put my seatbelt on and turn to Connie. "Put your seatbelt on, please." She does as I ask and I start the car and pull away from the curb.

Mr. Baker directs me, telling where to turn and we end up on the westbound highway. It's almost six and it's starting to get dark out. It's also rush hour. Traffic is a gridlock and we are moving slowly. I have to talk to him. I have to persuade him to let us go. How do I do it? What do I say? I just know that the longer I stay in this car and remain under his capture, the better the worse my odds are. He'll succeed with this insane abduction and I don't know where I'll end up. He doesn't want me, he wants Connie. I'm unwanted baggage.

I muster enough courage to talk to him. "Mr. Baker, you're taking Connie against your custody order. You could go to jail for up to ten years." If I can convince him that he might get caught, he might give up. I try to keep the fear out of my voice.

He turns back to look at Connie and then reaches over and turns on the radio. "Shhhh. I told you not to say anything."

I try to connect with him on a more personal level. "Martin, I just don't know if you're thinking straight. It doesn't matter that she went willingly with you. You will still be charged." I reach out to touch his arm.

He shows me the knife again and I flinch and withdraw my hand quickly. "Don't try your hokey shrink stuff on me. I love my daughter. She needs to be with me."

"If you let us go now, I won't say anything. I'll tell everyone that going for a drive is a part of Connie's therapy." I don't think anyone will believe me, but it's worth a shot.

"I'm not stupid. You fucking shrinks think you're all high and mighty and above me. Fuck you." He glares at me.

His eyes look through me and the hair on my arms stands straight up. I look quickly away. I understand that he is a desperate father with strong emotion, but there is something more. He is a dangerous. There may be some sort of mental illness or defect too.

"Now stop talking." He sits up a bit straighter and points to the right. "Get off here."

I take the off ramp and at the red light, he makes a call from his cell phone. "I'll be there in one minute," he tells whoever is on the other end. He points to the right and I turn again. After a couple more corners, we are in a residential neighbourhood just outside of Toronto. He tells me to pull into a driveway and I see a man waiting by the house. He takes the keys from the ignition.

"Do you have to go to the bathroom, sweetie?" he asks Connie.

"Yes. Is mommy here?"

"No, she's not. Let's go to the bathroom and we can be on our way." He scowls at me. "Come on. You too."

I am beginning to realize that he has planned this out pretty well. The other man opens the door to the house and stares at me, unsmiling and creepy. Please do not leave me with this creepy man. I look down and inch my way into the house, trying not to touch him as I walk by. When I am safely past him, I latch onto Connie's shoulders, as if for protection or safety. Mine or hers, I'm not too sure. We stop at two sets of stairs. One set going up and one going down.

"Go up the stairs and turn right. It's the first door on your right," Mr. Baker says.

"Go ahead, Connie. I'll be right here," I tell her. She walks into the bathroom and closes the door. I turn around and Mr. Baker's chest is in my face. I wish I went into the bathroom with her, but instead I try to plead with him.

"Come on, Mr. Baker. You are an intelligent man. You can leave us here and go no further with this abduction. You won't get into any trouble. I won't tell."

Mr. Baker steps even closer to me, and I almost have to turn my head away to take a breath. He looks down at me menacingly. He has the knife in his hand and he points it to my heart. "Stupid shrink. You need to stop talking," he hisses.

I try to get away and take a step backwards, but my back is now against the bathroom door. He takes another step forward and this time my cheek hits his chest. He could crush me easily. Then I feel his hot breath at my ear and I shudder.

"You are coming with me until I don't need you anymore," he whispers roughly. I can feel the tip of the knife against my neck.

His breath is revolting. He smells of booze and decay. "W-w-what do you need me for?" My heart is about to leap out of my throat. I feel very light-headed and weak, as if I'm about to pass out.

He steps back slightly and I am able to take a deep breath. "I need you to keep Connie happy. I need her to like me and trust me again."

I want to tell him that she might never trust him, but Connie opens the door. "Your turn," he says as he steps back.

I walk into the bathroom, shut the door and try to lock it, but it looks like the mechanism has been removed. Holy fuck. I take a couple of deep breaths to calm myself. I can hear him talking sweetly to Connie. Mr. Baker is smarter than I gave him credit for. I put the lid down and sit on the toilet, trying to think. I look around for something to take with me. To protect me. The bathroom has been cleared out. Nothing is the shower stall. No plunger. No waste basket. The mirror is even gone on the medicine cabinet. I stand up and open the cabinet. There's nothing inside of it, just a couple of cotton swabs. How long has been planning this?

43.

"Hurry up," I hear him say through the door.

I run the water and wash my hands and splash some on my face. I use toilet paper to dry off and then flush it down the toilet. I take a deep, calming breath and open the door.

"Let's go, girls." Mr. Baker escorts us outside and the creepy man is still there, staring at me.

"Everything is in the trunk and the cooler is on the back seat," the creepy man says.

The two men shake hands and we are ushered back into the car. I'm in the driver's seat again. Mr. Baker puts the keys into the ignition. "Let's hit the road."

I pull out of the driveway and he starts giving me directions again, leading me to the westbound on ramp of the highway. What is his plan? Where is he going? Maybe he has a hideout somewhere in western Ontario. My safest bet would be to do what he says, but the further we get, the worse off I am. If Connie trusts him again, how will he dispose of me? Will he just let me out on the highway? Will he kill me? He wouldn't do that in front of Connie, would he? I'm thinking of worst case scenarios and I'm freaking myself out. I need to calm down. I think of blowing bubbles and try to slow my breathing tempo.

Connie is being surprisingly good. She sings quietly to the songs on the radio and doesn't ask any questions or say anything. I understand why. During Connie's therapy, she told me that her dad yells at her when she's too loud. She's learned a valuable lesson. She's such a smart girl. I have to remember to praise her for her behaviour.

"I'm hungry, daddy," she says innocently. This is good news. Connie doesn't know it, but she may have just saved us. We will have to pullover at a rest stop with a restaurant. And people. I start looking ahead for the next one.

"There's a cooler beside you with peanut butter and jam sandwiches and some cheese sandwiches. All with the crusts cut off. Pick which one you would like. I also brought chocolate granola bars, fruit and juice boxes."

My heart drops. He anticipated this. I despise him.

"Thanks, daddy."

"Can you open it, sweetie?" He asks.

"Yes. Doctor Cousineau, do you want something to eat?" Connie asks.

"No thank you, Connie. I can't eat and drive at the same time."

"You will have to learn how pretty quickly, if you don't want to starve," Mr. Baker seethes.

I shudder and keep my eyes of the road. I don't dare look at him. I look at the gas gauge and it reads half empty. I roll my eyes. I cannot get a break. We could be travelling for another two hours at least, with this much gas. Maybe Connie will have to go to the bathroom again soon. All I can do is pray.

I've been driving awhile now and it's dark. I keep stretching my neck from side to side, hoping to relieve some tension in it. It aches, as do my hands and forearms. I guess I've been gripping the steering wheel rather tightly. So this is what stress does to a person. It's not a good feeling.

I can't see anything except car lights. I drive carefully, staying in the slow lane. What else can I do? What would Steve do? He might be able to overtake Mr. Baker, but Steve is shorter than him. I'm not sure if Steve would have enough strength. Jack could definitely do some damage to Mr. Baker. I smile at that thought. If Jack is in my thoughts, maybe I'm in his.

Oh my god! Jack! He was supposed to stop by the office! We were going to have dinner together. But our phone call ended badly. Would he still have come to the office to talk about our argument? Maybe he did and found Margie and Mrs. Baker. I breathe a sigh of relief, but then quickly start thinking the worse again. What if he didn't come to the office? Margie and Mrs. Baker could have gotten out of the bathroom by themselves. There are two of them. They could have helped each other. If they couldn't get out, the morning's patients will be sure to find them. But that's a long time to wait until the morning. Poor Margie. Poor Mrs. Baker. Stop! They are fine. You are not!

It's been about two hours and I notice the light indicator on my gas gauge has lit up. I'm not going to say anything to Mr. Baker. Maybe we'll run out of gas and we'll have to flag someone down for help. Now my eyes are starting to strain. I'm becoming a mess, physically now.

"It's getting late. I can't drive all night." I look in the rearview mirror and see that Connie is sleeping.

"We're almost there, but we'll have to stop for gas first."

Dammit. He saw the gas gauge. But then I get excited. Gas pumps mean people. I'll get to see people! I might be able to signal someone for help. I see a sign for the next rest station, but it's still thirty kilometers away. We don't have enough gas to get that far. That's ok! That's ok! When we run out of gas and we're stuck on the side of the road, it'll be my chance to get away.

My hope is crushed in an instant. "If you think we're going to stop at the next service centre, you're wrong. We'll never make thirty kilometers. There are gas cans in the trunk of your car."

Of course there are. I feel tears welling up in my eyes. He's planned this too well. I am not getting away from him. He has me captive. I'm hopeless.

"Pull over here."

"Here?" I squeak. Mt throat hurts from holding back the tears. We are on a stretch of highway with overhead lights. I put the signal on and start slowing down. I pull onto the shoulder and turn on my four-way lights.

Mr. Baker takes the keys out of the ignition. The blinking lights go out. So much for my safety concerns. "Don't get out of the car. I will chase you down," he threatens. I believe him. "Pop the trunk."

I obey and he exits the car. I try to stretch my body while seated. I'd love to stand up and stretch my legs too. The hours of tension has really taken a toll on my body. I look at Connie and she has woken up. She's leaning against the window, watching the cars speed by. I couldn't escape and leave her alone with him anyway. We're stuck here. I am a physical and emotional disaster. I shake my head pathetically. I can't believe how this situation has changed me. I was a strong woman and he has whittled me down to a pitiful, powerless subordinate. I am sickened by my new insignificance.

A minute later, bright lights shine through the crack of the trunk and onto the dashboard. I think a car has pulled over behind us. I turn around and try to get a better look. Seconds later, I hear voices. Someone is there!

"Do you need some help?" It's a man's voice.

What do I do? Do I make noise and alert the stranger? What if it is the creepy man? How can I tell?

"No. Thank you. I don't need any help. You can go on your way." That was Mr. Baker.

I need help! I wriggle around and look in my side mirrors. I still can't see very well. I have to do something quickly, before he leaves.

"I can help you with that. I see you have passengers in your car. Do they need anything? I have fresh coffee and cookies in my car."

"I said that I do not need help. Leave me alone." Mr. Baker slams the trunk and I can only make out a dark outline of the man because the headlights of his car are so bright.

I don't want the stranger to leave. I am desperate. I solidly press on car the horn, honking over and over. I look back and I see them pushing each other. They're fighting! Someone stumbles backward and falls down into the ditch. Is it Mr. Baker? I pray that it's Mr. Baker. I reach for my door handle.

All of a sudden, Mr. Baker rushes into the car, jams the keys into the ignition and yells, "Go!"

I hesitate, looking outside frantically. He holds up the knife to my throat and snarls, "Now!"

44.

I step on the gas and quickly swerve back out onto the highway. His thunderous voice echoes in my ears. I start crying. I hear Connie crying too.

"Faster." Mr. Baker grumbles.

I accelerate past the maximum limit. "If I go too fast, we could be pulled over by the police. Do you want that?" I don't want to get into an accident. I can barely see through my tears.

"Just drive." He keeps looking behind us. I hope the stranger follows us or calls the police. When is this going to end?

I sniff and wipe my tears away. "Connie, it's ok. Go to sleep." I say, trying to soothe her. I glance cautiously at Mr. Baker. "Do you have a blanket for her?"

"Uh. No."

You didn't think about that, did you? You big, dumb idiot?

But he takes off his coat, removing a flask from a pocket first, and turns and places it over his daughter. "It's ok, sweetie. Everything is fine."

Connie quiets down and he turns back around. He opens the flask and takes a swig.

I shake my head and think about Steve to calm me down. I touch the wedding band on my keychain, but quickly pull my hand away. I don't want Mr. Baker to see it. He might steal it and hock it for money.

Thoughts of my wedding day help to soothe me. I was so happy. I married the man of my dreams. We were so in love and had so many plans for the future. We were going to travel the world when we got older and make love in Paris. He was everything to me. But now that's over.

Nothing I have done lately has gotten me closer to getting Steve back. I've been selfish. Sleeping with all those men. What made me think that fucking random strangers would get Steve back? It has done nothing, but made me realize why Steve left me. I never satisfied him. He's been with other women way more sexually experienced than me. I know that now. He's moved on. He moved on even before we separated. There's no way we can get back together.

I'm not the same woman anymore. Steve would never forgive me for sleeping around. I've ruined my chances to reconcile. I think I'm just going to give up. Give up on Steve. Give up on my sex project. Just give up. Hell, I might never get home anyway.

"Exit here," Mr. Baker interrupts my thoughts.

I exit the highway and follow his directions. I notice a sign, *Welcome to Windsor*. Steve came here for work once or twice, but I've never been to this city before. Mr. Baker tells me to park on the side of the road. I do and turn off the car. He takes the keys from me.

"Get out." We both get out and he points at me. "Stay." I stand near the trunk of the car. He opens the back door, puts his coat back on and pulls Connie out, carrying her. Poor thing is so tired. She barely stirs.

We walk across the street and I see that we're going to a hotel. I scan the street. It's empty. No one is on it. No cars passing by either. The door to the concierge automatically opens and I start to walk to the front desk.

It's a run-down hotel. The kind of hotel that I would never stay in. Ever. But it's the kind of hotel that a crazed lunatic kidnapper can only afford. The forest green paint is chipping, the old-fashioned wallpaper border is peeling and the overhead fluorescent lights are buzzing and blinking sporadically.

"Come here," Mr. Baker says roughly. I turn back and he's nudging his head towards a chair across from the front desk. "Sit."

I sit down and he gently places Connie on my lap. I hold her tightly. She's still asleep. He gives me a stern look as if to say, 'don't move', and he goes to the front desk.

The lady at the front desk is old and tired-looking and has probably seen worse looking people than Mr. Baker come into the hotel. I watch the interaction. It sounds like he didn't have a reservation, but it doesn't seem to be a problem. He pays with cash. The lady looks at me briefly, and I scream in my head, 'Help me!', but she goes back to her front desk duties.

He walks back to me and takes Connie from me. "Let's go. To the elevator."

I walk to the elevator and we wait. When it opens he motions for me to go in first. "Press eleven," he says.

Just as I do, a man quickly slides in just before the doors close. He turns around to face the door and presses eleven, too. He's tall and looks muscular, wearing a hood on his head. I can't see his face. I want to scream at him. He could help me. But what if he's a worse delinquent than Mr. Baker? What other type of person is out this late in a seedy hotel? I try to see his reflection in the elevator doors, but they're too dirty and dented.

I look at Mr. Baker and he seems a bit nervous. Good. Feel nervous, you shit.

The door opens at the eleventh floor and hoodie gets out quickly. I watch him go to the ice machine. *Please don't go!* Mr. Baker turns right and waits for me. I consider my options. I could get back on the elevator and hope that the doors close quickly. But I can't leave Connie. I have no choice. I turn right and start walking.

"1121." He has the room card key in his hand. "Take it."

I do and slide it through the lock. The light flashes green and I open the door. The room is a suite. There is a living area with a television and a kitchenette. Behind a pair of French doors is the bedroom. He walks to the bedroom and rests Connie down on the bed, covering her up with the blankets.

"You're sleeping in there, too."

Sleep? I don't think so. How could I possibly sleep? I just stand at the hotel room door.

Mr. Baker opens the drawers in the kitchenette and closes them. He then goes into the bathroom, looks around and comes back out. What is he doing? What is he looking for? He walks back into the bedroom and I hear him fumbling around. He comes back out with the telephone in his hand. He unhooks the one in the living room, too, and throws them both on the couch. He then starts pushing the couch towards me. I have to move out of the way. He barricades the door with it. I'm trapped. It's clear to me that I'm not going anywhere.

"Might as well go to bed," he says spitefully. He sits on the couch, pulls out his flask and takes a long drink. He stares at me while he does.

His black, unfeeling eyes burn into my mind. I loathe him. I have never had this much hatred for anyone. The more I look at him, the more it consumes me.

I stand there for another minute, scrutinizing him, and then I head to the bathroom. I close and lock the door. There's a second door that leads to the bedroom. I close and lock that one too. I look around for something to hit him with or cut him or hurt him and I don't find anything. Maybe that's what he was doing when he came in here. Oh! Now I realize that he was looking for utensils or knives in the drawers in the kitchen too.

I turn on the water and use the facilities. I had been holding my bladder for too long. It was starting to hurt. I flush and wash my hands, splash water on my face and take a drink from the tap. For a moment, I hope that the tap water in Windsor is drinkable, but then I scoff at myself. Does it even matter? Will I even be alive tomorrow?

I look at myself in the mirror. Strands of my hair have come out of the bun. It's a mess. Mascara has run down my cheeks. I'm pale. I look and feel pathetic. I'm so weak. Last week, I had control of my life. I was following a plan that I created. I was trying to reach a goal. Today, I am a pawn in a frightening and chaotic game. I have no power. I feel hopeless. But there's that little girl sleeping in the next room. She's so at peace and so defenseless, and I know I need to remain strong. I need to look after Connie. I can only do that by not fighting back and being here for her. I can't take Mr. Baker on. It's the only thing I can do.

I can start by taking care of myself. I clean up my face, redo my bun and take long gulps of water. I should have eaten something earlier. I need to keep up my strength. I take long, deep breaths and stand up straighter. I am still a strong woman.

I unlock both doors and go to the bedroom. I peek out at Mr. Baker and he's still drinking from is flask. I don't think there's enough booze in that tiny bottle to make him drunk. I'm sure his tolerance surpasses eight ounces. Unfortunately, I don't think he'll pass out, but will he stay awake all night?

I take off my shoes and crawl in bed beside Connie. It's been such a long and emotional day. I am exhausted, but my mind starts up again. Maybe Mr. Baker is going to try to take Connie over the border. Detroit, Michigan is right next door to Windsor. He might have Connie's passport, but he doesn't have mine. Are we going to hole up here? For how long? He needs money for that. What's his plan? Connie's deep, even breathing is soothing. Can I sleep? I probably should sleep. It will help me to recuperate. I try to push the thoughts away and relax.

I am suddenly woken up by loud knocking. I don't even know where I am for a few seconds. I quickly remember and wonder how long I was actually sleeping. I get my bearings and sit straight up. It's two in the morning. Connie is still sleeping and I see Mr. Baker standing up by the door. Did the knocking wake him up too?

"Who is it?" Mr. Baker asks coarsely, trying to look through the peep hole.

"The front desk," a male voice says.

"What do you want?" I see him look through the peep hole.

"I'm very sorry, but we put you in the wrong room. This room is reserved for the night."

"Fuck you. We're not moving."

"I'm so sorry, sir. We will pay for your room tonight if you move to a different room."

Mr. Baker seems to like that idea. He turns to me, "Pick up Connie." He then starts moving the couch out of the way.

With Connie in my arms, I walk towards the door. He opens the door slightly, waiting for me.

Suddenly, the man on the other side of the door shoves it open harshly and the door hits Mr. Baker causing him to stumble backwards. I rush quickly back into the bedroom, but keep watching. My heart is racing. What is happening? Who is this man? Is he here to rescue me or hurt all of us?

Mr. Baker is quick to regain his composure and attacks the man. It's the man in the hoodie. I try to stay back, but if that doorway clears, I'm going to make a run for it.

Mr. Baker pushes the hooded man, but he holds his stance. He puts one hand on Mr. Baker's chest and punches him in the face with his other fist. Mr. Baker falters slightly and the man throws a second, harder punch. It lands on his jaw. They are in the hotel room now, but I still can't make it past them safely. Mr. Baker seems off kilter and swings blindly. He misses the hooded man. I still can't get a clear view of his face.

The man ducks down a little and goes at Mr. Baker full force, like a linebacker. He crushes him in the chest and Mr. Baker stumbles backward. They both hit the wall on the other side of the room.

Now is my chance. I take off with Connie still in my arms. I realize that I left my shoes in the bedroom, but I don't care. I'm definitely not going back to get them. I run as fast as I can with fifty pounds in my arms. I hit the elevator button over and over, cursing it, waiting for the doors to open. I keep my eyes down the hallway, praying that Mr. Baker doesn't win the fight. I start banging on the elevator doors, willing them to open. I feel awful for that man, whoever he is, but I have to get to the police.

"What's wrong, Dr. Cousineau?" I look down. Connie is awake.

"Shhh. It's ok, Connie." The elevator doors finally creak open, achingly slow. I step inside and push the close button over and over. The doors are so sluggish.

"Colleen!" A voice yells from down the hall.

Oh my god. It's Mr. Baker. Come on doors! Why is this elevator so god damned slow? I feel like I'm going to vomit. Fucking close already!

A hand appears on the doors, just before they close and I start to sink down onto the floor with Connie in my lap. I collapse into a puddle of utter frustration and despair. I'm crushed. Completely defeated. We were so close. We were almost free. He's going to be livid. He'll want vengeance and he'll take it out on me. I know what he did to his own wife. I know that I am not immune to his rage. I am shaking profusely and sobbing uncontrollably.

I feel a hand under my chin and I pull my head away. I don't want to look at him. I can't believe he's putting us through this.

The voice I hear is calm and soft, "Colleen. It's me. Jack."

45.

      What? I look up. Jack crouches down in front of me and he pulls his hood off. I see that he has a bloody nose. But it's Jack. I don't understand how he is here. How he knew? How? I grab him over top of Connie and pull him to me and hold him close. I am a mess of emotions. I am relieved, but shocked and still scared.

      I push Jack back slightly to look at him again. It's Jack. I smile faintly, completely confused. It must be the exhaustion. I can't piece anything together. I still can't believe he's here. I start to finally relax knowing them I'm finally safe. I kiss him hard. At first he hesitates and then he responds with equal fervor.

      He pulls away first. "Not that I want to stop kissing you, but we should really get downstairs. I knocked that guy out, but I don't know for how long. We should get to the police. They should be here by now."

      I start crying even more. "How did you find me?" I hug Connie tightly, who is just staring at us now. She has absolutely no clue what is happening or what has happened.

      "I've been following you since Toronto." He stands up and pushes the elevator stop button. The elevator comes to a halt and I hear a faint buzzing below us.

      "Since Toronto?" I am baffled.

      He squats back down to my level, cups my face and wipes my tears with his thumbs. "I wanted to return your watch, but that was just the excuse I was going to use see you. I mostly wanted to apologize for our telephone conversation. I am so sorry for lashing out at you and hanging up. I was being stupid and immature. Anyway, I saw that guy push you into your car. I saw his knife. I saw everything. I knew you were in trouble, so I followed you. Who the hell is he?"

      "He's Connie's father." I look down at Connie and she hides her face. "Without getting into it too much, he just wanted to be with his daughter, but the law was against it. Was that you on the highway when he stopped to put gas in my car?"

"Yes, that was me. It was dark. I didn't see him coming. He pushed me and I fell into the ditch." He takes Connie from me and stands up. "Come on, let's get out of here." He releases the stop button and the elevator begins to descend.

I don't want to move. I want to stay in the elevator with Jack. He's taking care of me and I feel completely safe. I know that I have shut down. I am running on pure emotion. I'd be happy to have all of my thoughts and actions completed for me right now. I rise up tentatively, still unwilling to do anything. I stand close to Jack and latch onto him as best as I can. I can't let him go yet. I wish I was Connie, lying in Jack's arms. She must feel completely protected and secure.

When the doors of the elevator open, there are six police officers waiting for us in the lobby. As soon as they see us, they draw their guns on us. "Step out of the elevator, slowly."

Jack can't put his hands up, so he tries to explain, "Mr. Baker, the man you want, is upstairs on the eleventh floor. We fought and I knocked him out. You might want to get up there quickly." Jack explains. "I am Jack Fraser, the man who has been calling 911 for hours."

"Ma'am? Is this true?"

I begin to snap out of my emotional coma. "Yes. This is my friend, Jack. What he said is all true."

The officers holster their guns. "Are you ok, ma'am?" An officer pulls me to the side. Another female officer takes Connie. Jack is pulled away too.

"Yes. Mr. Baker abducted Connie and me. Jack saved us. Mr. Baker is still upstairs. Room 1121." One officer goes up the elevator and another leaves to go up the stairs. I look at Jack. "Oh my god. We have to send someone to my office. My secretary Margie and Mrs. Baker are locked in the bathroom." They've been in there for the entire night. I panic again. I hope they're ok.

The officer standing with me asks, "What's your office address?" I tell him and he speaks into his radio to tell dispatch to get the Toronto Police Department to my office.

"Did you call Steve?" I ask Jack.

He stares at me blankly.

"Did you tell him?"

"No, I didn't call him," he says quietly.

"Do you need me to contact someone, ma'am?" An officer asks.

I shake my head. There's no need to worry Steve. I'll tell him all the details later.

The female officer brings Connie back to me. "She wanted to see you."

I crouch down to her. She has been crying and I hug her tightly. "We're going to go home soon to see your mom." She smiles softly. She looks so tired.

Two officers come out of the elevator. "There was no one in room 1121. We couldn't find him."

I look at Connie and then Jack. I feel sick. Jack puts his arm around me and I immediately feel safe, but Mr. Baker is still out there somewhere. He's going to be furious. He abducted us because he thought he was going to lose Connie. Now that he has lost her again, he might go on a more serious and more violent rampage.

The officers go to the front desk and I hear them say, 'lock down.' Are they really going to do that now? It's too late. There was plenty of time for him to get away already. He could still be hiding in the hotel. He could be watching us from somewhere close. I look around and a tremor runs up my spine.

An officer tells us that we have to make our statements at the police station. I want to go home, or at least to a different hotel to sleep. We are told that it's their basic procedure. They need all of the details to find Mr. Baker. I agree and when we are escorted out of the hotel, I realize that my shoes are still up in the hotel room. I explain and one officer turns away and talks into his radio. I still have to walk outside in my socks.

"And that's my car there," I say, pointing. I feel sick. I never want to see that car again. It probably smells of booze. "The keys to it could still be in the room. You might want to find those, too. I'm sure that he put some things in my trunk that might be of interest." I don't think Mr. Baker would be stupid enough to come back for my car.

"We will check it out," an officer says.

They take us to police headquarters and we are introduced to a Detective Jeffery. "I will need to take your statements separately in this office. I'll start with Connie. Dr. Cousineau, you can come in with her."

I look at Jack. I don't want him to leave. "It's ok," he soothes. "I'll be right here when you are finished."

They want to hear from Connie and I don't think she should be alone, so I go with her into a room with just a table and four chairs. When Connie answers the detective's questions, I realize that she has no idea of the level of danger she just faced.

When it's my turn, they lure Connie out of the room with the promise of donuts and hot chocolate. I get asked the same questions and I tell my version of the dreadful story. When I am finished, I step outside and I see Jack sitting alone in a chair, just like he promised.

"It's your turn." I say and Jack walks by me, but I stop him and hug him again. "Thank you so much for everything."

He hugs me back and when we pull apart he looks into my eyes and shakes his head at me. "I told you once that I would do anything for you. When are you going to open your eyes and see that?" He walks into the room.

I sit down in the chair that Jack was in and reflect back on all that has happened. I understand what Jack is saying to me. He wants to be with me. Why else would he follow a maniac across the province? He knew I was in danger and he wanted to rescue me. He is an amazing man. I feel so indebted to him at this moment, but I also don't desire or deserve his affection. He needs a strong woman, not me.

I thought I was confident and composed, yet when I'm put in a crisis, I can't even function. I break down. I was supposed to help Connie and I did absolutely nothing. I'm ashamed of myself. I'm a weak and pitiful woman in both my career and in my personal life. No wonder Steve left me. I was oblivious to his needs and he saw me as a pathetic and frigid neurotic. And what do I do to combat his allegations? I do insane things that aren't even me. A sex project? No one in their right mind would do that. I can't believe that this is where my ambitions and dreams lead me? What a mess I have made of my life. I give up.

46.

I jolt awake, panicked, but I am momentarily confused. I'm in a car. Whose car?

"Hey. It's ok. Colleen, you're safe." Jack reaches out and touches my thigh.

I jump at his touch and look at him. I nod. Right. I'm in Jack's car driving home from Windsor. My heart is still beating furiously. I was dreaming about Mr. Baker and it felt like I was still living that nightmare.

Jack and I had to stay in Windsor until late that afternoon. The police questioned us both and then cross-referenced our abduction details. They searched my car and the hotel room, too. They returned my shoes and found Connie's passport, the cooler and the gas cans, but not much else.

I asked if they had found any evidence as to where they thought Mr. Baker was going to take us. Detective Jeffery assumed that Mr. Baker was going to cross the border with his daughter, only because Connie's passport was found. He didn't say anything about me, but I knew that my passport was at home in Toronto, so I wouldn't have been able to cross the border. I thought it redundant to ask the detective what he thought my outcome would have been.

The police didn't want to release us until they were positive they had all of the evidence and facts they needed. It was a lot of sitting around for us and poor Connie. They left us in the waiting room with gross coffee and stale donuts. They didn't even have any tea.

Mrs. Baker arrived at the police station three hours after we were found. She held Connie in her arms, stroking her hair and whispering to her. I didn't think she'd ever let Connie go.

She hugged me too and said that she was glad it was me with Connie, but she had also apologized profusely for her estranged husband's behaviour. Unfortunately, we then had to wait for Mrs. Baker to tell her account of the story to the police.

Apparently, it took Margie and Mrs. Baker a couple of hours to tear the duct tape off of their hands. Then Margie took the toilet tank cover and smashed the door knob of the bathroom door. When that didn't work, they kept kicking the door until the wood trim split and they forced it open. They called the police, but had no idea where Mr. Baker had taken us.

In Windsor, the police searched for Mr. Baker in a ten mile radius and actually closed off some streets and the Canadian-United States border. There was a report earlier in the morning of a stolen car near the hotel, but it was ditched in Detroit, closer to the border. The police didn't know if it was Mr. Baker who stole the car or not. The car had been wiped clean. No fingerprints. Both the US and Canadian police departments issued a nationwide APB on Mr. Baker and they were following any and all leads.

When we were released, Jack said that he would drive me home because the police hadn't been able to locate my keys. I had to leave my car in Windsor. I didn't care too much about that. I'm going to donate my car to a family in need. I don't ever want to see that car again.

"Are you ok?" Jack still has his hand on my thigh.

I wipe the sweat off my brow and sit up straighter. "Yes, I'm fine. I just had a weird... and bad dream." Obviously, the entire event will bother me for a while, but Mr. Baker eluding the police scares me a great deal.

"I guess that's to be expected." He squeezes my leg. "At least you slept. You needed it. You were actually out cold. I even stopped for gas and you didn't budge."

I just look at his hand softly stroking my thigh, not knowing what to say. I turn and look out the window. It's pretty dark outside. I look at the dashboard clock. It reads 9:03. I don't like driving in the dark on the highway anymore.

"We're almost home. Just another ten minutes."

"Thank you so much for driving. I feel awful. I know that you didn't sleep at all either. I'm so sorry." There are a lot of things that I feel and regret, but I know that I should speak only of my gratitude.

"Hey! I'm happy to do it. I'm glad you're safe." He touches my hand this time.

I slowly pull my hand out from under his, pull my coat collar up and stuff both hands in my pockets.

"Are you cold?" He reaches over and starts pushing buttons and I feel a blast of heat.

I'm not cold. I just don't want Jack touching me. I want to be alone. I am so thankful that he saved me. I don't know where I would be right now if it hadn't been for Jack busting in the hotel room and kicking Mr. Baker's ass. I'm very lucky. However, I have never felt so helpless and worthless in all of my life. I don't know how to deal with it.

"You're home." He pulls into my driveway and as I look around to collect my things, he gets out, walks around the car and opens my door.

I look at him, extending his hand to me. I take it out of respect, but I've had enough of this helpless maiden nonsense.

"Thanks again, Jack. I can take it from here."

"Colleen, I can't let you go in your house alone."

I threw my hands up in the air. "Oh my god! Why on earth not?"

He looks at me strangely and calmly says, "Your key ring had your house key on it. Mr. Baker could be in your house."

"Oh." I'm embarrassed about my outburst. But then I realize something awful. "Oh no!"

"What's wrong?"

"I had my wedding band on that key ring too!" I can't believe that bastard. Not only did he kidnap Connie and me, and make me a physical and emotional mess, he took something so important to me. I curse and kick some rocks to take out my frustrations.

Jack lets me continue for a minute, watching me quietly. "Listen, you stay out here and keep doing whatever it is you're doing and I will figure out how to get into your locked house."

"I'm sorry. I am so pissed that that prick took my ring. He'll probably sell it. How am I going to explain it to Steve?" I wail.

Jack explodes, "Fuck Colleen! Who the fuck cares? Steve certainly doesn't. You make me so angry!" He starts to walk away and then comes back. "Stay here!"

I stand still, watching him walk away, with my mouth agape. I don't need that crap. I just went through a crazy, traumatic experience. I need support, not more stress. I pace back and forth, fuming.

"Colleen! Your house is open!" Jack is standing with my front door open.

I storm up the walk and straight past him. "Goodbye Jack."

"I'm not leaving."

I stop in my tracks and turn around. "What? Why?" I want him to go home.

"Just because Mr. Baker is not here now, doesn't mean he won't show up. When you have your locks changed tomorrow morning, that's when I'll leave. My buddy is coming first thing in the morning. He's a locksmith and he owes me a favour."

I growl under my breath. I know that I won't be able to talk him out of it. "Fine. I am going to take a shower. I do not feel myself. If you want to clean up, you can use the guest bathroom." I point, without looking at him. "Everything you need should be in there." I stomp my feet all the way up the stairs.

47.

He is so pushy. I forcefully turn on the shower. I don't want to entertain him. I throw my clothes on the floor. I wish he would leave. I step into the shower and the hot water washes over me. It feels amazing, but the water releases something inside me and I begin to sob uncontrollably. The tears don't stop.

I felt so helpless when Mr. Baker held the knife to me. I never want to feel that fear and insecurity again. But I can't even stay in my own house without Jack looking after me and protecting me. I feel so useless. Worthless. I watch the tears mix in with the water and pour down the drain. I let the hot water soothe me and massage my upper back and shoulders. So much tension has built up there. I eventually stop crying and finish up in the shower.

I twist my wet hair into a tight bun, put on comfortable pink leggings and a white fleece hoodie and head downstairs. I feel better, but I think that Jack might induce some more stress again.

I find him on the couch watching television. It's blaring. He must have showered because is hair is wet, but he's still wearing the same clothes. I wish I had some of Steve's old clothes that I could give him. I don't like that hoodie. I picture Jack barging into the hotel room, wearing it, knocking Mr. Baker down. Then later in the elevator, when he pulled the hoodie down and I saw his bloody nose. I shudder.

But now, Jack looks completely relaxed, with his feet up on the coffee table and a bottle of beer in hand. The beer was stuffed in the back of my fridge. They were Steve's. I never got around to throwing them out. Or maybe I didn't want to.

"Hey! You look one hundred percent better. Are you hungry? I just ordered some pizza."

I feel awkward. Why is Jack so comfortable in my home? I stare at him for a minute, not knowing what to say.

Jack is uneasy. He sits straight up, takes his feet off the table and starts talking quickly. "I made you some tea. I figured you like it because you have so much of it. Your mug is still in the kitchen. I didn't know how you take it. Or maybe you want a beer?"

I open my mouth and close it. That was really nice of him to make the tea, but it was still weird. "Thank you."

I turn around and walk into the kitchen. I see that he used my yellow sunflower tea pot. My Aunt Anna and I used to make our tea in this very same teapot. We would have tea together at least once a day. I really miss her. She might not give me affection and comfort, but she would get me back on track. I place the teapot on a tray, along with my mug, milk and sugar. I carry it all back to the living room.

Jack stands up quickly. "Here, I can take that for you."

I let him, but I'm upset. "Jack, I'm not broken or hurt. I'm not an invalid. I don't need special treatment or to be treated like a child. I just want everything to be normal."

He places my tray on the coffee table. "I'm sorry, Colleen. I don't mean to be treating you any differently than I normally would. I was just trying to help you with your tea tray." He sits down at one end of the couch, looks at me and then looks away.

I feel like I should apologize. Instead, I sit down at the other end of the couch and start pouring my tea. I told him how I feel. There's nothing wrong with that. I can't help thinking that he is babying me. He's doing everything for me and he's being way too nice. Oh my god. Did I just hear myself? I am such a horrible person. Jack *is* a great guy. He always has been.

When Jack would come to our dinner parties, he would always bring a date and she would end up sitting with Steve the whole night because he would be helping me in the kitchen. Jack would slice vegetables for the salad, help me set the table and open the wine for me. We'd talk about current events and our mutual love of travelling. Steve would sit on the couch, drinking beer and watching football on the television. Steve would yell at Jack to watch the game with him or call him a pussy, but Jack would keep me company. Jack's girlfriend would always get so mad. I'd tell him to go entertain her, but he'd end up in the kitchen again, helping me with the dirty dishes.

I sneak a look at him. He is watching some detective series on the television and has the volume down really low. The controller is between us. I grab it and turn the volume up.

He looks at me. I smile and shrug, "I can't hear it." He smiles back.

We are watching the show for only a few minutes when the doorbell rings. We both get up at the same time. I look at him thinking that this is *my* house.

"I'm sure it's the pizza. I'll get it." He leaves to answer the door.

I can feel the tension creeping up again. I sit back down. I'm not very hungry anyway.

I hear the transaction take place and the door closes again. I hear him in the kitchen, opening and closing cupboard doors, probably trying to find the plates. What man uses a plate for pizza? Then I hear the drawers rolling open. Forks too? Finally he comes out holding two plates and offers one to me. I take it. There are two slices of cheese pizza. It does look good. He then gets the forks and knives from his back pocket.

I laugh, "Not enough hands?"

"Sorry." He hands me the utensils.

I take them, but put them on the coffee table in front of me. I smell the pizza. My mouth waters. When was the last time I ate? I had a bite of a donut at the police station. And sushi yesterday afternoon with Margie, before everything happened. Ok, I'm hungry. I put the plate in my lap, hold a slice in two hands and take a large bite. So delicious.

I'm totally absorbed in my pizza, when I realize that Jack is staring at me.

"You took me for a fork and knife kind of a girl, Colleen." He laughs, puts his utensils down, and takes a huge bite of his pizza.

We smile at each other and continue to devour our pizza, while we watch a new reality series. I quit eating after two slices, but Jack goes back to the kitchen a couple more times.

"I would like to pay you for the pizza," I say.

"Colleen, you ate two slices. I had seven. It's fine."

"It's not about how much I ate. It's about you staying here over night and making sure that I'm safe."

"You're not going to yell at me again, are you?"

Did he need to bring that up? I sigh. "No. Just let me pay for the pizza."

"Sure. Whatever."

I get up and take my plate to the kitchen and stick it in the sink. I don't feel like washing it. The pizza box is empty, but it won't fit in the small recycling bin under the sink and I don't feel like taking it to the bins in the garage. I leave it on the counter. I find my purse and take out money to repay Jack, placing it on the pizza box.

I don't know what to do next. I just stand there, leaning against the counter, looking around. I feel out of place somehow. Maybe I'm just tired. I look at the clock. It's 10:30. I should probably go to bed.

I walk back toward the living room and am reminded that Jack will be staying over.

"Jack, there's a spare bedroom right beside the bathroom. Please make yourself at home. I'm going to bed."

"I'd like to stay here on the couch, if you don't mind. I, uh…" He looks towards the door. "I would feel more comfortable out here."

I know he's thinking about Mr. Baker and my keys, but I don't say anything. I don't want to think about it. Plus, I'm sure I'd be fine by myself. "I'll get you some blankets and a pillow."

I can hear him utter a response about not needing anything, but I ignore him and get him what he needs from the linen closet. I walk back and place his bedding on the couch beside him.

"Thank you." He half-smiles. "You must be exhausted."

"I think so." I pat the pillow. "I hope you can sleep on this couch. You seem too tall for it." It seems silly that he's giving up a perfectly good bed down the hall.

"I'll be fine."

There's a moment of awkward silence. I think he wants to say something, but he doesn't. And I should probably thank him again or tell him how much I appreciate him staying the night, but I'm not sure that it would come out pleasantly. I don't need a babysitter.

I finally say, "Good night, Jack."

He drops his eyes and then looks up again, "Good night. Sleep well, Colleen."

As I trudge up the stairs, I can feel Jack watching me.

48.

    That night in bed is as terrorizing as the actual abduction. I am hugging Connie and Mr. Baker glares at me with his impenetrable dark eyes. He thinks that I want to take her from him. I see the glint of the knife as he holds it high above my head. I barely get away as he stabs it into the air in front of me. He chases me and yells at me with his rough voice, "You're dead."

    I try to run away, but he keeps finding me and pushing me down. I try to scream at cars and people as they pass by me, but they can't hear me. I keep crying and begging him to let me go. He makes me feel completely helpless all over again. I feel like I am trapped down a deep, dark hole.

    I must have been making a fuss in my sleep because I wake up to Jack throwing open my door and running into my room. He sits beside me, lifts me gently, and cradles me in his arms. I am wearing a scant nightdress and he is shirtless. The warmth of his bare skin feels nice. His affectionate gesture triggers an emotional release from me and I begin to sob uncontrollably. I want the ache inside me to go away. There's so much fear and pain that I need to let out.

    I melt into his strong, gentle arms. I haven't felt this kind of intimacy in a long time. I'm not sure if I'm crying about the abduction or about being alone. He brushes the hair out of my face and tells me that I am safe. I let him hold me while I sob.

    I begin to calm down, but Jack continues to hold me, rubbing my back and arms. I tuck my head into his bare chest and continue to savour the warmth and tenderness. I listen to his heart beat and feel his soft breaths in my hair. He lulls me back to sleep.

49.

The doorbell wakes me early the next morning. Jack is not in my bed. When did he leave? Or was that a dream? No, I wouldn't dream of Jack like that. How am I going to handle seeing him after comforting me like that? It was so personal. I get up and search for my bathrobe. I put it on quickly as I head down the stairs. I'm not embarrassed. I can do this.

Jack already answered the door and he's shaking hands with a man who has come into my house.

"Tony, this is Colleen," Jacks says. "He's my buddy, the locksmith."

"Good morning." Tony nods.

"Hi." I wrap my robe around me a little tighter.

"Is there anything in particular you'd like to see in a new lock or would you like the standard deadbolt that you already have?"

"The same is fine. Thank you."

"I'll get to work on it now."

"Thanks, buddy. I appreciate this," Jack says.

"No problem."

Jack turns to me. "Come on, Colleen. I'm going to make you breakfast."

"Let me get changed and brush my teeth first." I still have the skimpy nightie on under my robe. I blush knowing that he saw it.

I quickly go upstairs and brush my teeth, put on some deodorant and dress in some yoga pants and a soft, purple tunic. My hair is still in a bun from yesterday, so I take it out and finger style it into soft waves around my face.

I notice Jack's blanket spread out on the couch as I pass by the living room. He slept there all night. Well, only until I woke him up because of my nightmare. Do I say something? Ok, maybe I'm a little embarrassed.

On the kitchen counter, I see that Jack used my aunt's teapot again. It's strange having him make me tea. Steve never once made me tea. Ever. It's really sweet that Jack has done it now twice.

Jack notices me in the doorway and smiles. "You look beautiful. Now sit." He pulls out a chair and I sit down at the table. "Tony is going to do both your front and back doors and fix the living room window that has a broken lock." He brings over the tea tray with milk and sugar.

I had forgotten about that window. "Good idea. Thank you so much." I start pouring my tea, it smells delicious. There's something about black tea that comforts me.

"No problem. You slept better the second half of the night, eh?" He walks away from me and comes back with a spoon. He looks concerned.

"Uh. Thank you. Um…yes. No more dreams after that, I guess."

He pats my shoulder. "I'm sure that your dreams will eventually subside."

"I've read about a technique for re-dreaming the end of a nightmare. It's called dream re-entry. Basically, if you have a nightmare, you're supposed to relive the dream, but act differently to make the events more favorable. You know, change it while you're awake."

"I get it. Maybe it'll change the outcome of your dream the next time you have it. Good idea. I guess you are the expert when it comes to the mind."

I smile and cradle my warm mug in my hands.

"Can I make you breakfast?"

"Jack, I can do that." I start to get up.

"I know that you can, but I would like to make it for you."

I look down at my tea and back up at him. "I wouldn't feel right. You've already done so much. I should make you breakfast."

"I'm making you breakfast. Sit." I sit down again. "I'll make you my famous waffles. I saw your waffle maker and you have all of the ingredients that I need. You enjoy your tea and watch me in action."

"Thank you." I smile shyly and look away. He has been wonderful, but that feeling of incompetence is creeping up on me again. I liked how he cared for me last night. His arms around me felt amazing. I swirl the tea around in my mug. But it's Jack. I don't want Jack. I roll my eyes. I guess that tells me how lonely I really am. It's strange. I don't think I've ever felt lonely. Even when my parents died and I moved in with my aunt. I always had my studies and my goals to work toward. I've always been so independent. I don't like this needy side of me. I would rather have Steve caring for me, but he can't see me like this. I don't think he'd like this side of me either. I need Jack to leave so that I can feel better about myself.

I watch Jack mixing the batter. He actually separates the eggs, which is a great feat for a man. He knows his way around a kitchen. My kitchen. He's opens cupboards and drawers like he lives here. I shake my head and take a sip of my tea. I do not want to get angry again. Instead, I look out the kitchen window at the gray sky and the bare tree branches.

My eyes fall to the table and I see my Sex Project notebook. I grab it and thumb through it. Am I going to continue with this? I learned a lot. Maybe it's time to try it all out on Steve. But I have to get my shit together first.

"What's that?" Jack comes up beside me with a plate of perfectly shaped waffles. He tries to read the notebook, but I slam it shut.

"Nothing." I bury it under a pile of magazines and mail.

He places the plate in the middle of the table. "Your warmed syrup and butter are right here. Help yourself." He places an empty plate in front of me and one in front of himself. "Dig in."

I use my fork to stab at a waffle and place it on my plate. I take a bit of butter and pour syrup over the entire waffle. After one bite I murmur, "So good." I look at Jack and he smiles.

We eat in silence. When I'm done my first waffle, I take one more. They are delicious.

I don't even get to start the second one when Tony interrupts us. "I am done," he says, coming towards me. "These are your new house keys. They open both the front and back doors. I fixed the window lock, as well."

I take the keys and stand up to find my purse. "Thank you so much. How much do I owe you?"

Tony looks at Jack. I frown and look at Jack. Jack looks at Tony. I put my hands on my hips and look back at Tony.

"You don't owe me a thing," Tony says. "I owed Jack a favour."

I look at Jack again. "You can't do that."

Jack ignores me and shakes hands with Tony. "Thanks man. I appreciate it. Try not to mess up your shoulder again."

"I think you fixed it, Jack. I haven't had any trouble with it."

They leave me standing in the kitchen. Jack walks Tony out the front door and I hear them talking on the front porch. I am angry.

When Jack comes back into the house, I start cleaning up the table and putting the dishes on the counter. I furiously scrape my second waffle into the trash. I feel bad that I didn't eat any of it. I throw the utensils into the sink, cursing under my breath.

"Here, let me do that. You sit down, Colleen."

"I am not a maiden in distress anymore. I am perfectly capable of washing my own dishes and paying my own bills. I am not helpless." I continue to rinse off the plates, with my back to him.

"I know that, Colleen. I feel his hand on my shoulder, but I shrug it away.

"While I appreciate everything that you have done, I can't accept any more help from you. I can get on with my life from here."

"I'm not here to help. I'm here to be with you. You went through something horrible and I don't want to leave you alone. You shouldn't be alone."

I dry my hands off on a towel and back away from him. "I'm fine."

Jack walks towards me and places his hands on my crossed arms. "I want to be here for you."

Tears spring to my eyes. "I'm fine."

He pulls me to him and his arms wrap around my body. "You're not fine."

I let my cheek rest on his chest and start crying. I don't need anyone to help me. I am not helpless. Why does he think I need to be comforted? His arms feel so warm and strong. It feels so nice.

"No, no, no." I push him away. Why am I crying? "Thank you for everything. God! I feel like a broken record! I am going to take a shower. Could you please be gone when I get out?" I start to walk away.

"Really?"

I turn around. "Yes, really. I need to be alone because… Because I can be alone."

"Fine," Jack says quietly, staring softly at me with his crisp, blue eyes.

"Thank you." Without another word, I turn and walk upstairs. Am I doing the right thing?

End of Book One

Made in the USA
Charleston, SC
26 August 2015